BLURRY

AN OFF-LIMITS NOVEL

MICHELLE HERCULES

INFINITE SKY PUBLISHING

Photography: Michelle Lancaster
Model: Chad Hurstt

Editor: Hot Tree Editing
Proofreader: My Brother's Editor

Paperback ISBN: 978-1-950991-65-5

1

CHIARA

Plastering a fake smile on my face, I power through the courtyard, greeting whoever is in my way with a cheery hello. The huge box in my hands is heavy, but it serves as a shield since I'm about to enter a mine zone.

Inside my grandparents' villa is chaos central. Italians as a rule can't congregate under one roof without mayhem. Add in wedding preparations and earplugs are required if you don't want to go deaf. The cacophony of several voices competing to be the loudest is not what bothers me; it's the people responsible for the noise. A viper's nest is a great analogy to describe the Moretti family.

Distant family members and strangers alike greet me as I stride toward the double doors that lead to the back of the main house. Before I take the steps down and join the fray of people working furiously to make sure my cousin's wedding is perfect, I pause to take in the sight. The breathtaking view of the Tuscan mountains is one of the few positive aspects of coming to Villa Moretti. If only this place wasn't spoiled by my rotten family.

The loud voice of Aunt Laura giving hell to someone brings me back from my reverie. I quickly find her shouting at a poor caterer. Her arm shakes as she points a chubby finger at the guy's face. I don't know what he did, but it's released the vicious beast that lives inside dear Auntie. I'd better stay the hell away from her.

Quickly taking the steps down into the backyard, I set the box with flower arrangements on a table nearby and search for the only thing that will help me cope with today's festivities. *Alcohol.* I scan the outside area, finding my favorite cousin, Max, already behind the temporary bar set up for the occasion. The corners of my lips twitch upward when I see what's in his hand —a bottle of prosecco. He wastes no time. I make a beeline in his direction, and, as if sensing my approach, he raises his head. His full lips twist into his trademark smirk, the one that makes him one of the highest paid male models in the world.

"Oh, hello there, Chibi."

"Starting early, aren't you?"

Max shrugs right before he pops the bottle of prosecco open. "What can I say? I need liquid courage to endure events like these."

He grabs two glasses and fills them up, almost to the brim. Practicality over classiness is Max's motto, much to his mother's dismay.

I roll my eyes. "Oh, give me a break. You love weddings. All those desperate single women, hoping to find their Prince Charming. It's like an all-you-can-eat buffet."

Max grants me a toothy grin. "Not this time. I think I've slept with all of Paola's friends."

Before I can open my mouth, Max continues. "The fuckable ones, I mean."

"You're horrible. One day you'll find the girl who will bring you down to your knees. I hope I'm around to witness your fall."

Bringing the glass of prosecco to my lips, I drink the whole thing in one gulp. The cool, fizzy beverage relieves my parched throat, but it does nothing to ease the pang in my chest. I should have told Pietro how I felt before my cousin Paola swooped in for the kill. He was one of my closest friends, after all, but I choked, mainly because he's five years older than me and probably only sees me as a child till this day.

"You'll be waiting a long time." Max pauses and stares intently. His scrutinizing gaze unnerves me, and I have an inkling of what he's thinking. "So, how are you holding on, coz?"

Pretending I don't know what he's talking about, I frown, signaling with a wave of my hand for him to fill my glass again. "What do you mean?"

"Don't play dumb with me. I know you better than you know yourself."

I scowl at Max before I bring the refilled glass of prosecco to my lips. I'm glad the alcohol is already helping me relax. Today is going to be murder, just as expected.

"Listen, he doesn't deserve you," he continues.

"I don't know what you're talking about." I turn my back to Max, pretending to watch the wedding preparations. Irritation simmers just below my skin. Why does he have to be such a busybody?

"You don't need to pretend with me, Chibi. I'm not blind. Pietro had all the chances in the world, and he chose Paola over you. He's not your guy. He has never been your guy. You're amazing, and he's second-rate."

Max's words make something clench in my chest, and tears prickle my eyes. I want to believe his words, but today it's almost impossible. If I'm all that, then how come Pietro is marrying Paola?

Fuck. What's up with Max and this sensitive bullshit conversation?

"I know I'm amazing, okay?" I reply feebly.

I'm so full of shit. My only consolation in this whole mess is that Max is the only one in my family who paid enough attention to see my true feelings toward Pietro. Everyone else, including Paola, seems oblivious.

"I've told you before, I'd tap you if you weren't my cousin."

Whipping my face in his direction, I glare at him. "Ew. Why do you have to be so gross?"

"Chiara? Is that you?"

"*Cazzo!* It's Mother." I scramble to finish my drink before going to her.

It's best if she doesn't interact with Max. He loves to antagonize her, and then I'm the one who has to deal with the woman.

My face is probably flushed when I stop in front of Ofelia Moretti, a former Miss Italia who still retains her pageant-days poise and beauty. Her perfectly arched eyebrows would furrow if her forehead wasn't frozen by Botox. But the pinch of her lips and the displeasure in her gaze are enough hints that I'm about to receive some negative comment.

With a tsking sound, she grabs a strand of my hair. "You look ghastly. Instead of drinking with Max, you should have done something about your appearance."

I take a step back to get out of her reach. "What's wrong with my appearance?"

"The question is what's *not* wrong with it? The hairdresser has finished with your cousin. Maybe he can do something about your hair. As for your attire...." Her gaze drops to take in the length of my body. "Well, there's nothing that can be done about it."

I want to tell my mother to go fuck herself. The insult obviously dies in my throat. She wouldn't hesitate to slap me across the face in front of all these people. She's done it before. There's nothing wrong with my fifties-inspired strapless dress. Sure, the tight bodice emphasizes my girls more than she deems appropriate, but there's nothing I can do about it. Does she want me to bind my breasts so I look like flat-chested Paola? Probably. I could tell her I'm wearing vintage Christian Dior, one of her favorite designers, but what good would it do? She'd probably say I make everything look trashy.

Mom makes a grab for my arm, but I sidestep her. "I have to use the restroom. I'll meet you inside."

I run back into the house as fast as my high-heeled shoes allow, veering toward the stairs. Once I reach the landing, I hear animated female voices coming from the master suite. I skid to a halt. The prosecco I just downed burns in my belly while hurtful memories assault me. Among other awful things, my cousin is a bully. Together with her friends, she tormented me through school. She's a couple of years older than me, but instead of bringing me into the fold when I joined their snobbish private school, she took pleasure in making my life a living hell. If Max hadn't been there, I don't know if I would have survived. Things only changed when I grew older and boys started to take notice of me. Suddenly, Paola wanted to be my best friend, and I was naïve enough to believe her bullshit.

Pietro, her fiancé, was my first friend there and the object of my affection. He was an awkward teen during high school, super tall and gawky, a little nerdy too. He didn't turn hot until he was in college. That's when Paola made her move and my crush died a sudden and painful death.

Maybe Max is right. I should have told Pietro how I felt sooner, but I was terrified of losing his friendship then and never confessed. Besides, he never would have really taken me seriously. Fat good that did me. I lost his friendship anyway when he started dating my cousin. In fact, this is the first time I'll have seen him in six months. But the good old saying "out of sight, out of mind" doesn't apply to me if the constant pain in my chest is any indication.

Forcing my feet to move, I veer in the opposite direction of

Paola and her phony friends, locking myself in the restroom down the corridor. I stare at my reflection in the mirror, holding a strand of my blonde hair between my fingers. I'm not ugly, but compared to Paola—who's tall, thin as a model, and gorgeous —I'm plain, and there's no way to hide my curves. No wonder Pietro picked her over me, but damn it, Paola isn't even nice unless she's faking it for him. I should have been braver and confessed I liked him before Paola was ever in the picture.

Get a grip on yourself, Chiara. Despite all her flaws, Pietro still picked her over you. It's time to move on.

I apply a fresh coat of lipstick and try to redo my curls using my fingers. No way in hell I'm going to let Paola's stylist touch my hair. Running a hand down the length of my dress, I attempt to smooth out the barely visible wrinkles, thinking about my mother's comment. The dress is perfect and completely appropriate for a summer wedding. I don't know why I'm surprised she disliked it. She has criticized everything I've worn since I was old enough to pick my own clothes.

My shoulders sag forward as I let out a heavy sigh. *It's just one day, Chiara. You can do this.* I straighten my back and raise my chin, ready to face the music, when the door bursts open.

I let out a yelp as Pietro stares at me wide-eyed. "Oh, so sorry, Chiara. I didn't know you were in here."

My heart takes off in a mad race. Why does the man have to look ten thousand times more appealing in his wedding tuxedo? His curls have been tamed with some gel, and his eternal five-o'clock shadow is nowhere in sight.

"That's okay. I was just freshening up my makeup. I'm all done."

He gives me an elevator glance, his gaze dropping to my shoes before slowly traveling back up the length of my body. "You look stunning, Chiara."

My heart does a backflip at his compliment. *Traitorous muscle.*

"So do you."

"Did you bring a date?"

"No. I'm not seeing anyone at the moment."

Why did I tell him that?

"It's really hard to believe a gorgeous girl like you is single. I would have snatched you up in a heartbeat if I had the chance."

Uh, what?

He did not just say that.

"What are you talking about, Pietro?"

He frowns, and it could be the prosecco here, but I think I catch a glint of guilt in his gaze.

"Sorry, I shouldn't have said anything. It must be the pre-wedding jitters."

Feeling bold and angry as well, I take a couple of steps closer. "Pietro, were you ever attracted to me?"

"Come on, Chiara. Let's forget I said anything, okay?"

"No, you can't take those words back."

His thick eyebrows furrow, and his lips turn into a thin, flat line. It's his trademark expression when he's feeling cornered.

Shit, I can't believe this is happening, but I can't back down now. I have to know.

"Answer me, Pietro!" I raise my voice, not caring if we're overheard.

"All right. I had a huge crush on you when we were at All Saints. God, I thought you knew."

My stomach bottoms out. I feel like I've been sucker punched. With wobbly steps, I reach for the granite top of the sink, fighting to get air into my lungs.

"Shit, Chiara. I swore to myself I would never say anything to you. I felt like such a perv for crushing on you. It doesn't matter anyway. I eventually moved on. Then Paola came along, and, well, the rest is history."

I can barely hear what he's saying over the loud sound of my pulse hammering in my ears.

"I-I can't be here."

Pushing him out of my way, I run out of the bathroom as if the devil is after me, rushing down the stairs two steps at a time. It's a miracle I don't twist an ankle. I veer toward the front door, ready to bolt and skip this fucking wedding. No way in hell I'll be able to stand aside and watch my hateful cousin marry the man of my dreams. Knowing it could have been me in her place if Pietro and I hadn't been such cowards and concerned about society makes it a thousand—no, a billion times worse.

I bump into Grandpa outside, struggling with his cane as he tries to get into the sporty convertible I know doesn't belong to him.

"Where are you going, Nonno?" I ask.

"Your useless father forgot to bring the cigars. I'm going into town to get them."

"No you're not, Dad." My mother's voice rings out right behind me, making my skin crawl. I don't want to deal with her on top of everything else.

"We can't have a wedding without cigars."

"You just took your medication, and you know how woozy it makes you. You'll get into a car wreck."

Grandpa, being the proud man he is, glares at his daughter, who does the same in return. Stuck in the middle, I see that as the perfect opportunity to get out of here.

"I'll get the cigars for you, Nonno."

"Nonsense. We'll send someone from the catering company. You're needed inside, Chiara."

With a quick glance in her direction, I see that if I don't go now, she'll drag me back to the house by my hair if necessary. I search for my car and notice it's been moved and is now stuck between two catering company vans. *Shit!* Needing to make a hasty exit, I veer toward one of the villa's Vespas because Grandpa is still halfway inside the little convertible.

As usual, the key is already in the ignition. The engine turns on with a creaking noise, and before my mother can do anything to stop me, I take off.

2

ALISTAIR

I'm such a fucking moron. Slamming my palm against the side of the car, I look ahead at the deserted road. It stretches on for miles without a sign of life nearby. I can't be that far from the winery.

Glaring at the useless phone in my hand, I feel tempted to break it to pieces. Forgetting to charge the blasted thing last night was exactly what I needed on top of a flat tire. Now I can either walk back to town or wait for someone to drive by and hope to score a ride.

I should have checked if the rental car had a jack before I accepted it. What good is a spare tire if I can't lift the damn car off the ground to change it? I rub my face and fight the urge to scream from the top of my lungs. This was supposed to be a stress-free trip, a reward to myself after all the bullshit I went through in the last year.

Coming to Tuscany had always been on my bucket list, but I never imagined I'd be here alone. Bitterness pools in my mouth. I thought I'd bring my two-faced, soon-to-be ex-wife here. I've always believed that when I married someone, that would be it. Now I'm twenty-six and getting a divorce.

In hindsight, I'm glad I never had the chance to bring Nadine here. At least this gorgeous place won't be tainted with memories of her.

I arrived in Siena two days ago, and everything went well—I mean, as well as things can go when you travel to a country where you don't speak the language. Custom differences aside, the trip met all my expectations until today. I should have known nothing good could happen after I was dumb enough to check my emails this morning and became aware of the shit-storm that's waiting for me back home.

Not only did I receive an email from my lawyer with Nadine's new demands, but my replacement fell through, and I have to teach my class next semester after all. The plan was to take a year off. I could say the hell with the job, but the school's principal is an old friend of mine. I can't fuck him over.

I'm not sure if I'm ready to go back to LA though. Traveling and doing different things is what kept my head above water, what prevented me from going apeshit on the asshole Nadine was cheating on me with—one of my friends.

My hands curl into fists by my sides. Now that the shock of discovery has worn off, I'm mostly angry at myself. *How could I have been so blind?*

"This is hopeless."

I lock the car and veer toward town. Staying here and hoping for a miracle won't cut it. I'm not looking forward to the long haul on foot though.

Two seconds after I make the decision, I hear the sound of a scooter approaching. The first thing I see come up the hill is a mop of blonde hair flying wildly in the wind. Then my gaze drops to the billowing skirt that reveals a pair of very nice legs. The driver slows down, stopping completely just a few steps away from me.

"*Ciao. Problemi con la macchina?*" the young woman asks.

I don't speak Italian, but I can guess what she's saying, so I nod. My tongue is stuck in my mouth. I lost the ability to speak because I'm too busy admiring the stranger. The only words that pop in my head to describe her are "achingly beautiful."

Shit. I must be losing my mind. I shouldn't be having such visceral reactions to attractive women.

She continues in Italian, and I soon become lost. I only know the basic words to get around. "Sorry, *no parlo Italiano.*"

"Ah, you're American. Let me guess, the rental company forgot to add the jack?"

"Yes. Is that a normal occurrence here?"

"I don't know. It was just a guess. You have the spare out, but you weren't changing the tire. I doubt the reason is lack of knowledge or physical ability."

I can't help but raise an eyebrow at her as the corners of my lips twitch upward. God, when was the last time I felt such easy amusement?

I cross my arms in front of my chest and say, "How do you know I'm not an overly pampered ass without any hand skills?"

Her blue gaze makes a quick scan of my six-foot-three frame before she smirks. "I seriously doubt that's the case. Where were you headed? Maybe I can give you a lift?"

My heart kicks up a notch, and I feel like a fucking teenager suffering from my first major crush. This is absolutely insane. Despite my body's reaction, I frown at her. Hasn't anyone taught her how unwise it is to offer rides to strangers, especially pretty girls like her?

But I'm not an idiot. I'll take the lift. "Winery Della Vecchia," I say.

Her delicate eyebrows arch as her plump, cherry-colored lips make a little *O* shape. I'm hit by a sudden urge to kiss the hell out of her, and in the same breath, I berate myself for having such inappropriate thoughts. I'm not a caveman.

"Oh, they aren't open today," she says.

"They don't open on Saturdays?"

"They usually do, but today they're closed." She pauses and seems to be deep in thought before she peers at me from under her thick eyelashes. "Do you feel like crashing a wedding party?"

The sudden change of subject takes me by surprise. "What?"

"I know it sounds crazy, but if you were looking to taste some amazing wine, my cousin's wedding is the place to be."

"I wasn't going to the winery for wine tasting alone."

"Oh, you were hoping to talk with the Della Vecchias?"

"Yes."

"Then you should definitely come with me. They'll be there."

Staring hard at the gorgeous woman in front of me, I can't believe I'm actually contemplating her offer. I was hoping to chat with the Della Vecchias about a particular grape they grow, and a social event would be the perfect opportunity to introduce myself and pick their brains without being too obvious. Visiting their winery was a last-minute, impulsive idea, and it didn't even occur to me to call beforehand.

She doesn't cower from my intense gaze; instead, she stares right back at me with a glint of amusement in her eyes. Cocking her head to the side, she smiles. "You're not afraid of me, are you? I promise I'm not a psycho."

I chuckle, running a hand through my hair. "What if *I'm* the psycho? Did you consider that?"

Her bright smile turns into a smirk as she narrows her gaze. "Nah. You're not a psycho. You look more like a cuddly bear."

I do something I haven't done in a long time—I throw my head back and laugh loudly, as a feeling of euphoria spreads through my chest.

"See, you're already having fun, and we haven't even gotten there yet."

The laughter is gone, but the excitement is still coursing through my veins.

"I don't think I'm wearing appropriate clothes to attend a wedding." I stare down at my jeans and Iron Maiden T-shirt.

"I can find you clothes. Come on. Where's your sense of adventure?"

The sassy smile that blossoms on her lips is what seals my fate.

"What the hell. Why not?"

3

CHIARA

A spike of adrenaline shoots up my veins as the American hunk hops behind me on the Vespa, looping his strong arms around my waist. He's so big, he barely fits on the small scooter.

I try not to think about what I just did. This is most definitely not one of my smartest ideas. Despite my bold talk that I know he isn't a bad guy, he could very well be a psychopath.

Tonight, I'm willing to take the risk. I can't face that stupid wedding by myself. I need a distraction, and Mr. Cuddly Bear couldn't be more perfect. He doesn't really look like a stuffed toy, more like the opposite. He's so rugged with those tattoos on his arm, that scruff on his face, and massive body; he's sure to give my mother a heart attack. Plus, he's the complete opposite of preppy Pietro. I need different. Maybe it's high time I forget my cousin's fiancé.

Aside from the American's sinful good looks, it was his deep voice that made my blood course faster through my veins and ultimately throw caution out the window.

"Do you make a habit of inviting strange men to join you at family parties?" he asks near my ear, giving me goose bumps.

"No." I laugh nervously. "I'm Chiara Moretti, by the way. What's your name?"

"Alistair Walsh."

Hell and damn. Even his name is sexy.

"That's not a common American name, is it?"

"Nope. My parents are Irish with Scottish blood."

"Hmm, how *Outlander.* Well, nice to meet you, Alistair. See, now we're no longer strangers."

I rev the engine and take off, needing to work extra hard to keep the balance with the increased weight.

This is, by far, my craziest stunt. I'm sure I'm going to receive a lecture from my father, and he usually looks the other way when I do something that pisses my mother off. It's too late now. Besides, knowing Alistair will be there has already managed to dissipate the anxiety that had been crushing my chest an hour ago. I'm actually giddy, and I don't even know why exactly.

"So, Alistair," I scream to be heard over the wind. "What brings you to beautiful Tuscany, business or pleasure?"

"Neither," he shouts near my ear, his warm breath fanning over my skin and doing crazy things to my body.

My nipples are as hard as pebbles now, and the little hairs at the back of my neck stand on end.

Ah, shit.

As of now, I've only slept with two guys, and neither of them was a real man like Alistair. They were boys really, inexperienced as hell.

"Well, that's a first. I assume you're here alone?"

Please be alone. Please be alone.

"Yup."

Relief washes over me.

"Gee, do you always answer in monosyllables?"

"Nope." He chuckles, and I find myself smiling as well. This will be fun. "I'm sorry. It's a bit hard to talk with the wind blowing on my face."

That's true, but I'm enjoying him shout-whispering near my ear. He has no idea the effect he's having on me right now. It's a miracle I can hold a conversation when I'm so aware of his hard chest pressed against my back, of his strong arms wrapped around my waist. Even though I'm the one driving the Vespa, he's controlling the ride. I might need to change my underwear when I get to Villa Moretti. My panties are soaked. I've never gotten so turned on so fast by any guy before.

When my grandparents' villa finally appears on the horizon, I let out a sigh. Staying this close to Alistair for another minute would have me combusting on the spot.

The building at the top of the hill is a typical stone construction, dating back centuries ago. To strangers, this must seem like an idyllic location, but I never enjoyed coming here. It always involves family affairs, and besides Max, all my cousins are odious.

The first thing I notice is the number of cars parked in the courtyard has doubled.

Alistair whistles as I park the Vespa. "That's a big party."

"Not really. Most of the guests are family and close friends."

I wait until he hops off before I do the same, smoothing my dress. I try to tame my hair next by combing it with my fingers. "Be honest, how close is my hair to resembling a bird's nest?"

Alistair moves closer, and I have to crane my neck to keep staring at his face. He's so damn tall, and I'm five foot nothing. To my surprise, he runs his hand through my loose strands, and I have to suppress the moan that threatens to escape my lips. His eyes capture mine, and I begin to drown in the depths of his azure gaze. The color of the Mediterranean Sea. Tiny flecks of turquoise in his irises give an extra depth to an already mesmerizing stare. My breath hitches right before the tip of my tongue darts out to moisten my suddenly dry lips. Alistair's eyes drop to them, and his Adam's apple bobs up and down. He wants to kiss me, and I'm dying for him to do so.

"Chiara! Where have you been?" my mother yells from the front door, breaking the spellbinding moment.

Alistair takes a huge step back and turns toward the house, finding my mother there with fire spitting from her mouth.

Fuck, I'm in so much trouble.

"I went to town like I said I would." I open the Vespa's storage compartment, retrieving two bags filled with the most expensive cigars I could find.

My mother's sharp gaze diverts to Alistair, who stays rooted to the spot, watching her warily. I bet he's regretting his decision right now.

"And who is that man?" my mother asks bluntly.

Ah, shit. I haven't thought of an excuse to justify Alistair's presence. Stupid me. I'm glad Alistair doesn't understand Italian, but I know he couldn't miss the sharp tone of my mother's voice. She narrows her eyes at me when I don't answer right away.

"Um, he is—"

"*Ecco*, he's my friend, Aunt Ofelia." Max joins us in the courtyard to save the day.

Where the heck did he come from?

"Yes, he's Max's friend from the US," I add quickly before my cousin starts speaking in Italian to the poor guy.

I don't miss the eyebrow raise Max gives me, nor the upturn of his lips.

"Hey, buddy. Glad you could make it." He pats Alistair's back as if they are indeed friends.

"Thanks for inviting me." Alistair doesn't miss a beat, following along with the charade.

Phew. A good sign. Looks like he wants some booty, and I'm all too happy to oblige. The thought of having a one-night stand with Alistair makes my core throb in anticipation. *Crap.*

I'm not prone to bouts of insta-lust. I usually require some major flirting and alcohol before I even contemplate sleeping with someone. That explains why I've only had a couple of hookups. Most of my friends from school have lost count of the number of casual sex encounters they've had. I'm the most prudish eighteen-year-old at All Saints, despite what the rumors say. And I have Paola to thank for that. Before she graduated high school, she made sure to tarnish my reputation just for kicks.

Max turns to me with a glint of mischief in his gaze. "Say, Chibi, how did you find my friend?"

I blink a couple of times to clear my mind from my stray thoughts. "Oh, he had car trouble. I found him on the side of the road with a flat tire and no jack."

Max glances up and down at Alistair's clothes. "Come on, let me get you something to wear. My family will flip out if they see you come in wearing jeans and a T-shirt."

Alistair throws me an uncertain glance.

I nod in encouragement. "I'll catch you later. It was very nice to meet you, Alistair."

He follows Max inside, and as soon as they disappear over the threshold, my mother grabs my forearm and pulls me closer. "If you think I buy for one second that half-baked excuse Max concocted, you're sorely mistaken, Chiara."

"It's not an excuse. Alistair is Max's friend from New York."

"Do you think I was born yesterday? I know you very well. I'm sick of your shenanigans. If your father hadn't already paid for your year abroad, I wouldn't let you go to California. You may fool him into believing you're going for your education, but I know all you care about is parties and sleeping around."

I pull my arm from her grasp and rub the sore spot. I'll have an angry red mark there, but that's not what's making my eyes burn. "Go ahead, Mother, just call me a whore."

"You sound so offended," she sneers. "I know very well what

you were up to in Milan. Your cousin filled me in on the sordid details."

"Paola is a fucking liar!" I finally lose control of my emotions.

Fury flickers in my mother's eyes. She grabs my chin, digging her long nails into my skin painfully. "You'd better watch your tongue. I'll not tolerate that kind of filthy language."

I step back, freeing myself from her sharp talons. There are so many things I want to say, but the words get lodged in my throat. Yes, I have ulterior motives for going to California. I want to escape all the fucking stares and gossip from All Saints. Thanks to my cousin's lies, everyone thinks I'm a nympho. The distance is also a great motivator. Maybe with an entire ocean and country between us, my family will forget I exist.

"Don't worry, Mother. I'll make sure to keep my profanities to a minimum." I turn on my heels and flee back to the house. I won't give her the satisfaction of seeing me cry.

I don't find Max and Alistair anywhere, and for that, I'm grateful. If Max sees me in this state and the mark on my arm, he's going to lose his shit. He's another one who hasn't been very lucky in the parental department. While my mother abuses me mostly with words, Max's father enjoyed using him as a punching bag. Thank fuck that asshole is now in jail.

I veer toward the kitchen, where the caterers are in full swing preparing food for the party. I spot what I'm looking for right away, and before anyone can say anything, I wrap my fingers around the bottle of Chianti and bolt out of the room.

But the problem is, where can I hide? If I manage to slip outside unseen, I can take the track down the valley and find a spot out of sight.

I veer in that direction but stop after a couple of steps when I hear the sound of overly cheery female voices approaching the house.

Paola's friends. Ugh.

Looking left and right, I make a split-second decision and enter the first room to my right.

It's not empty. Alistair is there wearing nothing but his boxer shorts.

My jaw drops while my heart jumps up to my throat, getting stuck there.

Mamma mia.

I don't care that my reputation is already in the gutter. I'm so riding that tonight.

4

ALISTAIR

I freeze when I hear the door open, finding Chiara standing there with a bottle of red wine in her hand. The deer-in-headlights look on her face tells me she didn't come looking for me. On instinct, I place my hands in front of my crotch to cover the sudden arousal her presence has caused.

Jesus fucking Christ. I'm not a perv. Why is my body acting like I'm one?

Her gaze drops below my waist, and I fight not to squirm where I stand.

"*Madonna Santa!* I'm so sorry. I thought the room was empty," she says but makes no motion to leave.

"I was about to change into the clothes your cousin brought me."

"Right."

She closes the door behind her and ventures farther into the room, making me even more tense. What is she playing at here? I'm not naïve when it comes to women and their games. I've seen plenty of them in action before. However, instead of preparing to rebuff her if she tries to come on to me, I'm actually looking forward to it.

Maybe Nadine and her betrayal did irreparable damage to my brain and turned me into a perv after all.

"Starting the party early?" I eye the Chianti in her hand.

Chiara cradles the dark bottle with both hands and stares at it, almost absentmindedly. "Yes. We love our wine."

She sits on the edge of the bed, curling her smooth legs under her. I swallow hard as my cock twitches inside my boxer shorts. *Fuck. I'm so screwed.*

She seems oblivious to what she's doing to me when she raises her lovely blue eyes to mine. They're a little red. Has she been crying?

"I'm sorry my mother was rude to you. She's stressed with the wedding."

I know bullshit when I hear it. I've never seen a woman look at her daughter with so much venom in her gaze.

"Don't worry about it."

Narrowing my eyes, I notice redness around Chiara's chin. *Fuck. Are those nail marks?*

She tucks a strand of her hair behind her ear, and the movement draws my attention to her forearm. There's an angry mark there too, as if someone grabbed her by force. Sudden anger unfurls in the pit of my stomach, making me see red.

"Did she do that to you?" I grit out.

Chiara's face turns ashen before she glances down, curling her fingers tighter around the bottle of wine. "This is nothing."

I clench my jaw hard as I fight the urge to seek out her mother and give her a piece of my mind. I don't know where this overwhelming need to protect Chiara is coming from. I just met her, but something about the petite blonde has managed to rekindle a fire in my heart that I thought had gone out forever.

Shit. I must be losing my mind.

Chiara notices I'm still staring and clears her throat. "I should go. You probably want some privacy."

"You can stay. I don't mind." My voice is thick, and I don't know if it's because of anger or desire. Probably a mix of both.

Chiara looks down at the bottle in her hand and frowns. "*Cazzo!* I forgot to bring the bottle opener. What a rookie mistake."

While she's distracted, I reach for the pair of slacks Max lent me and put them on quickly. They're an inch too short, but they fit nicely around my waist. Standing there wearing almost nothing was unnerving me.

"I'm sure there's one here though," Chiara says to herself before jumping from the bed to search the room. She opens drawers and cabinets, completely ignoring me.

While she's on her mission, I finish getting dressed. I'm in the process of fastening the last button of my shirt when she pivots on the spot, brandishing a small object in her hand: a corkscrew.

"Aha!" Victory is etched on her face, and I catch a glimpse of a much happier woman. It mollifies the anger from before.

She proceeds to open the bottle, and I watch her as if I'm in a daze. I've met my fair share of beautiful women before—God, I was married to one for four years—but none of them captured me in this foreign way. I can't make sense of it.

What kind of bullshit am I thinking now? If I'd been drinking, I would attribute my idiotic thoughts to alcohol. But I'm stone-cold sober.

Chiara finally opens the bottle with a pop, throwing the opener with the cork still stuck to the screw onto the bed before bringing the rim to her lips and taking large gulps from it. Before she can drown in red wine, I reach her in a couple of long strides and pull the bottle away from her.

"Whoa, easy there."

She stares at me wide-eyed before she bursts into giggles.

"What's so funny?"

"Nothing." She giggles again before she wipes her lips with

the back of her hand. It's such an unappealing move, but she somehow makes it look sexy. My rock-hard cock agrees.

A knock on the door saves me from doing something very stupid, like pushing Chiara against the wall and kissing the hell out of her. No matter how tempting the idea is, I can't let myself go there. It's clear that she's going through some rough shit, and I refuse to be the asshole who takes advantage of that.

"Come in," I say.

The door opens a fraction, and Max's head pops through the crack.

"Rea—Chiara, what are you doing here?"

"I didn't come looking for him, if that's what you were thinking." She turns to glare at her cousin.

Max doesn't seem happy with her answer by the way his eyebrows furrow together. "Sure you didn't. Hey, I'm all for sticking it to your mom, but don't you think bringing a complete stranger to her favorite niece's wedding party was a bit much?" He glances in my direction and adds, "No offense, dude."

"None taken. For the record, I usually don't accept random invitations from strangers. I was on my way to the Winery Della Vecchia, and Chiara mentioned the owners would be here."

"Ah, so you don't want to sleep with my cousin?"

Max raises an eyebrow at me, putting me in a very tough spot. I wasn't expecting him to be so fucking blunt. It's almost like I'm dealing with my lawyer, Enzo. It must be an Italian thing. Most of the people I know would wait until Chiara left the room to ask me that question.

Like an idiot, I blurt out the first thing that comes to my mind. "Good Lord, no."

Chiara winces as if I slapped her, making me regret my careless outburst. It sounded like I'm repulsed by her, which couldn't be further from the truth.

"Ouch. That was a solid burn, man," Max says.

"I didn't mean it like that. It's not that I don't find you attractive, Chiara. I—"

She raises her hand, speaking over me. "You don't need to apologize. Enjoy the party."

Pivoting on the spot, she shoves Max out of the way so she can escape the room.

"You really did put your foot in your mouth, didn't you?" He smirks.

I run a hand through my hair, frustrated with my inability to salvage the situation before Chiara left.

"How mad is she at me right now?"

Max shrugs. "I don't think *mad* is the right word. Her ego is probably bruised purple now. Our cousin Paola is marrying the guy Chiara has been in love with for years and—ah, *cazzo*. I shouldn't have told you that. Chiara will kill me if she finds out."

A spike of jealousy spears my chest, which is completely absurd. I rub my face, feeling worse than I did before.

"It wasn't my intention to make her feel bad. I'm not blind. Chiara is gorgeous, but I didn't accept her invitation thinking I would get some in the end."

Max scoffs. "Right. I'll pretend I believe you. Chiara is an adult, and I'm her cousin, not her keeper. She could use a distraction today, and if that's you, I don't care."

5

CHIARA

I must have done something terrible in my previous life, and the universe has decided to make me pay for all my sins today. I don't think my poor heart can take another rejection before I become a blubbering mess. The way Alistair answered Max's out-of-line question left me reeling. He sounded so appalled by the mere idea of sleeping with me that it felt like a punch to my gut.

Tell me how you really feel, why don't you?

I can't go back to the party outside, so I head to the second floor, hoping not to bump into anyone. My cousin and her bridesmaids are still enclosed in the main suite, waiting for the signal to head down. I veer in the opposite direction, going to Grandpa's office instead, the only place in this house where I feel relatively safe. It was my hiding spot when I was younger and my cousins were being extra mean to me. I was the youngest and the easiest target for their wicked games. Maybe if I didn't take every insult they aimed at me to heart, they wouldn't pick on me so much. I guess the old saying is right: if you stand for nothing, you fall for everything.

The office is mercifully empty—I can't believe I didn't think of coming here before. I let out a sigh of relief as I close the heavy door behind me.

After taking a couple of deep breaths in an attempt to calm my nerves, I walk to the window and watch the party downstairs for a few minutes. I spot my mother asking guests to take their seats, which means the ceremony is about to start. I have no plans to move from my spot. I'll stay right here. I don't care if there will be hell to pay later, or that I'm leaving Alistair alone down there to deal with the wolves by himself. I'm beyond the point of caring.

What a fool I was to indulge in fantasies about the man. I'm not unattractive, but the guy is sex on a stick, an Adonis among men, and way out of my league. He would never go for such a silly girl like me.

What am I doing? I promised myself not to allow those low self-esteem thoughts to enter my head anymore. Maybe Alistair was feeling disarmed and thought it would be disrespectful to tell Max he wanted to bang me.

I'm lost in my thoughts when the door opens. *There goes my privacy.* Turning around, I find Pietro standing at the entrance. *Oh fuck. What now?*

"Shouldn't you be downstairs already, waiting for your blushing bride to walk down the aisle?" I can't help my sarcastic tone.

Pietro closes the door behind him with a resounding click, making me swallow hard. *What is he doing?* My heart kicks up a notch, not from excitement, but from apprehension.

"I don't think I can go on with the ceremony until we finish the conversation we started earlier."

My heart lodges in my throat. "What?"

"I need to know something, Chiara." He stalks my way, and I feel like prey all of a sudden. I don't like the strange look in his gaze.

"We have nothing to talk about, Pietro." I try to sidestep him, but he blocks my way, grabbing my wrist.

"That's bullshit, Chiara. Why did you bolt out of that bathroom when I confessed I had a crush on you during high school?" He watches me with a fire in his gaze I've never seen before.

"You made me uncomfortable. You're about to marry my cousin, after all."

"Is that all?" His voice is strained, as if he's fighting some inner turmoil. "How come I have the feeling you're lying?"

"I'm not lying. Why does it matter anyway?"

"I need to know if you felt the same way about me. Otherwise I'll go insane." The confession comes out of his mouth as if it pains him to say it.

Too fucking late.

I pull my arm from his grasp. "Are you kidding me right now? You need to know? Why? Is your ego already in need of a boost?"

"No. You don't understand—"

"It doesn't matter if I did or not, Pietro," I cut him off. "Time has passed, and like you said, you've moved on, and you're about to marry my cousin."

"You're wrong. So very wrong, Chiara."

He moves closer again, wrapping his arm around my waist and bringing me flush against his body. I've lost count of how many times I dreamed about this moment, but in none of my fantasies was disgust present, and that's the overwhelming emotion jamming in my heart right now. I don't melt into his embrace; I feel repulsion instead. He's about to marry my cousin and he's coming on to me? But I'm frozen on the spot as he caresses my cheek.

"What are you doing, Pietro?" My voice is feeble; it's vapor.

"I want to know, Chiara."

He brings his lips to mine, almost too forcibly. I squirm against his hold, fighting to get him off me.

"Stop!" I finally manage to shove him off, wiping my lips with the back of my hand. "Are you out of your goddamn mind? You are minutes away from marrying another woman, you asshole!"

"A woman who was a second choice," he replies weakly, and I want to punch him in the throat.

Sudden fury bursts through my veins. "If you liked me so much when we were younger, you should have made your move. You choked, and now it's too late. You've made your choice. And to answer your question, yes, I did have a crush on you back then, but I would never get involved with you now. Do you seriously believe I would have my cousin's sloppy seconds?"

Pietro winces as his face turns ashen. I take that opportunity to dash out of the room, only to hit Alistair smack in his chest. He grabs my forearms, stopping me from falling on my ass.

"Whoa, easy there." He takes a good look at my face, probably noticing I'm about to crumble. "Do you wanna get out of here?" he asks.

With trembling lips, I say, "Yes, please. Take me away."

I FORGO the Vespa this time and borrow Max's car instead, letting Alistair drive. I can always count on my cousin to leave the spare key inside. I've had too much wine, and even if that wasn't the case, I'm in no condition to drive. My mind keeps going back to the scene in Grandpa's office. Did Pietro really kiss me? The notion is almost too far fetched to be believable. But I'm not losing my mind. He *did* assault me after he confessed Paola was his second choice.

I get angry all over again as my hands ball into fists on my lap. Does he think saying he's marrying my cousin even though I was his first choice makes his decision better? Ugh, I can't believe I wasted years of my life pining for him. I thought he was different than the other guys. I thought he had honor. I guess I didn't know him that well, or maybe I was just projecting what I wanted to see.

Alistair hasn't spoken much since we left the villa, but when he covers my fist with his warm hand, some of my anger dilutes a bit. I stare at our joined hands for a couple of beats before I raise my gaze to his face. He's still looking straight ahead at the road, but he does glance at me briefly with a smile that says "I'm here for you."

My heart beats faster. The anger dissipates completely to be replaced by a deep yearning. It's crazy how at ease I feel in Alistair's presence, even after his careless words hurt me more than they should have.

He continues to drive in silence through the charming countryside of the Chianti region, a magical landscape of cypress trees, vineyards, and olive groves that fails to impress me today. The picture-perfect scenery pales in comparison to the man sitting next to me.

I've gone back to fantasizing about him, to wanting his mouth everywhere on my body. I rub my legs together, trying to get rid of the sudden ache between them. *Shit.* I shouldn't have let my mind go there, not after Alistair made it crystal clear he has no intention of sleeping with me.

He takes me to Monteriggioni, a completely walled medieval town sitting on a small natural hill. It was built in the thirteenth century by the overlords of Siena, and it attracts tourists galore in the summer. I've been here just once as a young child and remember being enchanted by the medieval castle.

After he parks, I turn to him. "Why did you bring me here?"

"I planned to stop here on my way back from the winery visit. I figured you wouldn't mind accompanying me."

"Ah, *cazzo*. You didn't have the chance to meet the Della Vecchias, did you?"

"No, but it's okay. It wasn't a wasted trip."

I don't know what to make of his statement. Is he saying it wasn't a wasted trip because he met me?

"Thank you for saving me."

He frowns. "What happened back there? You left that room like you were running away from a ghost."

I sink against the leather seat and face forward. "I guess I was."

"Your cousin's fiancé?"

I whip around to face Alistair. "How did you—Ugh, never mind. Max opened his big mouth, didn't he?"

"He did mention something by accident."

I stare ahead again. "I can't believe I've wasted years of my life idolizing Pietro. He's just like the other guys. A big disappointment."

"We're not all bad."

Glancing at Alistair again, I find him staring at me with the most enigmatic glint in his eyes. "I'm sorry. I didn't mean to offend you. I haven't had the best luck with guys. I guess the problem isn't gender specific. People are just assholes as a rule."

"I can agree with that."

He touches my arm and gives me a crooked smile that almost makes me melt like a popsicle under the sun. My heart gallops at a thousand miles an hour as I prepare to make a complete fool of myself. I unbuckle my seat belt, but instead of opening the door, I launch myself at him, attacking his mouth like a deranged woman. There's only a moment of hesitation on Alistair's part before he wraps his arms around my waist and pulls me all the way across until I'm straddling his lap.

His tongue darts inside my mouth, taking complete control

as he digs his fingers into my hips. In this position, my throbbing core rubs against his slacks, or better yet, his rock-hard erection. I've never kissed a guy with scruff before, and at first, it tickles. But soon I get used to it because what he's doing with his tongue is already short-circuiting my brain.

I grind my pelvis against his, trying to increase the friction down below, and I end up eliciting a grunt from him. I pull away slightly to capture his lower lip between my teeth. He groans before his hands leave my hips to disappear under the skirt of my dress. His deft fingers slowly travel up my legs until they curl around the sides of my panties.

"Is this okay?" he asks.

I close my eyes and hum an affirmation. He kisses me again, slower this time. With a featherlight touch, he traces the edge of my underwear, getting closer and closer to where I so desperately need his fingers to be. He cups my pussy with his palm, and I swear to God, I almost come right then and there. I lock my hands together behind his neck and try to bring my body even closer to his. Alistair rubs my core with his palm first before he pushes my panties aside to brush his thumb against my clit.

"Oh my God. Yes."

He chuckles against my mouth before he slides one finger down my entrance and teases the spot. "You're so fucking wet already, Chiara."

I rotate my hips, trying to impale myself on his finger. I won't sit quietly here while he tortures me.

He removes his other hand from under my dress to let it travel up my side. When his fingers brush the underside of my breast, I moan against his lips again. He deepens the kiss, cupping my breast with his large hand. Even so, my girl can't quite fit inside his palm. He squeezes it slightly through the fabric of the dress at the same time as he inserts two fingers inside me. It's just too much stimulation going on all at once, and I can't fight the wave of pleasure that rushes over me. If it weren't for his mouth on mine, I would have screamed at the top of my lungs.

It's still pretty bright outside, and anyone walking nearby could see what we're up to, but in this moment, I don't care. Alistair keeps fucking me with his fingers until the tremors racking my body dissipate. I'm left boneless and suddenly mortified by my actions.

He moves his hand, pulling his fingers from inside me, before putting my underwear back in place. I try to get off his lap, but he keeps me there, resting his hands on each side of my hips.

"Don't move just yet." His voice is thick with need.

"Sorry, you probably want to, uh, finish as well, huh?"

He stares at me and runs his left hand through my hair. "No, it's not that at all. I just want you in my arms for a bit longer. It feels nice."

I drop my gaze to the base of his throat, unable to withstand the intensity of his stare. "I'm sorry I jumped you, even though you said you had no intention of sleeping with me."

He places a finger under my chin and forces me to look into his eyes. "That was a lie. I've been walking in a state of semi-arousal since you rescued me. God, you must know how sexy you are, Chiara."

I can't help the elation that spreads through my chest, but at the same time, I'm scared that the feeling isn't real, that it's only a reaction to the shitty day I've had.

"I'm sorry I hurt your feelings before," he continues. "This is all a bit unusual for me. I'm not a spur-of-the-moment kind of guy. This trip to Italy was my attempt to loosen up a bit."

"You may find it hard to believe, but I also don't do things like this."

"Like what? Taking advantage of stranded guys you find on the side of the road?"

I hit him on the chest, getting a deep chuckle from him in return. "No, hooking up with a man I barely know, even though my cousin Paola will say differently."

Alistair's expression turns serious, right before he tucks a loose strand of hair behind my ear. "I want you to promise me something."

"What?"

"Promise you won't think about your cousin, your mother, or anyone else who made you sad today. For the next couple of days, I want you to be one-hundred-percent happy."

"Next couple of days?" I raise an eyebrow at him while my heart jams against the confines of my chest and the butterflies in my stomach turn into ninja insects.

He rewards me with a crooked smile before capturing my mouth for a long, toe-curling kiss. When he finally lets go of my lips with a pop, I'm a little light-headed.

"Yes," he answers. "I have two days here in Siena before I head back to Florence to catch my flight to the States. I'd love to spend them with you. I do need someone who speaks the language, after all."

"Oh, so you just want me around for my oral skills?"

His heated gaze drops to my lips. "Yes, among other things."

6

ALISTAIR

I'm going to hell for this, but I couldn't resist Chiara, not when her delicious mouth covered mine, bringing forth a deep-rooted desire I didn't know I was still able to feel. I've slept with other women since Nadine, but all those encounters were meaningless, hollow. With Chiara, it's different; it isn't about taking care of a physiological need. I don't even know why that is. Maybe it's the place or the circumstance of how we met. In the end, it doesn't matter.

I never tasted anything sweeter than her tongue, and as I walk side by side with her, I have to fight the urge to stop every few minutes to attack her mouth again. My cock is straining against the seams of my borrowed pants, and I know I won't find proper release until I'm buried deep inside her.

Our hands are fused together as we roam the streets of this medieval town. Chiara points at things she finds interesting or offers a little bit of historical information whenever she can. I said before that I wanted her to be truly happy in these two days we spend together, but what I didn't factor into the equation was being happy myself as well. And I am. I haven't felt this way since I caught Nadine fucking Wade in our own bed.

With a silent groan, I quickly banish the image from my head before it sours my mood.

I focus on Chiara instead. The shadow that dimmed her eyes earlier is gone. She pulls me toward a particular store with several trinkets and shiny objects on display. Pointing at a twisted wire silver bracelet with an opal stone as the focal point, she explains something about it. I'm only half listening because I'm too distracted—staring at her instead. Finally giving in to my urges, I turn her around and capture her face between my hands to claim her mouth. She makes a small sound in the back of her throat while her body melts into mine. I can't help but think she fits perfectly into my arms. I pull back after a while, fearing getting carried away and doing something completely inappropriate in public.

"Wow! What was that for?" she says, a little out of breath.

"Nothing. I was hit by sudden withdrawals. What were you saying about the bracelet?"

She looks at my mouth with flushed cheeks and hooded eyes for a few seconds before she replies, "Oh, that my great-grandmother used to have one just like this. She'd let me play with it and promised I could have it once I was older. When she passed away and the women in the family got together to go through her stuff, Paola said Bisnonna had promised the bracelet to her instead, which was a bold lie. My mother obviously didn't believe me, so Paola got what she wanted."

"Your cousin sounds lovely."

Chiara snorts. "She's awful, but she's not the worst in the family."

I eye the bracelet and commit it to memory. The store is already closed, but I'll try to sneak back here tomorrow and get it for Chiara. I know she didn't tell me this story to get me to buy it for her, but I want her to have it just the same.

"Come on, I'm hungry. Let's find a place to eat." She yanks my arm, and I let her drag me away.

I'm not exactly hungry for food, but I don't voice that out loud. I'll need sustenance to do what I have planned. Chiara finds a hole-in-the-wall restaurant, or *charcuteria*, as she calls it, a place specializing in cold cuts, cheese, and wine. After a fast exchange in Italian between Chiara and the manager, we're ushered all the way to the back of the already busy restaurant to the last table available. The waiter removes the Reserved sign from it and helps Chiara to her seat.

After he leaves to grab our menus, I turn to her. "Did you just convince them to give their reserved table to us?"

Chiara laughs and shakes her head. "No. They usually keep one or two tables available for last-minute VIP patrons."

I raise an eyebrow at her. "Oh?"

"Well, I'm not exactly VIP, but the Moretti name carries weight in the area. I just used it. If I have to suffer being related to them, I might as well take advantage of the perks."

Even though she tries to sound nonchalant, I hear a slight catch in her voice. Who are those people, and why do I get the impression Chiara is the anathema in the family?

The waiter returns with menus and a jug of cold water. He doesn't speak any English, but Chiara is happy to play the interpreter for me. I sit back and let her choose the wine and the appetizers. Watching her talk with confidence and make decisions without hesitation is a hell of a turn-on. Well, not that I'm not walking at half-mast already.

I lean closer and stroke her cheek, pausing at her lips. "So, what did you get for us?"

Chiara's tongue darts out, right before she sucks my finger into her mouth. Jesus fucking Christ. She's going to be the death of me.

Finally letting go of my finger, she says through a wicked smile, "It's a surprise. I hope you're a meat lover."

Staring at her lips, I say, "You have no idea."

Our server comes back once more with wine, but there are

no glasses in sight. Chiara smiles at me when she catches my confused look.

She flips the ceramic bowl that was already on the table—that I honestly thought was meant for soup—and lets the waiter fill it up.

"We drink wine in these like in the good old days."

The waiter fills my bowl with an amused twist of his lips. He must get this confused reaction a lot from tourists.

Chiara raises her bowl after the guy walks away. "What shall we toast to?"

"How about an unforgettable weekend?"

She smiles, and her entire face lights up. I feel a sharp pang in my chest, and suddenly I understand why I'm having such a visceral reaction to her. She reminds me of Jamie, the best friend I lost when I was a teen. Only Jamie was a guy, and I wasn't remotely attracted to him. He and Chiara share the same vulnerability masked by a happy-go-lucky personality though. I grin at her in return, trying not to show how much this revelation is doing my head in.

"Cheers to that."

Chiara places the bowl back on the table, laces her hands together, and rests her chin on top of them. "So, shall we establish some ground rules for this epic weekend?"

I lean back and cross my arms. "Okay. Rule number one, we won't speak about your family."

Her eyes flash with an emotion I can't discern before she says, "Deal. My turn. We won't trade specific details about our life, like jobs, where we live, etcetera."

I stare at her through slits but with a smirk on my lips. "Why? Are you afraid I'm going to turn into a stalker after all?"

Chiara shakes her head and smiles ruefully at her wine. "No, it's not that." She pauses to lick her lips, looking at me again from under her eyelashes. "I have the feeling that the more I know about you, the harder it will be to let you go."

I clench my jaw hard and don't say anything for several beats. I can tell Chiara is interpreting my silence the wrong way by how her eyebrows furrow together, marring her otherwise smooth skin. I reach for her chair, pulling it across the floor with a loud screech until she's sitting next to me.

"Now, that's better. You were too far from me." I touch her cheek with the back of my hand as I stare deep into her eyes. "I agree to your rule only because it's going to be hard for me as well."

Her breath catches at the same time her lips part, making it impossible for me not to shorten the distance between us and kiss her again. But I'm greedy, and kissing her doesn't satisfy my hunger. I want more.

I slide my hand up her thigh and under her dress, stopping just a few inches away from her warm pussy. I don't dare go any farther, not in the middle of the restaurant anyway. Instead, I make lazy circles with the tips of my fingers, smiling against her lips when I feel the goose bumps form on her skin.

A throat clearing nearby makes me pull away, and I level the waiter with a glower, not appreciating the interruption.

"*Il antipasti*," he says before he places the tray of cold cuts in front of us.

"*Grazie mille*," Chiara replies without making eye contact with the man.

Ah shit. I made her uncomfortable. I better behave until I can get her alone.

We eat our food and drink our wine, but we both have the same sense of urgency. We don't linger.

Back in the car, it's a Herculean effort to keep my hands to myself, but I push through the urge to stop on the side of the road to steal a few more kisses from her.

"I thought today was going to be the worst day of my life," Chiara says as she sticks her hand out the window.

"I'm glad it didn't turn out that way. It will only get better from here."

I sense her stare, so I peel my gaze off the road for a second.

"Cocky, aren't you?"

"Nope, just being realistic, babe."

Her nose wrinkles, and she pouts. "Don't call me that. I hate that endearment."

"Sorry. What should I call you, then? *Chibi*?"

"No!" she shouts, and I have to glance at her again.

"Isn't that what Max called you? I thought it was cute. It fits you."

She crosses her arms in front of her chest and levels me with a glare. "No, it doesn't. *Chibi* means small in Japanese, and it's also a style of caricature where the characters are super cute and tiny."

"See? It fits you." I laugh.

"*Stronzo!*" She hits my arm. "Keep calling me Chibi and you won't get any booty tonight."

"Okay, okay. I won't. What does *stronzo* mean? I know it can't be anything good."

She faces forward and says under her breath, "Asshole."

I reach out and squeeze her thigh through the skirt of her dress. "I promise I won't call you Chibi again."

"Uh, I don't know. I think you need to grovel a bit more."

"Is that so? What would you have me do?"

"You'll have to wait and see. How far are we from your hotel, anyway?"

We both stare at the car's GPS. We're ten minutes away from our final destination.

Still too fucking far.

7

CHIARA

Despite the red wine making my head fuzzy and the excitement rushing through my veins from being alone with Alistair, when he opens the door to his hotel room, my stomach twists in knots. I can't control the sudden shaking of my body. I've never done this before. Well, I've had hookups but with guys I already knew from school, never with a complete stranger.

Walking into the room, the first thing I see is the massive king-size bed. I swallow the lump in my throat and peel my gaze away from it. All the bravado from before disappears in a cartoonish white cloud. *Poof.* Gone. I also notice his room is immaculate. God knows the mess I make in my hotel room whenever I travel. I'm not an organized person.

"Would you like something to drink?" Alistair asks.

I turn around and shake my head. "I think I've had enough wine to last me a month."

He stares intently at me before he runs a hand through his hair and says, "Listen, we don't have to do anything. I'm more than okay if you just want to crash here. I'll drive you back to your grandparents' villa tomorrow morning."

I stop breathing for a second. *Did he change his mind?*

My expression probably shows my disappointment. He moves closer and brushes my face with a featherlight caress. "Hey, what's the matter?"

"I-I'm just nervous," I whisper as I stare at the collar of his shirt.

God, he's probably noticing the age gap now. As a matter of fact, I don't know how old he is, but he's definitely not eighteen anymore. He'd probably run for the hills if he knew my age.

"Chiara, look at me."

Taking a deep breath, I bring my face up to his, only to be ensnared by his eyes.

He laces his fingers with mine and brings my hand up to his chest. "Can you feel how fast my heart is beating for you?"

"Yes. It's beating as fast as mine."

"Why don't we just talk for a little bit?"

Shaking my head, I take a few steps back until my thighs touch the edge of the bed. Without taking my eyes off him, I reach behind me and pull my dress's zipper down, letting it drop to the floor in a heap of silk and tulle.

"I've had enough talking."

Alistair's eyes turn molten as he drops his gaze to my feet before slowly traveling up the length of my body again. In silence, he unbuttons his shirt, revealing steely abs and tattooed chest as he parts the fabric. He shrugs it off, dropping the piece of clothing to the floor. The slacks go next, but he keeps his boxer shorts on. A lump forms in my throat, because there's no hiding his size. He's huge.

He shortens the distance, stopping only when there's no gap between our bodies. Staring at my face, he runs his hands up my arms slowly, leaving a trail of goose bumps behind.

I close my eyes and say his name. It sounds more like a moan than anything else.

"Open your eyes, Chiara."

I do as he asks. He rubs his thumb over my lips, and I bring it into my mouth, sucking it gently. His breathing changes, turning shallow as his gaze becomes hooded, hungry. I realize I haven't touched him yet, so I explore his body, running my hands across his washboard abs. I glide my long nails over his taut skin, making slow circles that keep going lower and lower. When my hands reach the seam of his underwear, Alistair makes an animalistic sound in the back of his throat right before he pulls his thumb from my mouth, replacing it with his tongue.

I open to the demanding invasion as I curl my hand around his shaft. He grabs a handful of my hair to keep me in place as his feverish kiss intensifies, turning almost feral. I rub the soft tip of his cock with my thumb, spreading precum over it before going up and down his length.

Without breaking our connection, he picks me up, only to throw me on the bed in the next second. I laugh when I bounce on the soft mattress.

"Eager, aren't you?" I say.

"Sorry about that."

I scooch backward to make more room for Alistair. He joins me on the mattress, crawling my way like a jungle cat that just cornered his prey. My core throbs in anticipation. Alistair wraps his hand around my ankle, then kisses my calf. I part my legs for him as he glides his hot tongue up my shin and thigh, eliciting a moan from me. This is just the worst possible torture. And yet the best kind. He stops inches away from my underwear, sprawling his hands over each of my hip bones.

"I'm about to explode here, but I have to taste you first."

"Yes, please," I croak, my voice already raw with desire.

He rubs his nose on my center right before he licks me through the thin fabric of my lacy panties. I curl my hands around the bedcover, arching my back, the tingling sensation almost too much to bear.

"Alistair," I moan.

"Never tasted anything sweeter," he says before he pushes the fabric aside with his tongue and sucks my clit into his mouth.

Holy fuck. I won't last a minute like this.

While he sucks my nub, he teases my entrance with the tip of his finger, slowly inching his way inside. I try to control the pressure building below, wanting to prolong this amazing sensation for as long as I can, but Alistair is a magician with his tongue and fingers. I soon find myself spiraling out of control as the orgasm hits more intense than before.

"*Dio Santo*," I scream as he keeps sucking and pumping through my waves of pleasure. With one hand still sprawled over my hip, he keeps me from bucking out of his reach.

When I'm finally back into my body, it's boneless. I keep my eyes closed because I'm afraid to wake up in case this is a dream.

Alistair kisses the inside of my thigh, his scruff tickling me a little, and I try to move away.

"Are you okay?"

"Yes, more than okay." I open my eyes and see him kneeling between my legs, sporting a raging hard-on.

I lean on my elbows, and the movement makes my tits bounce inside the confinement of my bra. Alistair's gaze drops to the girls, and I panic, covering them with my arm.

He gently pushes it out of the way and caresses the skin just above the bra line. "Don't hide them from me, Chiara. They're amazing."

He's looking at my breasts like he wants to eat them up. I always thought they were too big for my petite frame, but here is Alistair, the sexiest man I've ever met, completely turned on by them.

Feeling courageous, I sit up and reach for the clasp behind my back, deftly unhooking my bra using only one hand. My girls spill free, and I get a warm feeling in the pit of my belly when Alistair's eyes turn as round as saucers.

"Fuck, you're gorgeous." He covers my mouth with his before I can protest and cups my right breast with his rough palm. I reach for his erection, resuming what I started.

He abandons my mouth to trail wet kisses down my chin, my neck, and collarbone before going straight for the kill. When his warm tongue swipes against my nipple, a shiver runs down my spine. Alistair makes lazy circles around the tight bud while I keep a steady pumping motion on his cock. I can tell he's on the verge of losing control completely. I never thought I would say this, but I love the feel of his scruff against my sensitive skin.

He lets go of my nipple with a loud, wet sound and leans back, breathing hard as if he just ran a marathon. He stares at me for a few intense beats before jumping off the bed.

"Where are you going?"

He looks over his shoulder with a smirk on his lips. "Patience, Goldilocks."

"Goldilocks?"

"Didn't you say I looked like a cuddly bear earlier today?"

I cross my arms in front of my chest and pout. "I'm not sure I like that nickname either."

Alistair laughs and heads to the bathroom, returning a few seconds later with a box of condoms in his hand.

This is it. We're really doing it.

The jitters take over again, and to hide my reaction from him, I lie back down and stare at the ceiling. I hear the sound of foil wrapping being torn, and a moment later, Alistair is between my legs again. Placing his forearms on each side of my head, he stares at me as if he's committing every detail to memory.

"You're beautiful, Goldilocks. I could stare at your face all day."

I shake my head while my fragile ego rejoices at the compliment. I bet he says that to all his conquests.

He leans closer, and I feel the tip of his erection at my entrance.

"You can say no."

I frown. "Why do you keep trying to make me give up having sex with you?"

"Because I'm damaged goods, Chiara."

I see it then, the glint of vulnerability in his gaze. Someone hurt Alistair deeply, and I feel a crazy urge to find the woman and kick her ass.

Capturing his face between my hands, I bring his lips to mine. Now it's my turn to start the assault. His tongue dances with mine, but he's still holding back. I raise my knees and cross my legs at the ankles, trapping him. He loses the battle, and with a precise push, he's inside me, filling me completely. He waits a couple of seconds, giving me time to get used to his girth before he pulls away, only to slam back inside. I would have cried out if my mouth wasn't occupied. I do manage to make some kind of sound, and Alistair asks me if I'm okay.

"Yes. Please don't stop. You feel so good."

"You're so tight. I could stay inside you forever."

He kisses me again, his tongue matching the rhythm of his hips slamming into mine. He's as good as his word and stays with me, pounding into me over and over until I have the most intense double orgasm of my life.

"That's it. Come for me, Goldi." He bites my shoulder to muffle his groan, not hard but enough to shoot a spike of pleasure down my spine.

Shuddering, he brings his face to the crook of my neck as he rides the wave of his own release. After one final thrust, he rolls off me and pulls me against his chest. We stay in that perfect lover's embrace, frozen as we wait for our shallow breathing to return to normal. I snuggle against him, closing my eyes and pretending we'll have many nights like this, even knowing I'm probably nothing more than a summer fling to him.

8

CHIARA

The morning light comes streaming through a crack in the curtains, waking me from the most peaceful night of sleep I've had in a long time. My fuzzy brain takes a few seconds to remember the events of yesterday, and Alistair comes to the forefront of my mind. My nipples pucker and my pussy clenches remembering last night.

I reach behind me but find the spot empty and cold. Frowning, I turn around and lean on my elbows. He isn't here. My heart jolts forward, twisting painfully inside my chest as my eyes begin to burn. Did he leave me?

"Alistair?"

No reply. He's not in the bathroom either. I look at his pillow, finding no note there.

I throw my legs to the side of the bed, beginning to suspect Alistair has left me. The idea brings tears to my eyes. I'm so stupid. I don't find my clothes scattered on the floor where I left them last night. At least he had the decency to pick them up and fold them before he bailed. They're in a neat pile on the chair in the corner of the room. A lonely tear rolls down my cheek—more because of shame than anything else—while I put my clothes back on with jerky movements.

I'm halfway through zipping up my dress when the door opens and Alistair enters, carrying a brown paper bag in his hand. I freeze on the spot, noticing the glint of surprise that flashes in his eyes.

"Going somewhere?" He strides across the room, setting the bag on the table before he stops in front of me. He takes note of my flushed face and wet cheeks and frowns. "Do you want to go home?"

Heat rushes to my face, and I hastily wipe the tears with the back of my hand. "I thought you bailed on me."

"You didn't see my note?" He points at my nightstand, and sure enough, there's a handwritten note there. God, I feel like an idiot.

I drop my gaze. "No. You must think I'm a drama queen now."

He places his finger under my chin, forcing me to look into his eyes. "No I don't. I shouldn't have left you alone. I went to get some breakfast, but it took longer than I expected. I'm so sorry."

His apology is heartfelt. I can read the guilt in his eyes while he keeps staring at me as if I'm about to break. Warmth spreads through my chest while my heart soars.

Don't get attached, you fool.

Curling my lips into a grin, I ask, "What did you bring? I'm famished."

He rewards me with a wide smile before turning around and pulling me with him to the table. "I got all kinds of pastries at a bakery nearby. I didn't know what you liked. I wanted to bring coffee too, but they didn't have to-go cups."

I open the bag to peer inside. "Yum. Croissants filled with Nutella, my favorite. Thanks."

I rise on my tiptoes to plant a soft peck on his lips, but he wraps an arm around my waist, keeping me in place while he deepens the kiss, his hot tongue sneaking into my mouth with focused intent. Heat pools in my core, and my legs turn to jelly. I hold on to his arms to keep from collapsing to the floor.

When Alistair pulls back, I follow him, not wanting to end this toe-curling kiss. He chuckles against my lips. "I thought you were famished."

"Suddenly, I find myself hungry for something else entirely."

He narrows his gaze as his eyes flash with a dangerous glint. Before I can say anything else, he picks me up and takes me to bed once more. I let out a yelp when he pivots and falls backward, letting me be on top of him this time. His hands skim my sides before they brush the underside of my breasts.

"I don't think I got to play with them enough last night."

Through our layers of clothing, I feel his bulging erection, so I grind my pelvis against his, trying to soothe the ache between my legs. He hisses before yanking my strapless dress down to cup my boobs.

"Somebody is naughty this morning." I curl my hands around the hem of his polo shirt, pushing the fabric out of the way so I can admire the beauty that is his torso.

Leaning forward, I run my tongue over the ridges of his abs, loving how, with each stroke Alistair seems to lose more control. His hands are now under my dress, palming my ass. Scooching backward, I finally reach the seam of his jeans and pause my ministrations to glance up.

"You're not the only one who didn't play enough last night."

"Goldilocks...."

I unzip his jeans, pulling them down eagerly, like a kid unwrapping a gift. Curling my fingers around his dick, I free it from the confines of his boxers. I lick my lips in anticipation, dying for a taste of him. Alistair leans on his elbows, and I peer at him from under my lashes. Without taking my eyes off him, I stroke the tip of his cock, tasting the saltiness of his soft skin. He moans but keeps staring at me. I tease him with my tongue again, stroking the side of his length this time before wrapping my lips around his head.

"Oh my God. That feels so good." He tangles his fingers in my hair, curling around a section and yanking it slightly.

I dive in, swallowing his entire length until the tip of his cock hits the back of my throat. Alistair's groans become louder, spurring me on, and I repeat the same movement slowly, loving the taste of him. But I can only torture him for so long at this snail's pace, and soon he starts to fuck my mouth. I curl my fingers around the base of his cock, noticing how the pumping and sucking combination drives him wild. It's intoxicating to realize I have this much power over him. I feel beautiful and sexy. He gets harder under my tongue, and I know he's moments away from coming.

He shouts my name as his warm seed fills my mouth, and I drink every single drop of it.

After his tremors subside, I let go of his still hard cock with a wet sound and stare at the expression of ecstasy on his face. His eyes are still closed when I crawl up his body to place soft kisses on his jaw. He squeezes my ass before opening his eyes to gaze at me.

"I knew you had a devious mouth, but that was fucking incredible."

"I told you I was famished." I grin like a fool, loving the compliment.

He slides his fingers down my ass, moving my panties out of the way to play with my soaking pussy.

I close my eyes and shudder. "Alistair."

"I love how wet you get for me, Chiara."

Opening my eyes again, I search the vicinity for the box of condoms, finding it on the nightstand. I stretch my arm toward it, grabbing a foil packet from inside. His cock twitches under me, and I know he's ready for round two.

"I'm riding you, cowboy."

Alistair gives me a wolfish grin right before he unhooks my bra. "Works for me, Goldilocks. I'm loving the view."

He runs his thumbs over my already hardened nipples and I shudder. I make quick work of the condom, rolling it into place before I bring the tip of his cock to my entrance. Lowering my hips, I impale myself on Alistair slowly, loving the fullness of him.

"Fuck. I can't get over how good your pussy feels wrapped around my cock."

I hum a response, clenching my internal walls as I begin to move. Alistair runs his hands down my sides, gripping my hips now, trying to increase the pace.

I grab his wrists, stopping him from trying to control things.

"Not so fast, mister. I'm in charge now."

He makes a sound that's all male, and I almost come on the spot. I bite my lower lip to keep it from happening this time. I want to make this moment last, as if I have all the time in the world. The reality is completely different though, but I banish those sappy thoughts to a dark corner in my mind. I don't want to think that today is my last day with Alistair and most likely I will never see him again. He didn't mention keeping in touch, agreeing to my stupid rule too fast.

"Goldi, you're driving me insane." He tries to fuck me from his prone position, lifting his hips to meet mine.

"You're terrible." I laugh, but I don't try to stop him. It feels too good.

I lean forward to give Alistair a long, hard kiss, loving the feel of his scruff against my face, while I let him take control down below. He grabs my tits and squeezes them hard, eliciting a loud moan from me.

"God, I'm coming," I yell as he increases the speed, kneading my breasts almost painfully before he pinches my nipples without mercy.

He lets out a guttural sound while his swollen cock throbs inside me. A few more seconds go by before the wave of our combined orgasms begins to dissipate. When they do, I fall on top of him, completely spent. My face is pressed against his shoulder. I can hardly breathe like this, but I don't care. I'm incapable of moving.

Alistair's hands are now covering my ass, but instead of squeezing it, he makes lazy circles with the tips of his fingers. His cock twitches inside me, and I know it's my signal to move. We definitely don't want an accident ruining our last day together.

I roll off and lay my head against his chest, noticing for the first time how smooth the skin is. "Why do you shave?"

"Who says I do?"

"You're not saying this is your natural look, are you?"

He chuckles, and my stomach ties in knots.

Ugh. Settle down, Chiara.

"I get too hot in the summer. Shaving my chest helps."

"What about your scruff?"

"What about it?"

"That can't be good in the summer either."

There's a noticeable pause before Alistair continues. "No, it isn't, but shaving it is out of the question."

I lean on my elbow so I can look at his face properly. "Why is that? Is it a bet?"

Alistair looks into my eyes, too serious for my liking, before he touches my cheek with his fingertips. "If I told you, I would be breaking rule number two."

I want to say I don't care about the rules anymore, that I

want to know everything about him, but it won't change the outcome. He'll still go back to the States tomorrow, leaving me behind without a glance back.

The truth is on the tip of my tongue, but I'm a coward, and the confession dies in my throat.

9

ALISTAIR

While Chiara takes a shower, I call the rental car company and explain what happened yesterday. She'd distracted me so much, I completely forgot to take care of that after we arrived at the hotel. Since the reason I got stranded in the first place was due to their negligence, they didn't give me a lot of grief for abandoning the car on the side of the road. I wrap up the call and decide to head downstairs to grab coffee for us, but this time, I let her know where I'm going before I leave.

Chiara is still in the bathroom when I return, so I pull the small gift box from inside the bakery bag. It had taken me so long to return before because I had to wait for the jewelry store to open. I had to get the bracelet before we left; otherwise, I wouldn't have had time to come back for it. I toy with the colorful packaging, considering the best time to give it to Chiara. I planned to do so during breakfast but think maybe it's best if I wait until the day is over. I'm not sure how she's going to react to it. She was the one who came up with rule number two, after all. At the time, it sounded like a smart idea. Now, I'm not so sure. I don't want to say goodbye to her.

Don't be a fucking moron, Alistair. She's young. This is just a summer adventure to her. The last thing she wants is to get involved with someone with enough baggage to fill a commercial plane.

I put the box away when I hear the door to the bathroom open. Chiara walks back into the room with an uncertain glint shining in her eyes, as if finding me sitting at the table waiting for her is unsettling. She joins me with hair still damp and smelling of soap. My cock awakens, and I send a silent order to it to calm the fuck down. It's no use. I want to strip her naked again and feast on her body. But if I do that, I'm afraid we'll never leave this hotel room.

"Oh, you found coffee." She eyes the Styrofoam cups.

"Yeah. I didn't know how you took yours, so I went stereotypical and got you a cappuccino."

Chiara leans over and kisses me softly on the lips. "That's perfect. Thank you."

When she pulls back, I follow, catching myself at the last minute. We're not starting this again.

Focus, Alistair. You do want to visit some vineyards today, don't you?

That was one of the reasons for this trip, to get ideas for my parents' vineyard business. It had been their dream to own a vineyard after retirement, and I was able to make it happen. Now I want to make sure it's a successful venture. My parents sacrificed so much for me, so it's the least I can do. It's too bad I couldn't visit the Della Vecchia vineyard—my lawyer, Enzo, said their wine is phenomenal. But I got to spend the weekend with Chiara instead, so I'm not too disappointed.

Somehow, I manage to control my urges and eat breakfast. In between bites, Chiara asks, "Where do you want to go today?"

"Well, I've already seen Siena, so I thought maybe we could head to San Gimignano and then Pisa."

Chiara smiles at me, her eyes twinkling. "Who can resist the charm of Val d'Orcia, right?"

I laugh. "That tagline was actually in a tour brochure."

"I bet. Did it go something like this? 'Who can resist the charm of Val d'Orcia, where locals and tourists stop every day to take a billion photos? The full-day tour will introduce to you not only the towns of X, Y, and Z but also the wine and local flavors,'" she says, going heavy on the Italian accent.

"You're cute."

Her delicate eyebrows scrunch together at the same time as she pouts. "I'm not cute."

"Right. You're not cute. You're sexy as hell."

Her bright blue eyes widen a fraction. "Do you really think so?"

Does she not know the effect she has on me? My cock is at full mast now, straining against my jeans. *Fuck me.* We need to get out of here fast before I have Chiara on her back again with my cock plunged deep inside her sweet pussy.

"God, yes. I would show you, but we really have to go. Are you ready?" My voice comes out strained.

With a smirk, she drinks the last sips of her coffee before wiping her mouth with the napkin.

"Yup."

When she stands up, my attention diverts to her party dress. Guilt sneaks up on me. "We could stop by your grandparents' villa for you to change clothes."

Chiara's expression immediately turns dark. "No. It's out of the way. The dress is fine. I wouldn't mind buying ballerina flats though. These Gucci shoes aren't the best for a touristic outing."

She eyes the high-heeled footwear, and I wince in sympathy. They look like a torture device.

CHIARA FOUND MORE comfortable shoes at a small boutique in the hotel. I paid for them, despite her protests, but I wouldn't back down on that.

"Doesn't your cousin need his car back?" I ask her once we're inside the vehicle.

"Nah. I bet he'll be nursing a hangover by the pool the whole day. Besides, there are plenty of cars he can borrow if he needs to go somewhere."

Chiara insists we don't need the GPS since she knows the area well, so I gladly let her be my guide. Her sexy voice is much better anyway. Instead of leading me toward the most direct path to our first destination, she takes me on a scenic drive through the hills of the Tuscan countryside.

We stop by one of the many Chianti vineyards first, where we take a stroll among grapevines, olive groves, and wine cellars before partaking in a traditional Tuscan lunch, which consists of more cured meats and delicious bread. When asked where we wanted to sit, there was no question about outside, despite the high temperature. How could we deprive ourselves of the breathtaking view of the Sienese hills? I honestly could stay here forever, but not because of the scenery or the food. The company is everything. I've caught myself staring at Chiara several times when she was distracted, and every single time, there's been a sharp twist in my chest.

I'm a grown man. I shouldn't be feeling whatever the hell I'm feeling, but fuck if I'm not getting drunk on this euphoria.

We head to San Gimignano next, where we roam the maze of cobbled streets and small squares. Chiara insists we grab a gelato before we walk between San Gimignano's famous fourteen towers.

The final stop is Pisa, and I go full-on tourist mode there, taking several pictures while pretending to be holding the leaning tower.

The day goes by too fast, and when we're on our way back

to Siena, I can't help but feel a little glum. I turn to Chiara, finding her staring out the window.

"Did you have fun today?" I ask.

She glances at me and smiles, but it doesn't reach her eyes. "Yes, loads. I'll remember this day forever."

"Me too." I reach for her hand, bringing it to my lips to kiss the back of it. "Spend the evening with me in Florence."

"What?" Her big doe eyes turn as round as saucers.

"My flight doesn't leave until the afternoon. I can bring you back in the morning."

She blinks a couple of times before she shakes her head. "Are you sure that's what you want?"

Chiara's doubtful tone almost makes me stop the car so I can show her how much I want to spend another evening with her. This has nothing to do with the amazing sex. I don't want to say goodbye just yet. I'm not ready.

"Yes it is. You don't want to? You won't hurt my feelings if you say no."

Bullshit.

Her breathing seems to stop. She bites her lower lip, really making me want to pull the car over.

"Okay. Why not? I love Florence."

Fuck yeah. I can't help the smile that appears on my face. My heart is going a hundred miles an hour. I feel like a fucking teenager who just asked the girl of his dreams out and she said yes.

I wish I was younger and didn't have this rotten crap fucking up my life. I'm not even officially divorced yet, and at the rate things are going, it will be a long and nasty process. I can't bring Chiara into that mess. Shit, if it weren't for that, I would say to hell with rule number two and beg to know everything about her. But that's not the case, and wishful thinking is just a waste of time.

After returning to the hotel in Siena to collect my stuff, I ask Chiara what we should do about Max's car.

"He won't mind if we borrow it for another night. Besides, I need a car to get back to the villa."

I'm not crazy about this arrangement. I hate taking advantage of anyone, so I ask Chiara to call her cousin regardless. She does so with a roll of her eyes, putting the conversation on speaker so I can hear the answer from the horse's mouth.

"Yeah, man. It's cool to keep the car for another day. It gives me the perfect excuse to borrow my uncle's Ferrari," Max says.

Chiara gives me a haughty look that says "I told you so" before taking the call off speaker mode and walking away to continue her conversation in private.

I watch her for a few seconds, noticing how tense she becomes. She keeps her voice low, even though I wouldn't understand what she's saying anyway. A couple of minutes later, she rejoins me, but the smile on her face is forced.

"Is everything okay?"

"As okay as it can be when my mother is involved. But let's not talk about her. That would break rule number one, anyway."

I reach out, pulling her into my arms to kiss the crook of her neck. When she melts against my chest, a sense of protectiveness takes hold of me. I wrap my arms around her body tightly, and I can't help thinking how right this moment feels.

Chiara pulls away first and stares into my eyes.

"Are you ready to go?"

"Yes."

The drive to Florence takes roughly one hour. When I pull in front of the centuries-old Antica Torre di via Tornabuoni hotel, I'm glad I decided to splurge. Besides comfort and a convenient location, it's as romantic as it gets—not that I was thinking about that when I made the reservation.

"*Mamma mia,*" Chiara says before looking down at her

clothes. "You know, as much as I love this dress, I think I'm ready for a change of outfit."

"Ah, Goldilocks, we should have stopped by the villa so you could grab your stuff."

"Are you crazy? That would have meant dealing with my mother sooner than I intended. I'm going to check out the stores nearby." She gets out of the car.

"Hey, I'll come with you," I say, following suit.

"You want to come shopping with me?" The question comes with an eyebrow raise.

"What? Is that so hard to believe?"

"Yes." She laughs, a sound so rich, it's infectious.

I break the distance between us, looping my arm around her waist and stopping inches from her face to run my thumb over her lips. "Okay, I won't enjoy it. Maybe I'm just afraid you'll take off and not come back."

"You're afraid I'm going to bail on you?" Her voice comes out as a breathless whisper.

"Yes, I am." I rub my lips against hers, dying for another taste.

She puts her hands on my chest, pushing me back. There's a deep V between her eyebrows, marring her lovely face. "The last thing I want to do is run away from you... unless we're role-playing. I'm Little Red Riding Hood and you're the Big Bad Wolf chasing me." Her lips twist into a grin.

"So, first you call me a bear, and now you want me to play the wolf? What's up with your obsession with wild animals?"

"I'm not obsessed!" She hits me playfully on the chest. "And first of all, I didn't call you a bear. I said you were a cuddly bear. Very different. But it was a bad a nickname. The Big Bad Wolf fits you better. Or maybe big bear."

"Gee, thanks?" I laugh. "Let me bring the bags to our room." I tug her hand, but she plants her feet on the ground.

"Uh-uh. I'm not coming upstairs with you. We might not

leave the room, and frankly, I'm starving. I'll ask the concierge to make us dinner reservations."

"You'd better be here when I come back."

She steps away from me with a wicked smile on her lips. "Hmm, I don't know. Maybe I'll find another hopeless tourist who needs my assistance."

I take a step forward while a guttural sound comes from the back of my throat.

"Easy there, big bear. I was just teasing." She spins around and swishes away into the hotel.

This girl has me ensnared, hook, line, and sinker. I follow her, not liking one bit the way the men in the hotel's lobby twist their necks to watch her walk by. I increase my steps and throw my arm around her shoulders, kissing her soundly on her cheek, marking my territory even though she's not mine.

She laughs at my enthusiasm, turning her face to mine and kissing me deeply. Dropping my duffel bag to the floor, I hold her closer and fuck her mouth with my tongue. I don't know how long we stay glued like two horny teenagers in the middle of the five-star hotel lobby. One thing is certain, I would have kissed Chiara longer if she hadn't pulled away first. She stares at me with swollen lips and hooded eyes, and I want to throw her over my shoulder and bring her to our room. I'm about to explode in my pants.

Shit, this girl turns me on like no one else.

"Me, dinner reservation. You, get us checked in." She steps out of my embrace, almost running toward the concierge desk.

I watch her leave like a lovesick puppy, wondering when the hell lust turned into something more.

When I return to the hotel lobby ten minutes later—I had to take care of my raging boner first—I find Chiara waiting for me and wearing a new dress. She stands up as soon as she sees me, and I track the length of her body, taking her in. The simple black dress she's wearing wraps around her like a glove, accentuating every single edge and curve, leaving me breathless.

"Do you like it?"

"I thought you were going to wait for me to go shopping."

"I was bored." She shrugs.

I step into her personal space and kiss her softly, whispering against her mouth, "I love it." Before I get carried away again, I step back. "Where are we going?"

"You'll see."

We skip the big tourist restaurants and go to a quaint side street mom-and-pop establishment so small, it only has four tables inside.

"This is the smallest restaurant I've ever been to," I say.

"It's one of the best restaurants in Florence and almost impossible to get reservations last minute. We got lucky."

Chiara orders *aperitivo* for each of us, which consists of a glass of prosecco accompanied by three small snacks. She hasn't led me astray so far. I trust her choices. Plus, I love seeing the confidence in her. It beguiles me.

"Do you have any plans for the rest of the summer?" I ask casually.

"Uh, yeah. Stay the hell away from my family." She laughs and shakes her head. "Actually, I'm going to Ibiza with a couple of friends next month."

"I heard it's a beautiful island."

"Yes, but we're mostly hitting the clubs," she replies, distracted as she nibbles on her snack while a spike of jealousy pierces my chest. Clubs mean other guys. Meat markets.

I finish drinking the prosecco and signal for the waiter to bring me another one. I would prefer something much stronger, but I don't think they have whiskey here.

"How about you?" she asks.

"Nothing as exciting."

Chiara furrows her eyebrows, and I realize my answer came across a bit standoffish.

I reach across the table and curl my fingers around her hand. "This has been one of the best weekends I've had in a long time. I'm glad the rental company screwed up."

She drops her gaze and stares at our joined hands for a couple of beats in silence. When she finally looks up, I notice her eyes are brighter than before while her lips pull into a tight smile.

"This has been a great weekend for me too. I'm sad it's almost over."

"We still have tonight."

Chiara raises her glass. "To tonight."

10

CHIARA

I've gone and done it. I have fallen in love with Alistair in less than twenty-four hours. That must be a world record. And the worst part is I don't know anything about him, so the swirling feeling inside my chest defies logic.

After we dive into a delicious homemade lasagna, we stroll back to our hotel along the river that flows through the heart of Florence, stopping to perch on the wall of one of the bridges along with locals to watch the sun go down. This all feels like a dream, but I know eventually I'll have to wake up.

The room he got is more opulent than I could have imagined, and it makes me wonder what he does for a living to be able to afford such luxury. It doesn't really matter to me though. I can testify that money means nothing, and it most certainly can't buy anyone happiness. You just have to look closely at my miserable family to see that.

I sit on the edge of the bed, and suddenly I don't know what to do. I'm afraid if he pays attention, he'll read the yearning in my eyes.

Alistair stops a little away from me, and he seems as unsure as I am. Does he also feel the shift in the air?

Impossible.

The hunger in his gaze is undeniable, and my body reacts accordingly. My heart is drumming so loudly inside my chest, it seems it wants to take flight. Heat pools between my legs just from thinking about what's to come.

Slowly, Alistair unbuttons his shirt without taking his eyes off me. The jeans go next. I remain frozen. Watching him strip is damn sexy and a little frightening too. I feel so out of my depth.

I swallow hard when he stands in front of me in all his naked glory. He's Adonis personified. His abs look Photoshopped. I know they aren't though. I've felt the hard ridges of his muscles under my fingers; I've tasted their raw power.

Slowly, Alistair crosses the room, dropping to his knees in front of me. Placing his warm hands on my thighs, he makes lazy circles over my skin with his fingertips. I forget how to breathe.

"Chiara," he says almost reverently before he pushes my dress up my legs, the fabric bunching up around my waist.

When his face gets closer to my pussy and his warm breath fans over the sensitive skin, I almost climax right then and there. Without removing my underwear, he rubs his nose over my clit, the friction too good to describe. I thread my fingers through his hair, grabbing at the strands.

"Alistair...."

"What, Goldilocks?"

"If you keep at it, I'm going to come."

"There's nothing wrong with that." He darts his tongue out, sweeping over my nub in one languid stroke.

A whimper escapes my lips, and Alistair laughs.

"I love the sounds you make."

I know he didn't mean anything by it, but I still tense up upon hearing the word "love." Alistair must have sensed it because he stops to look at me.

"Is everything okay?" he asks.

Not wanting him to see the angst in my eyes, I pull the dress over my head, tossing it to the side before getting rid of the bra. My plan works, and his gaze quickly drops to my chest. Like a kid presented with a buffet of candy, he reaches out to the girls with eager hands, kneading them before playing with my tight nipples. He pushes my body gently onto the massive bed and leans over me, bringing one nipple to his hot mouth while his hand plays with the other.

I don't know how long he spends lavishing my breasts with attention, but when he finally brings his face level to mine, I'm so close to the edge, one simple nudge will be enough to send me spiraling over.

He must have read the raw need in my gaze because he quickly jumps off the bed to retrieve a condom from the box on the nightstand. I've never seen a guy put protection on so fast in my life. Before I know it, Alistair is back between my legs. He brings one of them over his shoulder, rubbing the head of his cock against my entrance.

"Just a warning, Goldi. I might not be gentle," he says gruffly.

"Good. Don't."

He enters me with a swift move, and I get lost in oblivion.

ALISTAIR and I have sex three times before he collapses next to me, dead to the world. I, on the other hand, can't fall asleep at all and decide to get out of bed just before sunrise. I pick up my clothes and put them on as quietly as I can, not wanting to wake him.

Once fully dressed, I take a moment to stare at Alistair's sleeping form, committing every detail of his body to memory —the wide shoulders corded with muscles and the sexy ass that I made sure to scratch a little last night. But most importantly, I pay close attention to his face, partially hidden in the manner he's sleeping, on his belly with one arm folded under his pillow. His expression is peaceful and vulnerable at the same time.

It's hard not to caress his cheek, not to place a farewell kiss on his lips. But I can't risk waking him up. I refuse to stay to say goodbye because I'm afraid if I do, I'll beg him for more. It wasn't part of the agreement. The rules don't seem that important now, but I can't get past the fear that he'll reject me if I break them. So I won't.

11

CHIARA

After leaving Alistair in the silence of early morning, I don't return to Villa Moretti. Most likely, everyone has headed home, and I must do the same to deal with my mother's fury sooner rather than later.

I'm surprised she didn't call me while I was with Alistair. Her silence doesn't bode well. It means she's thinking of a punishment that will hurt me deeply. I don't regret my actions though. Spending the weekend with Alistair is something I will never forget. I connected with him on a deeper level than I ever thought was possible with any man, especially a stranger. I erroneously believed that this kind of rapport could only be built with time.

My heart is heavy when I park in front of my parents' upscale building in Porta Romana. It's lunchtime, and I hope Mom is out, eating with her snobby friends. But no sooner do I step out of the elevator onto my floor than I can hear Mom's raised voice. She's having an argument with Dad, and I bet a million euros it's about me.

Taking a deep breath, I unlock the door and walk in. From the entry foyer, I can't see much of the apartment, but if I could hear my mother's voice in the hallway, my parents must be in the living room.

"Chiara, is that you?" my father asks.

"No, it's a burglar here to rob you in broad daylight."

With heavy steps and a heavier heart, I join them in the living room. Mom is standing, cradling a glass of whiskey in her hand. Her eyes spark with fury when they land on me.

"Where the hell have you been?" she asks.

"Spending the weekend with a friend. Max told you, didn't he?"

Mom laughs without humor. "Do you mean slutting around with that American savage you found in the middle of the road?"

"Alistair is not a savage," I grit out. "He has more class than you, Paola, and that weasel husband of hers."

Mom takes a step forward. "How dare you speak to me that way?"

Dad stands up from his chair, getting between us. "Darling, calm down." He turns to me. "Chiara, apologize to your mother. That was uncalled for."

"Uncalled for? She's the one who called me a slut."

He pinches the bridge of his nose. "This silly war between you two is going to send me to an early grave."

Dad believes my fights with Mom are because we're too stubborn and similar. He couldn't be more wrong. We argue because Mom is a bully, and if I don't fight her from time to time, she'll crush me until I can't get up anymore.

"I'm sorry, Dad. You know Paola and I never got along. I didn't think she wanted me around, and, well, I figured no one would miss me at the reception."

"Sweetie, of course you were missed," he replies with kind eyes.

"Don't you dare go soft on Chiara now, Giovanni. She took off without a word to spend the weekend with a stranger. And she did that under our noses. How can we know she won't do something worse living alone in America?"

A sliver of fear pierces my chest.

"I've never done anything reckless like that in my entire life."

"So *you* say. Those are not the stories I've heard."

I ball my hands into fists, digging my nails into the softness of my palms until it hurts. "Whatever rumors you heard are all lies."

Her lips curl in a wicked grin. "Where there's smoke, there's fire. And your actions this past weekend only reinforce that. Your trip to California is canceled. You'll complete your final year of high school here in Milan where I can keep an eye on you."

"What? You can't do that." My eyes fill with angry tears. "Do you know how hard it is to be accepted at DuBose High? It has one of the best programs in the country for anyone interested in a career in the film industry."

"You should have thought about that before you pulled your latest stunt."

I turn to Dad. "Did you agree with this?"

"Chiara, perhaps you should stay. I don't want to worry about you while you are miles away from us."

"This is such bullshit. You know I'm responsible. I'm the top student at All Saints."

"I know, *tesoro.*"

Fuck. I knew Mom would aim for the punishment that hurt me the most, but I didn't think she'd convince Dad to not let me attend DuBose in California. I've been looking forward to it since I started high school.

Nothing I can say will convince him to change his decision now that Mom poisoned his mind against me. There's only one person who might have a shot, the one who triggered my flight response and sent me straight into Alistair's loving arms.

Pietro.

I head to my room, locking the door to avoid an invasion by my mother. Then I call Pietro, hoping he's not too distracted on his honeymoon.

He answers on the third ring. "Chiara, are you okay?"

"I'm fine."

"I was so worried about you. You disappeared and... I know it was all my fault."

"What you did was shit, Pietro."

"I'm so terribly sorry. You were right. What I did was caused by pre-wedding jitters."

"It doesn't change the fact that you kissed me."

"Please, Chiara. I beg you. Don't tell anyone that."

"I won't, but you need to do something for me."

"Anything."

"My father wants to cancel my trip to the States because of what happened this weekend. You need to tell him why I bailed from the wedding."

"What do you mean I have to tell him? You mean the truth?"

"Yes, Pietro. The truth."

"Chiara, I can't do that."

"It's either you confess to my father, knowing he won't tell a soul, or I tell everyone."

I'm hoping Pietro is dumb enough to not realize my word means nothing in my family.

"What if your father decides to tell Paola?"

"He won't. I'll make sure of it."

I wait with bated breath for his answer. If Pietro calls my bluff, I can say goodbye to California.

He sighs deeply. "All right, Chiara. I'll do it."

12

ALISTAIR

Two months later

I loosen my tie as I stride out of the brick building where the meeting with the mediator took place. What a waste of time. I couldn't sit in that room face-to-face with Nadine and listen to her five-hundred-dollar-an-hour lawyer try to convince the mediator that the bitch deserved half the vineyard I gave to my parents for their fortieth anniversary. He said I had no right to make such a gift without her signature on the deed, never mind that we had a fucking prenup in place.

My phone vibrates in my pocket, and sure enough, it's my lawyer calling. I send the call to voice mail. I don't want to talk to him either. I tried my best to keep things out of court, but Nadine is asking for it. She thinks my need for privacy will make me do anything to keep the sordid details of our divorce from reaching the press.

I snort loudly. That boat sailed a long time ago when I made the mistake of marrying her, a B-movie actress.

It doesn't matter anyway. Word on the street is she's looking for someone to sell her sappy story to. I can't think of anyone who would be interested in such garbage, but stranger things have happened, and this is Hollywood, after all.

It's my damn fault anyway. I should have left this dreadful town when I had the chance.

Grumbling, I get into my truck and text Lance, one of my oldest buddies from college, hoping he can meet me at the gym today. I need a good workout to get rid of the tension.

ME: Want to hit the tatami in twenty?

A minute later, he fires back.

LANCE: Fuck yeah. Just got out of a board meeting. I'm ready to punch something.

ME: Good. See you in a few.

I toss the phone aside, and with the click of a button, the engine comes to life and Breaking Benjamin blares through the speakers. I increase the volume, feeling the sound of bass and drums reverberate through my chest. As I tap the steering wheel in sync with the song, I wonder if Chiara would like this type of music.

Shit. Here I go again thinking about her. To be honest, there hasn't been a day since I returned from Italy that her image hasn't invaded my mind. I haven't been able to hook up with any other woman since either. I'm one of the few people who doesn't do social media, and it's the only reason I haven't searched for her yet. It's a good thing. She snuck out of that hotel room in Florence without a word or note for a reason. I have to respect that.

By the time I arrive at Ginga, a gym and martial arts center owned by another good friend of mine, I'm ready to do some damage. I have to get back to work on Monday, and if I don't get rid of this pent-up aggression, I don't know how I'll be able to do my job without ripping someone's head off.

It's close to lunchtime, so the gym is already packed. Most of the weight lifting machines are in use, and there's already a group of guys waiting to take their turn in the boxing ring. I veer toward the back of the gym, where the martial arts practice room is. When there isn't a class in session, this becomes a private room for Caio—the owner of this place—and his closest friends.

The door is wide open, and before venturing in, I can already hear the grunts and the muffled sound of flesh pounding against a punching bag. Lance is there, covered in sweat.

"How the hell did you beat me here?"

"I was on my way when you texted," he answers without stopping his routine of kicks and punches.

"Is Caio joining us?"

"I don't know. Haven't seen him today."

Shrugging, I head to the locker room to change. When I return, Lance has already moved on to solo exercises. I need to warm up first before I can engage him in hand-to-hand combat. Lance is a fucking beast on the tatami, fast as a cobra. The only person he can't beat is Caio, but the Brazilian is a legend.

It doesn't matter that most likely I'll have my ass handed to me today. As long as I can get some punches in, I'll be happy.

I take my frustration out on the punching bag, hitting that motherfucker as hard as I can. My muscles protest at first, but as I get into the zone, I don't even feel the pain. Time ceases to exist. I keep picturing myself from seven years ago, when I was dumb enough to fall for Nadine's bullshit. By the time exertion slows me down, I notice Caio has joined us.

The distraction costs me, and I'm hit in the face by the punching bag when I fail to stop its swinging motion. Pain explodes in my nose. With a grunt, I take a few steps back, woozy from the hit.

"Are you okay there, man?" Caio asks.

"Peachy."

I take a seat on the nearest bench, hanging my head

between my shoulders. Blood drips from my nose. *Fucking fantastic.* I hope it's not broken.

"Let me guess. The meeting with the mediator went as bad as I said it would?" Lance chimes in.

Without raising my head, I flip him off. Lance *did* warn me that the meeting would be a waste of time, but I'm really not in the mood to listen to his I-told-you-so speech.

"Thank fuck I'm single," Caio adds.

"I really didn't come here to talk about relationships." I look up to glare at my friends.

Caio narrows his eyes before his lips curl into a grin.

Ah fuck. I know that expression.

He waves me over. "Come on, Ali-boy. Let's see whatcha got."

Lance chuckles, something I rarely see him do. "Oh, this will be good."

I'm taller than Caio by a couple of inches, packing more pounds of muscle too. But that doesn't mean shit on the tatami. He's way more agile and precise than I am, which means in the next half hour, I spend more time flat on my back than landing blows.

"What's the matter with you, Alistair? It's like you're not even trying." Caio circles me with as much energy as when we started, I'm already winded. Fuck, I need to do more cardio.

Letting out a roar, I aim for the side of his head. Caio easily sidesteps me, sticking out his right leg to trip me. I don't fall this time, pivoting on the spot and, by some miracle, managing to keep my balance.

Lance chuckles from the bench, and I turn to him, missing the roundhouse kick aimed in my direction. The blow hits me directly in the face, knocking me down.

"Goddamn it, Alistair. Pay attention," Caio yells somewhere nearby, but with the ringing in my ears, I can't pinpoint his exact location.

Rolling on my back, I focus on my breathing as I stare at the ceiling. Dark spots fill my line of vision, and then Caio's face appears.

"Are you okay?" he asks.

"I'll live."

He offers me his hand and drags my sorry ass back up.

"I'm gonna have a massive bruise in a few hours, won't I?" I continue.

"Yep, sorry, man. You should never lose your focus during a fight."

The way the jiujitsu master keeps staring at me with a deep frown tells me he's more annoyed than sorry.

"Maybe your friend will finally decide to fire your ass," Lance says.

I groan before answering. "Unlikely."

"I don't get why you don't quit if you hate it so much." Caio shakes his head.

"I don't hate it, but I'm not as invested in teaching as I was before. I made a promise to Forrester that I'd stay another year, and I never back down on my word."

Both Caio and Lance watch me through narrowed eyes, probably not buying my story. It's not a lie, but it's also not the complete truth either.

John Forrester, DuBose's principal, was there for me in my darkest hour. His friendship saved me from going down a path that probably would have destroyed me in the end. I won't turn my back on him now.

13

CHIARA

I take a deep breath as I stand in front of the DuBose building, one of the most prestigious high schools in LA. It's a dream come true for anyone who wants a career in show business. The list of alumni includes top celebrities in Hollywood, from actors, directors, to movie studios' VIPs. I'm tempted to pinch myself to make sure I'm not dreaming.

Pietro came through after my little chat with him. He fessed up to my father that he was responsible for me running away. Dad was furious, wanted to punch the prick's face, but I was able to convince him to let things go. All that mattered to me was being allowed to study in LA, which he agreed would be for the best, much to my mother's chagrin.

I head in, not minding one bit that I don't know anyone here. That means they don't know me either. I receive curious glances as I go, but they aren't followed by malicious comments.

The email I received from administration told me a student would show me around before class starts. I'm supposed to meet him at the principal's office. I follow the signs until I turn a corner and find not only the office but also a tall ginger leaning next to the door with his eyes glued to his phone.

He glances up when I walk over. "Are you Chiara Moretti?"

"Yes, that's me."

He offers me his hand. "Robert Donovan. You can call me Robbie."

"Nice to meet you, Robbie."

He drops his eyes to my shoes and smiles. "Ah, you didn't disappoint me. Prada?"

It takes me a moment to grasp what he's asking me. I look at my shoes too, and then it hits me. "Yeah. How did you know?"

"I'm obsessed with fashion. *Project Runway*? Life. I want to be a designer for A-listers."

"That's cool."

"What about you? Why did you come to DuBose?"

"I want to work in the filmmaking business, though in what capacity I don't know yet."

"Not an actress?"

I twist my face into a scowl. "God no. I'd be a horrible actress."

He shrugs. "You have the face though. You look like a fresh Scarlett Johansson but way prettier."

His compliment makes me blush. "Thanks."

"All right. First, let me see what classes you have."

I pull my cell phone out, and after a few clicks, I show him my schedule.

"Oh, we have creative writing together, yay. And AP math. Meh. Those are back to back, by the way, and first and second periods. I don't need to show you their location right now, as you'll come with me." He pauses for a second and then continues. "We also have the same lunch period. Awesome. I'll introduce you to everyone who's worth knowing in this school."

"Uh, thanks?"

He lifts his gaze from my phone. "God, am I being awful by

saying that? My mothers always tell me I'm too blunt. I guess it's a Gemini thing. What's your sign?"

I'm still caught on the plural mother thing, so it takes me a moment to reply, "Aries. I'm an Aries. My birthday is April 14."

His lips widen into a bright smile. "Perfect. Aries and Gemini get along fabulously."

"I trust you. I don't really follow the horoscope."

"Girl, you should." He returns his attention to my phone, and after a moment, he says, "Okay, so we have four classes together and lunch. Are you good in math, physics, and biology, by any chance?"

"Yeah, I'd say so."

He presses his hand to his chest in a dramatic fashion and glances up. "Thank you, Lord. I'll be forever grateful."

His antics make me laugh. "What was that?"

He returns my phone. "One thing to know about me. I'm the shit when it comes to fashion, arts, and such. Exact sciences? Not so much. We're in math, physics, and biology together, which means you got yourself a side of rice."

"A what?"

"A side of rice." He shakes his head. "It's a Brazilian thing. Basically, I'll be stuck to you like glue, but I'll never be more than a side of rice to your steak because I only drink one type of wine and you're not it."

"That's an elaborate way to say you're gay."

"I know. What can I say? It gets boring after a while."

"Are you Brazilian?"

"One of my mothers is."

"Cool. I love Brazil. I've been to Rio and Salvador."

His eyebrows shoot to the heavens. "Shut up! My mother is from Salvador. You need to come for dinner. She'll love you. By the way, where are you staying?"

"At an apartment a block from here. The school helped me out."

"Oh, you're at Brandywine Hall, right?"

"Yeah."

"A lot of out-of-town students live there. That's cool. There have been some epic parties in that building. If the walls could talk." He shakes his head, laughing. "We'd better get started with this tour or we'll be late for class."

GOOD ON HIS WORD, at lunch break, Robbie introduces me to a bunch of people. Trying to memorize all their names is impossible though, even when I apply the trick of repeating their names back.

We grab our food from the cafeteria and then head out to eat at the beautiful park next to the school building. A couple of Robbie's friends from the drama program are waiting for us under the shade of a big oak tree.

"How do you like school so far, Chiara?" a freckled guy wearing thick-rimmed glasses asks me.

"I love it." I take a bite of my sandwich.

"Even AP math with Mr. Snoozeville?" The girl sitting next to me raises an eyebrow.

I laugh. "Even him. He wasn't that boring."

"Only because you're an ace in the subject," Robbie replies.

"What do you have after lunch?" the girl asks.

"Study hall and then writer's room elective. I'm really excited about that."

"Oh, that's cool," the freckled guy pipes up, and then he reaches inside his backpack. "Look what Mom sent, guys."

"Brownies!" the girl exclaims excitedly. "Those are the best. Gimme it."

He pulls the plastic container away from her greedy hands. "Wait. Chiara first since she's new here."

I shake my head. "Oh, I don't know. Eating sugar now would probably make me sleepy."

"Drink a shot of espresso," Robbie chimes in. "You need to eat one of these brownies. They melt in your mouth."

"All right. Twist my arm, why don't you?" I grab the smallest piece from the box and then take a bite. "Fudge. This is really good."

"Told ya." Robbie smirks and then grabs a piece too.

I devour my brownie in three huge bites, regretting going for the smaller piece. But I won't be a glutton and take another one.

Ten minutes later, we go back inside. Robbie and his friends head to their respective classes, and I go to the library to get some reading done and check my emails. I forget to buy coffee before, but I feel fine, which is surprising. Maybe I'll get sleepy later.

It's not until I have five minutes left of study hall that I begin to feel strange. I'm light-headed, and the library seems to be spinning out of control.

What the hell?

I think it's time for that coffee after all.

I pack my things, and when I stand up, I almost fall on my ass. Bracing my hands on the desk, I take deep breaths, waiting for the dizzy spell to pass.

It helps a little, and I manage to walk out of the library without kissing the floor. But once in the hallway, things become worse. I keep seeing everything double. I flatten my back against the wall and text Robbie.

ME: What the hell were in those brownies?

ROBBIE: Nothing. Why?

ME: I'm seeing double, FFS.

I wait for his response, getting more panicked by the second. Finally, the three dots appear.

ROBBIE: Harold thinks you might have eaten one of his special brownies by accident.

Porca miseria!

I have several choice words that I'd like to yell at Robbie and Harold, but that wouldn't make me suddenly sober.

ME: I have writer's room now. What am I going to do?

ROBBIE: Wear sunglasses and try to not draw attention to yourself.

Great. My first day of school and I managed to get high by accident.

Disaster seems to follow me wherever I go. Fate must hate me.

At least I know nothing will top that.

14

CHIARA

In my current state, it takes double the time to get to writer's room class, which happens to take place on the other side of the building. *Why not make my life more difficult, right?*

When I finally stop in front of my destination, I find the door shut because class has already started. I pull my sunglasses down and take a deep breath, hoping I can walk in without drawing too much attention. I open the door slowly, cringing when the hinges creak loudly. *Merda!*

This is an auditorium-style classroom, rather large for high school. This must be a popular class. I hug the wall, striding up the stairs without looking at the front of the room. I spot an empty seat in the last row, and I'm halfway there when the teacher's booming voice makes me stop in my tracks.

"I expect all my students to be punctual. Next time you're late, head straight to the principal's office."

My heart begins to drum madly inside my chest.

Holy shit. I know that voice.

No, it can't be. I must be hallucinating thanks to the magic brownie.

Pushing my sunglasses up my forehead, I turn slowly.

I wasn't imagining things. It's Alistair. He's writing something on the whiteboard and turns around a second later. When our gazes connect, I have to lock my knees tight to avoid collapsing to the floor. My legs have turned to jelly. The scruff, the intense gaze, it's all there, just as I remember.

Madonna Santa. Alistair is my teacher. And he now knows I'm still in high school.

I can't move. I can barely breathe. All I'm able to do is stare at him. His lips are slightly parted as he pins me with his gaze. It's like time has suddenly stopped. Memories of our time in Italy invade my brain, more vivid than ever. I want to do something, run into his arms, kiss him, but that's impossible. I spent so many nights wishing he would come back into my life. But not like this. What a cruel joke.

Somebody clears his throat, snapping me out of my stupor.

"I'm sorry I'm late. I got lost," I lie.

Without waiting for his reply, I continue my track up the steps until I reach the last row and practically collapse on the seat I had been aiming for. My neighbor fidgets next to me, but I don't look in his direction to ask what his problem is.

"Please make sure it doesn't happen again," Alistair finally replies.

He returns to business as usual, going on with his lecture as if everything is fine. Maybe to him it is, but fine is the complete opposite of what I'm feeling right now. I'm a mess on steroids. Or maybe it's just the brownie. But hell, by the end of the class, I have no fucking idea what Alistair said. I've missed it all.

The guy next to me taps his pencil on my desk, and I almost jump. "Shit, you scared me."

"Sorry. I just wanted to know if you would like to pair up for next week's assignment."

I stare at him like a moron as if I forgot how to speak. *Okay, I'm never touching a fucking brownie again.*

"Sure. Only if you tell me exactly what we're supposed to be doing."

"Having a rough day, huh?" He smirks.

Fuck. Can he tell I'm high? My face becomes hot from embarrassment. Despite all the rumors about me, I don't do shit like this.

"Something like that."

He stares at me for a couple of beats without saying anything, making me hella uncomfortable. I'm tempted to put my sunglasses back on my face.

"So, the assignment?" I press.

He blinks a couple of times. "Right. It's simple. Select three scripts of our choice and do a deep analysis."

"Ah, that's cool," I say absentmindedly.

I'm still reeling from the fact that Alistair is the teacher in this semester's elective class. I picked writer's room thinking it'd be a fun subject. I couldn't have foreseen my life was about to become worthy of its own screenplay.

"I'm Josh, by the way."

"Chiara. Nice to meet you."

He smiles, revealing small dimples on his cheeks. The pre-Alistair Chiara would have melted on the spot—dimples are my weakness—but it seems Alistair ruined all men for me.

Pulling his cell phone from his backpack, Josh asks for my number. We make plans to meet the next day to work on our assignment.

As I head toward the exit with my new partner, I avoid looking at the front of the classroom where Alistair is sitting behind his desk. I'm holding my breath as I approach the man.

Only a few more steps, Chiara.

"Miss Moretti, I'd like to have a word with you," Alistair says, and my heart stops beating for a second, only to kick-start in the next moment with a lurch.

I should have known I wouldn't be able to avoid talking to

him. But I'm still under the effects of the damn brownie. God. What a mess.

"I'll see you tomorrow, Chiara." Josh continues toward the door.

I want to beg him to not leave me alone, but that'd be strange as hell. My stomach bottoms out when the door clicks shut and I'm suddenly alone with the man I haven't been able to forget.

"Chiara."

Alistair's voice is much gentler now that we're alone. It almost feels like a caress, and it creates havoc in my body and my mind. Taking a deep breath, I turn. My mouth is dry and my tongue is stuck there while my heart feels like it's going to burst out of my chest.

"How can I help you, Mr. Walsh?" I force the words out.

Alistair swallows hard, but he doesn't move from his spot.

What did you expect, Chiara? For him to sweep you off your feet? He's your bloody teacher.

He opens and shuts his mouth several times before he finally decides on what to say. "How have you been?"

My jaw drops. *Seriously? He's asking how I am?* I thought he was going to yell at me for not telling him I was a teenager. Though to be fair, we agreed to not exchange personal information.

I don't answer for several beats until my brain is able to put words together.

"Honestly, I wish a hole would open in the floor so I could disappear."

Alistair's eyes become pained. "I had no idea, Chiara. If I had known, I wouldn't have—"

"Accepted my ride?"

Fucked me all weekend long back in Italy? I don't say it out loud, but I know we're both thinking about it.

He swallows hard. "Yes."

"I never thought I'd see you again. I'm eighteen. Hardly jailbait."

He sighs. "What's done is done. We can't erase the past, so we just have to find a way to move forward without making things worse."

I wince, feeling the rejection deep in my bones. *Worse than sleeping with me in Italy, he means.* To protect myself, I cross my arms. "How do you propose we do that? Pretend we don't know each other?"

"Yes," he says without hesitation.

I know he's right, but it hurts nonetheless to hear him say it in such a cold manner.

"Wouldn't it be easier if I just dropped out of this class?"

It's the coward's way out, but I have to protect my heart at all costs.

Alistair frowns, and his lips become a thin, flat line. "This is the most popular elective at DuBose. I don't want you to miss out on something because of me."

Dropping my gaze to the floor, I curse under my breath. He's right. I was looking forward to this class before I knew he'd be teaching it.

"Listen, you don't have to worry about my impartiality. I'll treat you the same way as I treat all my other students. I can separate things," he continues.

I nod without meeting his eyes. "Okay."

"Chiara, look at me."

No, I don't want to look at you because it's so damn hard. But I do as he asks, lifting my chin and staring at him in defiance to hide how much this is hurting me.

"What?"

"Are you working with Josh on the assignment?"

"Yeah. Why?"

Alistair seems mad, and I have no idea why. Is he jealous? *Don't go there, Chiara.*

"I just want to make sure you have a partner. I expect my students to be dedicated. This class requires you to spend at least two hours per week reading extra material and doing research. I want you to keep that in mind."

"I read the description when I signed up for the class. I know what I'm in for, or at least I knew. The teacher's last name wasn't Walsh though."

A muscle in Alistair's jaw tics. "It was a last-minute change. They probably forgot to update the registration portal."

My phone pings with an incoming text message. I glance at the screen and see it's from Robbie.

ROBBIE: Where the hell are you? Are you still alive?

Suddenly, a bubble of laughter goes up my throat. His question seems hilarious considering the new situation I'm in.

"It's rude to check messages while in the middle of a conversation with someone," Alistair retorts, and that only makes me laugh harder.

Damn it. I have the giggles.

"I'm sorry. But you have to admit, laughing is better than crying."

He frowns. "Chiara...."

"Don't. I'm fine with this. Totally, one-hundred-percent fine."

"You don't look fine. As a matter of fact, you look—"

"High as a kite?"

His eyebrows arch. "You're joking, right?"

I start laughing again. "Not on purpose. Oh God. I can't stay here and talk about this with you. You're my teacher!"

His blue eyes become stormy. Alistair is suddenly angry, and shit, if that isn't a turn-on.

Wait? What? I can't allow this to happen.

"You got high on your first day of school?" His voice rises.

"It was an accident, okay? I didn't know the brownie I ate at lunch was the special kind."

I realize I'm almost shouting, which seems to irritate Alistair more. In the back of my mind, I know I'm making a spectacle out of myself. If he didn't have regrets about hooking up with a high school student, he does now.

"Chiara, settle down. If school administration finds out you're stoned, you could be expelled."

"For real?"

He rubs his face. "You need to go home. Where are you staying?"

"At Brandywine Hall."

My phone buzzes again with another message from Robbie. He's coming this way. I can't let him see me with Alistair. He might be able to guess I had a summer fling with him. I don't trust myself to keep a straight face right now.

"I can take you."

I'd be tempted to accept his offer if only to spend a few more minutes alone with him. But his tone implies the task would be a chore for him.

"No need. My friends are coming."

I try to appear calm and collected as I walk out of the classroom, but I'm screaming inside. Alistair, the man who left a permanent imprint on my heart, is here, in the flesh, so close and yet unreachable.

How am I going to survive the semester?

15

ALISTAIR

I turn my cell phone off because I can't deal with anyone right now. I'm probably giving Enzo, my lawyer, premature gray hair. I'm sure he's going to mention it the next time he sees me.

This is a cosmic joke of epic proportions. Chiara showing up in my class, high out of her mind, was the worst thing that could have happened to me. It opened old wounds. It reminded me of when I was her age and utterly lost. I was torn between yelling at her for doing something so reckless and kissing her because I've missed her so damn much.

I can't help but notice the irony. I'm teaching screenplay writing while my own life just became a fucking soap opera. I'm a walking cliché. I have a soul-sucking villainesque ex-wife, and I'm crushing on a student. It was a miracle I was able to get through the class without making a fool of myself in front of my students.

I'm looking forward to a quiet evening in front of the TV as I head home, but it seems that isn't going to happen today. Nadine's car is parked in front of my condo.

Fuck me.

My jaw is locked tight as I park my truck in the designated spot. Without looking in her car's direction, I stride to my front door, body coiled with tension. But I know it won't matter how fast I walk.

Sure as shit, as soon as I hit the pavement, I hear her car door open and she calls my name.

I ignore her.

She catches me right before I open the front door, grabbing my arm. "Alistair, for fuck's sake, stop! I need to talk to you."

I glance at her hand on my arm, then level her with a glare. She swallows hard, releasing me and taking a step back for good measure. Her brown eyes are wide as she tries to portray deep sorrow. But I can see through her bullshit now. There isn't an ounce of regret in her soul. She's always been about the money and influence, things I still have despite not working as an actor anymore. Too bad I was just too blind to see before.

"I have nothing to say to you. I'll only deal with you through my lawyer."

"Please, Alistair. Let's not do this. Why can't you let bygones be bygones?"

"Are you serious? You fucked my friend in our bed, and you want me to simply forgive you?"

"I made a mistake. Showbiz was kicking my ass, and I was lonely. You were never there for me."

"Don't you dare pin your betrayal on me."

She sighs loudly and amps up the remorseful expression on her face. "I want us to reach an agreement. I'm broke, Alistair. I haven't worked on anything in months, and if I don't pay my rent, I'll be out on the street."

"Not my fucking problem. Call Wade."

She looks down. "I haven't seen or talked to Wade since you... you know."

"Like I said, not my problem. Now, if you'll excuse me, I have better things to do."

"Just give me half the vineyard and I'll be out of your life for good. You have the money, Alistair."

"Yes, I do have the money, but it's *my* money, and I'll be damned if I let you have a penny of it."

"You're so fucking selfish. I gave you the best years of my life!"

I roll my eyes. Here she goes with the over-the-top drama. She makes it sound like we were together for decades, not seven years, four of those as a married couple. Eight years older than me, she hated when gossip magazines mentioned our age difference, so "the best years of her life" speech isn't a surprise coming from her.

"Sorry, honey. This source has dried out. Good luck finding another idiot who believes your bullshit."

I walk around her and push the door open. Just before I shut it in her face, she says, "You'll regret this, Alistair."

Even her last words are unoriginal. What was I thinking when I married her? I can't even blame my mistake on a spur-of-the-moment bad decision. We dated for three years before I proposed. She's a very attractive woman; I can't deny that. The brunette version of Jessica Rabbit, I couldn't resist her voluptuous curves. But it was Nadine's drive to succeed that made me fall for her in the end.

Since there's no chance I'll be able to rescue my mood from the sour pit now, I turn my phone back on. Might as well deal with all my problems since I won't have any peace of mind tonight anyway.

I have ten missed calls from Enzo—no surprise there—plus a bunch of text messages. He left only one voice mail, which I don't bother listening to. I call him back instead. He answers on the first ring.

"About fucking time. Why don't you answer your damn phone?"

"I was working. What's so urgent?"

"Did Nadine contribute anything to the purchase of the vineyard?"

"Hell no. I paid for it with my money."

"Are you sure?"

"Yes, I'm fucking sure."

What is that viper playing at now?

"Well, her lawyer is claiming she paid for part of it. If that's the case, then she would be entitled to half according to your prenup contract."

"That's complete BS."

"I'll have to look at your bank statements. If her lawyer can prove you used money from your joint bank account to purchase the vineyard, he might have a case."

"You'd better make sure that doesn't happen, Enzo. That's why I pay you so much." I pinch the bridge of my nose because I can't remember if I used money from our joint account or not. *Fuck.* "Nadine was waiting for me in front of my house."

"Why?" I notice the change in Enzo's voice.

"What do you think? She wanted money, said she was broke."

"What did you tell her?"

"I refused."

"Listen, be careful with Nadine. I know the type. She's a snake, and she'll go to any lengths to get what she wants."

I scoff. Enzo is preaching to the choir. It might have taken me a while to figure that out, but now I know what kind of woman Nadine is, which brings my current situation to the forefront of my mind.

"I have to tell you something not related to Nadine."

"Do you want me to listen as your lawyer or as your friend?"

"Both."

"Ah shit. What did you do now, Alistair?"

I let out a long sigh, thrusting my hand in my hair. Shit, I can't believe Chiara is my student. My fucking student. I'm so screwed.

When I don't answer Enzo right away, he continues. "Your silence is making the lawyer side of me very nervous."

Not wanting him to start charging me for this call, I blurt, "I slept with one of my students."

"You did *what?*" Enzo screams so loudly, I have to pull the cell phone away from my ear.

"It's not as bad as it sounds. I met her in Tuscany. We spent the weekend together. She wasn't a student when we hooked up."

"But let me guess, she's a student now? In what class?"

I hesitate again. Shit, Enzo is going to love this. "Writer's room."

There's a moment of silence before he bursts out laughing. I wait a few seconds before I cut him off. "Are you done?"

"Sorry, man. But you have to see the irony in this."

"Yes, the irony is killing me. What the fuck do I do?"

"First, let's clear something up. How old was she when you fucked her?"

I sigh loudly. "I didn't know then. We didn't exchange personal information save for our names, but that was the first thing I checked after she walked into my classroom. She was legal."

"Thank fuck. But hell, Alistair. How can you be so fucking stupid?"

Enzo is not wrong. I wasn't thinking and completely let my attraction to Chiara take over everything. I had gone to Italy to forget all my problems, after all.

"She looked and acted older," I reply defensively. "I thought she was in her twenties."

"Well, technically, you did nothing wrong. You didn't break any rules. Can the girl keep her mouth shut?"

Anger surges out of nowhere. I don't like hearing Enzo

speak about Chiara with such a condescending tone. "Trust me. She wants nothing to do with me. I'm sure she'll have a boyfriend by the end of the week."

"Hmm, and does that bother you?"

"Of course not. She's a student and therefore off-limits."

"And if she wasn't?"

I open my mouth to reply but pause for a moment. The truth hits me then. If Chiara wasn't my student, I would go after her with everything I have, mindless of Nadine and the ongoing divorce.

"Hello, Alistair? You still there?"

"Yes."

"You didn't answer my question, but never mind. Your silence says it all."

I let out a heavy exhale. "What the hell do I do, Enzo?"

"You know what I would tell you as your lawyer, but as your friend? I say stay the fuck away from her. You can't afford that kind of rumor spreading around. That would give Nadine all the ammunition she needs to clean out your bank account."

Don't I know that? But staying away from Chiara will be a nightmare.

This semester is going to hurt like a mother.

16

CHIARA

Robbie and Harold took me home after Alistair's class, and Harold apologized a million times for the mishap. He'd packed the special brownie by accident. He seemed sincere, and I already have too many problems in my life to hold a grudge against the guy.

Once at home, I crashed, which meant fewer hours to worry about the sudden reappearance of Alistair in my life. But this morning, my chest felt heavy, yearning for someone I can't have. Pretending everything is fine while I navigate my second day at DuBose is the hardest thing I've ever had to do. I keep looking over my shoulder, expecting to see Alistair at a moment's notice.

I have lunch with Robbie again, but no Harold or Valerie, the other girl in the drama program.

"I still can't believe you ate one of Harold's magic brownies." Robbie shakes his head. "You have to write a comedy screenplay with that scene."

"Trust me, it wasn't funny."

"At least you didn't get caught by Mr. Greene."

I frown. "Who?"

"Jesus, you *were* high. Mr. Greene, your writer's room teacher."

"That's not my teacher. I got Alistair."

Robbie gives me a strange look, and it takes me a second to realize my mistake. "I mean Mr. Walsh."

His green eyes bulge out of his skull. "Shut up! You got Alistair Walsh? Oh my God. I can't believe it. I thought he wasn't teaching that class this semester. That's why I didn't sign up."

My stomach coils tightly. I should change the subject before I have another slipup. But my tongue has a will of its own.

"What's so special about him?"

"Uh, hello? First of all, the man is an Adonis. I'd so do him if he wasn't straight."

My face heats as I remember my time in Alistair's bed.

"He's okay," I reply.

"Okay? Woman, are you blind? In a land of mortals, the man is a god. But again, you were high, so you probably didn't notice. Wait until you get a load of him when you're sober."

This conversation is making me super uncomfortable. I don't want to hear Robbie objectify Alistair like that. I don't have any claim on the man, but I'm getting jealous nonetheless.

I glance at my phone and realize I'm late for my meeting with Josh at the library.

"*Cazzo*! I have to go." I jump off the bench.

"Where are you going?" Robbie asks.

"To meet someone to work on an assignment for Mr. Walsh's class."

"All right, girlie. See you later."

DuBose's library is semi-busy with a few empty desks available in the middle of the atrium. The school went with a modern-museum vibe for the interior, meaning the walls and furniture are all white with a few splashes of color here and there in the shape of modern sculptures and paintings. Floor-to-ceiling windows bring plenty of light into the open space.

Josh is waiting for me near the information desk, staring down at his phone. He looks up when I approach and smiles. Faded jeans hang low on his hips, and the comfy-looking sweatshirt can't hide the wide chest and taut abs underneath. He's positively yummy, yet the butterflies in my stomach remain dormant.

"I was beginning to think you would stand me up," he says.

"I'm so sorry I'm late. I spaced out and didn't check the time."

He narrows his eyes. "Are you sure that's all?"

I fidget where I stand. "What do you mean?"

"I know you were high yesterday," he whispers.

Merda.

"That was an accident. I didn't mean to get stoned. I'm not a pothead."

He lifts his hands. "Hey, I'm not judging. But I do take my studies seriously."

Josh's implication makes me mad. But I can't fault him for thinking the worst about me.

"So do I. Can we go now?"

"Sure. Ladies first." He motions with his arm for me to go forward.

I choose the nearest free desk, keen for this meeting to be over already. Pulling my laptop out of my bag, I drum my nails against the desk. I don't make eye contact with Josh while I wait for my computer to boot up.

"Chiara, I'm sorry, okay? I swear I'm not a jerk."

I glance at him, surprised by his apology. My irritation simmers down.

"I'm sorry too. First impressions are important, and you didn't have a good one of me."

He smiles. "Start over?"

"Yeah, I'd like that."

He extends his hand. "Hi, I'm Josh Flannigan."

"Chiara Moretti. Nice to meet you."

We both laugh at the silliness of this scene, but it does help lighten the mood.

My computer is finally on, so I open a browser window. "Do you have a screenplay in mind that you'd like to analyze?"

"I was thinking we could choose one from a successful blockbuster, an independent movie, and maybe a comedy?"

"All successful, right?"

"Yeah, I want to learn from the best."

"I have a movie in mind. I'm not sure it's considered independent, but it was super out there."

"What's the name?"

"*Eternal Sunshine of the Spotless Mind* with Jim Carrey and Kate Winslet."

Josh's eyes light up. "Oh, that's a great movie. And so different. Yeah, we definitely need to analyze that."

I download the screenplay from the school's database.

"What else?" he asks.

"Since I picked the first movie, why don't you choose the blockbuster?"

He groans. "You had to give me the hardest one."

I chuckle. "Why is that hard?"

"There are so many good ones. How about *Avatar*?"

"Really? You want a rip-off of *Pocahontas* as your pick?"

Josh frowns at me. "I don't agree, but okay. How about *Aliens*, then?"

"I've never seen it."

"What? That's a classic. Better than the first movie in the franchise—which was great, by the way. We're definitely analyzing that screenplay."

"Okay. That leaves us with the final pick. The comedy."

"How about *Election* with Matthew Broderick and Reese Witherspoon?"

I tense immediately. Reese's character has an affair with

her high school teacher in that movie. My thoughts wander to Alistair, and I feel a sharp pang in my chest. I haven't recovered from yesterday's encounter. He looks even more alluring in his serious teacher persona. Why does he have to make me feel like I might combust on the spot with a single glance?

Stop obsessing about him, Chiara!

"Don't you think there are better comedies?"

I so don't want to analyze *Election*'s screenplay. Too close for comfort.

"Probably. I just caught it on TV the other night, and it got stuck in my head."

We keep throwing names left and right, but we don't agree on anything. It seems we have different ideas about what's funny and not.

"This is impossible." Josh tosses his pen on the table in frustration and leans back in his chair. "We should change genre."

"No way. I want to analyze a comedy script. Let's search for a list of the top comedy movies and see if we can agree on something," I reply.

"Fair enough."

I click on the first link, which gives us a well-curated list from more recent movies to old classics.

I'm halfway through the page when Josh tells me to stop. "That's it. We should do *Napoleon Dynamite*."

I twist my nose as I read the synopsis. "It doesn't sound funny."

"Trust me. That movie is great. We could watch it together."

My shields go up automatically. His offer sounds innocent, but what if he sees it as an opening for more? I don't want to add another complication to my life.

"Nah, it's okay. If you say it's good, I trust you."

"You should watch it anyway, even if not with me."

Shit. Did I offend him?

Chancing a glance at his face, I find him staring at his laptop screen with serious intent.

I turn back to my own screen, wrestling with feelings of guilt. Maybe Josh didn't mean anything by inviting me to a movie session. But what if he did? The last thing I want is to lead him on. I came to DuBose looking for a clean slate, but somehow I found more drama here than I had back home.

I slept with my teacher. If that doesn't earn me a scarlet letter, what does?

ALISTAIR

I catch a glimpse of them in the library, and it feels like I've been sucker punched. Jealousy rears its ugly head, making me see red. It's completely wrong for me to want to punch a student in the face, but that's what I want to do to Josh Flannigan. They're not doing anything besides working on an assignment together, yet here I am, seething with white-hot rage.

That's it. I've gone insane.

I turn around and get the hell out of there, having forgotten why I went to the library in the first place. One thing is certain: I need to get my head straight; otherwise, I'll end up doing something stupid.

I pull my cell phone out and log into the dating app I downloaded after Nadine and I split. The app claims it will help me find my perfect match, but it's nothing more than a glorified booty call. The two women I found through it had nothing in common with me. I took them out to dinner, fucked them, and that was the end of it.

Since the last time I logged in, I've accumulated over three hundred invitations to start a conversation. Jesus fucking Christ. I didn't realize I was so popular.

I don't have time to go through them all, so I delete everything without looking and start a search of my own. When the filter results only show young, pretty blondes, I realize I entered Chiara's attributes in my search.

Fuck me.

Goldilocks has gotten under my skin, and I have no idea how I'm going to stop wanting her now that I'm forced to see her once a week.

I'm doomed.

17

CHIARA

Three Days Later

I watched the comedy Josh suggested alone. Did I enjoy the movie? Sure. Was it the best comedy of all time? Not really. We met a couple of times this week to work on our assignment, and there were no more invitations to do anything together later. A relief. With that unwanted complication out of the way, we were able to establish an easygoing rapport. He seems to be a nice guy, very dedicated to his studies.

I didn't bump into Alistair after his class. I'm glad writer's room is an elective and I only have to see him once a week.

The assignment is due on Monday. None of my other teachers gave out big assignments with such a short deadline, but Robbie said Alistair is known for being hard core.

Today, Josh and I work at the library again on the final edits. We're done in under an hour, and he doesn't linger. He says he has to pick up his brother and bails before I even finish packing my stuff up.

Since school is done for the day, and I have no desire to go back to my apartment, I decide to take a stroll through my neighborhood because I haven't had the chance to explore it yet.

My stomach rumbles loudly, and I remember reading somewhere that there's a donut shop that has the best treats in town. I pull up my phone and search on Google Maps. Sure enough, there's a big donut symbol on the commercial street behind my building. Ditzy Donuts. The name rings a bell.

I shoot a text to Robbie, asking if he wants to meet me there for coffee. He replies that he'll be there in ten. I arrive before him, and to kill time, I send Max a couple of selfies in front of the shop. Bending in the most awkward positions, I try to capture my face and the sign in the same frame, but without a selfie stick, it's almost impossible to get the right angle.

"Need help with that?" a voice that still evokes all sorts of wrong feelings asks from behind me.

Flustered, I almost drop my phone as I spin around with my heart now stuck in my throat. Alistair is standing too close to me in all his six-foot-three hotness, holding a box of donuts.

"What are you doing here?" I blurt out like I have the right to know.

I'm such a dumbass.

He raises an eyebrow, displaying a phantom of a smirk on his lips. "Getting sugar treats for a faculty meeting."

What a one-eighty change in attitude. He was furious with me on Monday after he found out I was high. Here he is now acting like the Alistair I fell in love with in Italy. My heart is fluttering like a hummingbird in my chest.

"Gotcha."

He points at the phone in my hand. "Do you need help taking a picture?"

I want to say no and run away. But that would be stupid as hell. There's nothing illicit about a teacher offering to help a student out. It's just an innocent picture.

"Yes, if you don't mind. Max loves donuts. I want to make

him jealous that I'm about to order the biggest one they have."

Alistair gives me a small smile before taking the phone from me, brushing his fingertips against mine in the process. A zing goes up my arm.

Nonsense, Chiara. You're imagining things. There's no such thing as magical, electric touches.

"What do you want on the picture? The sign?"

"Yes, please."

I stand in front of the shop and strike a lame pose. I can't relax when Alistair is the one taking the photo. I feel self-conscious and exposed.

"Come on, Goldilocks. You're not even trying."

My heart skips a beat, and I drop the fake smile. I can't believe he called me that out in public where anyone could hear him.

A second later, Alistair realizes his mistake. His easy grin vanishes as he lowers the phone.

Troubled, he says, "I'm sorry. I didn't mean to call you that."

"No, it's okay. Slipups happen."

He returns my phone. "Are you getting donuts to go? They have a special deal today. You'll get double your order if you buy a dozen. I suspect once this hits social media, the place will be packed."

"That's tempting, but I don't think I can eat twenty-four donuts by myself. I'll probably go into a sugar-induced coma, and who's going to rescue me?"

"I would," he says, and my heart decides to do the conga.

What the hell is going on here? Alistair just offered to be my knight in shining armor. I must be hallucinating. Sure, we're not on school property, but he's still my teacher. He'll lose his job if people suspect we were involved before.

I don't know what he reads on my face, but he suddenly clears his throat and says, "I'd better go or I'll be late. See you in class on Monday."

He walks away, leaving me bereft and cold inside. The silly girl in me is upset he didn't stay longer.

I'm still watching his retreating back when someone touches my shoulder, scaring the crap out of me.

"*Madonna Santa*! Robbie, you almost gave me a heart attack."

"Sorry. Hey, was that Mr. Walsh?"

"Hmm, yes."

"That man is sin incarnate."

"You really need to stop lusting after a teacher."

I'm such a hypocrite. If he only knew the wicked things Alistair did to me this summer.

Shit. My face must be redder than a tomato.

He sighs loudly. "I know. I hate the rules that students can't get involved with teachers. It's so unfair. Do you know how many hotties we've had at DuBose since I started? Too fucking many. All forbidden, which makes them even more appealing."

"If you're into older guys." I shrug, hoping I'm selling the lie that I don't find Alistair all that hot.

"Are you referring to Mr. Walsh? He's not *that* old. He's only twenty-six. No, wait. I think his birthday is coming up, so he'll be twenty-seven soon. But he's still hot."

"How do you know when his birthday is?"

"I googled it, of course." I stare at Robbie with a question in my gaze, and he adds, "Oh my God. You have no idea who he is, do you?"

A sliver of apprehension and excitement runs down my spine. "No. Should I?"

"Mr. Walsh is a former child star. He was on this super popular show called *The Lockharts* for a decade!"

"No way! We never got that show on Italian TV."

"Way! Let's grab some coffee and deep fried sugar treats and I'll show you. You're going to lose your shit."

We go inside and place our orders while I'm bouncing on

the balls of my feet. *Alistair used to be an actor? That's crazy.*

With our coffees and donuts in hand, Robbie pulls his laptop out and brings up Alistair's profile. I almost choke on my donut when the picture of little Alistair fills the screen. So darn cute.

"*Dio Santo.* How old was he there?"

"I think he was eight at the time, but his character was six years old on the show. So yeah, he totally grew up in front of millions."

"Did he work in anything else after the show ended?"

"Nope. During the last season, Alistair turned wild."

"What do you mean?"

"Oh, you know. The usual. He was partying too hard, probably doing drugs. The standard behavior for children who grow up in the limelight. But I think what triggered Alistair's reckless side was the death of his best friend."

Robbie types in another name on the Google search bar, Jamie Lewis, and the image of a cute dark-haired kid pops up. In the description, it says he died when he was only seventeen.

"What happened to him?" I ask.

"Suicide."

"That's awful."

"Yeah. Alistair was really tight with him. Anyway, after the show ended, he just disappeared."

My chest feels heavy now. Alistair is still a very good actor. He never gave any indication he'd carried that heavy burden with him. Unlike me, who had the woe-is-me sign flashing above my head the whole time we were together.

Robbie keeps scrolling through the pictures of Alistair until we get to a much more recent one. He has a beautiful brunette in his arms. My heart clenches so painfully, I almost can't breathe.

"Who is that?" I choke out.

"Oh, that's Alistair soon-to-be ex-wife."

"Wait. He's still married?" The donut I just ate burns in my stomach, and bitterness pools in my mouth.

"Uh, technically yes. Word on the street is that she cheated on him with one of his friends."

I keep staring at the photo while my pulse drums in my ears, drowning out all the other sounds. A huge sense of betrayal makes my cheeks turn hot. Alistair didn't make any sort of commitment to me. Still, I hate the fact that while he was screwing me in Italy, he had a wife back home.

"When did that happen?" I ask after a moment.

"Around eight months ago. He was a mess. Stopped shaving regularly, got grumpier than ever, and took a leave of absence. I was surprised to see him back at school. I thought he was going to be away longer. It's not like he needs his teaching salary to survive."

"And he's still married to her? Why?"

Robbie watches me through narrowed eyes. "Look who's interested in the teacher all of a sudden."

"What? It's good gossip." The lie is weak, and I think Robbie can totally see through my bullshit.

"I don't know why they haven't divorced yet. My guess is that she wants more money than is due to her. I met her once at a school function. She's a snobby bitch. I don't know what Alistair ever saw in her."

"She's gorgeous," I say with a pitiful tone, knowing I can't compete.

"Nah, she's not that pretty in person. Trust me. You're way hotter than her."

I lean back, crossing my arms. "Why would it matter if I'm hotter than her or not?"

Robbie smiles knowingly at me. "Maybe because you're hot for teacher?"

"You're crazy. I'm not into Mr. Walsh. *At all.*"

A bigger lie has never been told.

18

CHIARA

Without knowing it, Robbie shoved me into hours of obsessive and destructive behavior. I spent the weekend stalking Alistair online, even though it hurt like a mother learning how he met his wife and seeing pictures of them together. I read a bit about his friend too, but I was more interested in his relationship with his wife.

Glutton for punishment that I was, the more I read about his whirlwind romance with the Mexican actress Nadine Perez, the bigger the hole in my chest grew. Last night, I had to force myself away from the computer, but sleep eluded me. I kept seeing them together whenever I closed my eyes.

Lack of rest adds to my irritation today. Following my lessons in the morning is murder, and not even Robbie can help me with his humorous antics. To fight tiredness, I drink too many cups of nasty cafeteria coffee, and when I arrive in Alistair's class, I'm jittery as hell and ready to unleash the nasty bitch.

I'm ten minutes early, but I'm not the first student there. I consider for a brief moment sitting next to someone new, forcing myself out of my comfort zone and making more friends, but I don't think it's a good idea today. Maybe next time.

I take the same seat as before, deciding to kill time by checking my emails on my laptop. The top message in my inbox is from my mother, and I'm tempted to delete it without reading it. I skip her email for now because I really don't need to add her viciousness to my sour mood.

The next email is from Max, and it's a picture of him and his latest conquest. I swear to God he has a new girlfriend every other week. This one is an Asian beauty he met at a photo shoot in Thailand.

I click on the Reply button, but my fingers hover over the keyboard and no words come. For the first time, I don't know what to say to my cousin. I haven't told Max yet that Alistair is one of my teachers, and it feels wrong to write anything to him without revealing that bit of gossip. I'm not ready to spill the beans, mostly because Max is a shithead and he'll tease me to no end. Maybe I can wait to tell him in person when he visits at the end of the month.

"Good morning," Josh greets me as he takes the seat next to mine.

"Hey, good morning."

I close my laptop with a jerky movement, not knowing why. It's not like I was doing anything wrong. Josh doesn't seem to notice my fidgety reaction though.

"I uploaded our assignment last night," he says.

"Cool, thanks. When do you think we'll be graded?"

"Knowing Mr. Walsh's reputation, I'd say we've already been graded. I haven't checked the portal yet."

As if he was summoned by the mere mention of his name, Alistair walks in, looking sexier than ever. His button-down shirt stretches across his wide chest and clings to his biceps, making my mouth go dry. He seems well rested and relaxed, and here I am feeling like shit for losing sleep over him. The sense of longing hits me hard, but so does the anger that had been simmering low in my guts.

Remember, Chiara, he's still married.

"Good morning, everyone." His voice booms, commanding our attention.

He throws a cursory glance over the room but gives no indication he sees me.

"As of ten minutes ago, your first assignment grades have been posted. I wish I could say you all did well, but unfortunately, it seems not everyone here is taking this class seriously."

His gaze finally lingers on Josh and me as if he's implying we were some of the students who did poorly. That's impossible. Our essay kicked ass.

I quickly log into the portal via my phone and search for our grades. Josh must have gotten to it first based on the low curse that escapes his mouth.

The page finally loads on my phone, and I have to blink a couple of times to believe my eyes.

We got an F? What the hell?

I glance in Josh's direction.

"Is this for real?"

"I don't understand." He looks as confused as I feel. "I thought we nailed that assignment."

"If you have questions about your grades, please wait until the class is over to discuss it. Now, let's move on with today's lecture."

I'm so pissed that I can't see straight. I curl my hands into fists over my lap and grind my teeth. I've never received an F in anything in my life. I'm an A student through and through. That's why my father didn't even bat an eye when I asked to study in California. He knows I'm serious about my education. Who the fuck does Alistair think he is to fail me?

I'll show him.

I channel my frustration into paying extra attention to class, and for once I'm able to ignore how my heart hurts from being in his presence. I'm so in tune with the lecture that when Alistair asks me a question, I'm able to answer without hesitation. The arching of his eyebrows tells me he wasn't expecting me to be so assertive.

Jerk. I'm blonde, but I'm not dumb.

So it wasn't enough to give me an F, but he also wants to humiliate me in class?

Let's see who's going to have the last laugh.

As soon as the class is over, Josh makes a beeline to Alistair's desk. I follow him but let my classmate do all the talking, mostly because I'm afraid of what will come out of my mouth.

"Mr. Walsh, with all due respect, I don't understand why you gave us an F," Josh starts.

Alistair leans forward and laces his fingers together. "What grade should I have given you for a blank Word document?"

"What?"

Alistair turns his laptop screen toward us and shows an empty page where our assignment should have been.

Josh shakes his head. "There must be a glitch in the system. I uploaded a ten-page assignment last night. I swear."

Alistair frowns, and maybe I catch a flash of guilt in his eyes. I watch him through slits. So it did cross his mind that there could have been a technical error, and he still chose to give us an F. That's fucked up, and I can't keep my mouth shut any longer.

"I'm surprised you were so quick to fail us when it was obviously a system failure. Why would anyone submit a blank document?" I say.

"Someone who didn't finish the assignment in time and was hoping to blame a glitch in the system."

"*Dio Santo.*" I throw my hands up in the air. "That's ludicrous. Josh and I would never do something like that. How about innocent until proven guilty?"

"Miss Moretti, you'll soon find out that's the biggest lie ever told."

I openly glare at him. "I guess you should know all about lies and deception."

A vein on Alistair's forehead throbs as his eyes narrow.

Good. I managed to hit a nerve.

Josh, the poor thing, glances between Alistair and me without a clue of what's going on now. He must have sensed the sudden tension in the air though.

"Mr. Walsh, I swear that's not the case. I can show you the date the final file was saved," he says.

Alistair breaks the staring contest with me and turns his attention to Josh. "I suppose I could give you the benefit of the doubt. Send me the assignment as an attachment, and I'll grade it accordingly. But this is the only time I'll make an exception, system failure or not."

"Thank you, Mr. Walsh," Josh replies, clearly relieved.

I can't say the same.

I walk out of the classroom with Josh, still seething from the exchange with Alistair. A minute later, I hear a ping on my phone. A notification is flashing on my screen saying I have a new email from—*gasp*—Mr. Walsh. My heart is hammering inside my chest when I stop in the middle of the hallway to open the email. There's no subject line, and the body of the message only has one line: **Meet at my office in five minutes.**

What a jackass. Does he think my world revolves around him?

I'm tempted to blow him off, but the opportunity to yell at him is too good to pass up.

19

ALISTAIR

The moment I send the email to Chiara, I know I've made a mistake. I can't be trusted alone with her, but I have to know why she was giving me a death stare throughout the entire lecture. Sure, it could be solely related to the F I gave her, but her little speech about lies and deception had nothing to do with the assignment.

I leave the door to my office open on purpose and try to keep myself occupied. Five minutes never took so long to pass. It's possible she'll ignore my email or not see it at all, which doesn't make the wait any better.

I'm staring at my PhD diploma hanging on the wall, the one I never thought I'd receive, when a knock comes at my door, making my heartbeat kick up a notch.

"Miss Moretti. I'm glad you could make it."

She closes the door behind her with a soft click. I should ask her to leave it open, but my tongue gets stuck in my mouth. *Shit.* Chiara stays rooted to the spot, watching me with an indecipherable glint in her eyes.

"Why don't you take a seat?"

"I'm fine standing."

She's not mad—she's furious.

I stand up and walk around my desk, something I shouldn't be doing. I have to keep the distance between us. Just being in the same room alone with her is already wrecking my resolve to remain detached.

"I sense you have something you'd like to get off your chest. Come on, let's get on with it," I say.

"You failed Josh and me on purpose."

"No, I didn't."

"Don't you dare lie to me, Alistair. Even if you suspected we were trying to be sneaky, you could have given us the benefit of the doubt and asked us to resubmit the assignment."

She has me there.

"You're right. I should have done that, but I already rectified my mistake. Anything else you would like to say to me?" I take a step closer because I can't help myself.

She stares at me with such fury that I'm afraid to know what I did to get her so pissed off.

"You. Are. Married," she finally says in a strained breath while punctuating each word.

Ah fuck. I should have known she would find out about Nadine eventually.

"I'm separated."

"But you're still legally married."

"Yes, but not for much longer." I move closer, and Chiara takes a step back, lowering her gaze to my chest.

"It doesn't matter. You slept with me while you were still married. You cheated on your wife with me."

The fire is gone from her voice. She sounds hurt, and I hate that I'm the cause.

"Would it have made a difference if I had told you then?"

"Yes. No. I don't know."

Standing in front of her now, I place a finger under her

chin, bringing her face up so I can look into her eyes. There's defiance in them mixed with raw vulnerability. My gut twists.

"Chiara, I didn't tell you because I didn't want to ruin our time together. Yes, I'm still legally married, but I haven't felt bound to Nadine for a very long time, even before she cheated on me."

"It doesn't really matter, does it? We're not together. What we had was a meaningless summer fling."

Her words cut deeply, but I'm not sure I believe her, not when she's staring at me with her heart in her eyes.

"It wasn't meaningless to me," I say before I lean closer, brushing her tender lips with the tip of my tongue. God, I missed her taste.

I hear Chiara's sharp intake of breath right before she parts her lips and welcomes my invasion. She tastes like peppermint dipped in honey, waking a wild hunger in me no one else but her can satiate.

Goldilocks has unleashed the Big Bad Wolf.

With a groan, I deepen the kiss, bringing my body flush against hers. The craving intensifies tenfold, an uncontrollable sensation that spreads throughout my entire body. Warning bells are going off in my head, telling me this is a mistake. But I'm powerless to stop it. I'm taken over by a reckless fever.

The sound of my cell phone ringing snaps me from the madness. I pull away, taking a couple of steps back for good measure.

Chiara stares at me with cheeks flushed and wide eyes.

"Sorry, I shouldn't have done that," I say.

"I'm not sorry."

Her answer surprises me. It makes me ecstatic, but it doesn't change the fact that we can't continue what's going on here. She's my student. I'm risking not only my reputation but the school's. If Nadine finds out, she'll also ruin Chiara's life.

I run my fingers through my hair, frustrated as hell with myself for not being able to fight my crazy attraction to this girl.

"Chiara, this was a mistake. It won't happen again."

She narrows her eyes. "Do I look like a fucking blow-up doll to you? Some idiotic bimbo with big tits you can dry hump one minute and discard the next?"

"What? Of course not. Goldilo—"

"Don't call me that! My earlier assessment of you was right. You're nothing more than a washed-up child actor with a big ego. I wish I had never laid eyes on you."

She opens the door and is gone before I can stop her.

It's not the first time someone's called me that, but hearing the words from Chiara cut deeper than a knife. Her youthful cruelty should be enough to halt whatever it is I'm feeling for her, but it does exactly the opposite. I know the drill; I was once like that, so angry that the only way I could cope was to lash out at those closest to me.

My stomach churns as guilt sets in.

Fuck. What have I done?

20

CHIARA

I manage to hold off the tears until I'm outside the building, but then the water flow starts and I can't control it. I run off without direction. All I want is to put as much distance between me and Alistair as I can.

He kissed me. He fucking kissed me, then took it back like it was the biggest mistake of his life.

I don't know why I'm surprised. Hadn't I already established he's an asshole?

I can't believe I told him I wasn't sorry he kissed me. I left him in Italy without saying goodbye to avoid the heartache, but here I am, making a fool of myself at the first opportunity. I'm so stupid.

Cutting through the park to reach my apartment building faster, I bump into a solid chest. I would have fallen on my ass if the person hadn't held my arms.

"Whoa, Chiara. Where's the fire?"

"Hey, Josh. I didn't see you there."

He frowns and looks intently at me. "What happened?"

Ah shit. I forgot I was crying. I hastily take a step back and wipe the moisture from my cheeks. "Nothing."

"Chiara, come on. It looks like you've been crying your eyes out. Whatever it is, you can tell me."

I shake my head. "It's nothing. I'm homesick, that's all."

Josh narrows his gaze. He's not buying my bullshit.

"Fine. I'll pretend I believe you. It looks like you need a pick-me-up. Why don't you come with me to Ditzy Donuts? My treat."

I should say no and head back to my apartment. But I can't bear the thought of being alone right now.

"All right. I can't say no to sugary treats."

"*Andiamo*, then," he says, and despite everything, I laugh.

God, why couldn't I have met Josh first?

It turns out it's always busy at the donut shop, no matter the time of day. Josh and I have to wait ten minutes in line to place our order. Grabbing a table outside is impossible, so we head back to the park near school.

We manage to snatch a shady spot under a tree, which works out better than the donut shop would. At least here, there aren't a lot of people nearby to eavesdrop on our conversation.

"So, why do you think Mr. Walsh failed us like that?" Josh asks, and I groan to myself.

He had to bring up the man I'm trying to forget.

I shrug, ignoring the sharp pain in my chest. "Because he's a jerk?"

"I don't know. This is my third year at DuBose, and not once have I heard anyone say he was a douchebag, despite his colorful past."

"Colorful past?" I ask with a smirk.

Josh makes a dismissive gesture with his hand. "You know, his child acting past. He's known to be a serious and fair teacher, so I got totally blindsided by his attitude today."

"Well, at least he let us resend the assignment."

Why are you defending him, Chiara?

"Yeah, there's that. So, are you going to tell me the real reason you were crying earlier?"

I tense on the spot, my spine turning as rigid as a board. "I already told you. I was homesick."

Josh touches my knee, making me look at him. "Chiara, I know we've just met, but you can trust me, okay? If someone did something to you that you didn't want them to, you can tell me. I won't judge, but I'll kick his ass."

Dio Santo. I think Josh suspects someone sexually assaulted me. Well, someone *did* kiss me, but it was something I more than welcomed, even if later I regretted my weakness.

I cover his hand with mine and smile feebly.

"Thanks, Josh. I do appreciate your concern. Don't worry. It wasn't anything like that."

Relief washes over his face. I think this time he believes me. Good. I couldn't have him worrying like that.

"Do you have a boyfriend back home?" he asks.

Uh-oh. Dangerous territory. It never bodes well when a guy asks if you have a boyfriend. I don't owe Alistair anything, so there's nothing keeping me from finding a new guy, but Josh is one of the good ones. I can't string him along while I'm pining for someone else.

"Yes and no. It's complicated."

"Oh."

I hear the disappointment in Josh's voice, which makes me feel bad for my half-truth.

Trust me, Josh. You want to stay far away from this train wreck here.

"I met him in Tuscany last July. It was supposed to be a summer fling, you know, but it evolved into something more."

"Ah, I see. Now you're here and he's back in Italy, I assume?"

I almost reveal part of the truth that Alistair lives in LA. But Josh is too smart, and he would be able to connect the dots in no time. So I lie.

"Yes."

"Well, that sucks. But long-distance relationships can work."

"He's married," I blurt and then lower my gaze, cursing my big mouth. "I mean, he's separated, but he's still officially married. I feel betrayed in a sense, and also dirty. I'm not a home-wrecker."

Josh doesn't say anything for a long time, and when I look up, I catch him staring out in the distance.

"Josh, are you still here with me?"

He shakes his head and looks at me. "Yes, of course. I was just thinking about what you said. I don't think you should feel that way. You didn't know he was married at the time, and he's separated. A piece of paper linking him and his wife doesn't really mean much. The most important connection"—he points at my heart—"is what should matter. Do you love him?"

Wow. That was deep shit from an eighteen-year-old dude. I know I'm in love with Alistair, but do I love him? Those two feelings are not necessarily the same thing. How can you love someone you don't know?

"My legs turn into jelly, and I get butterflies in my stomach when I think about him. I think I'm in love with him, which is super crazy. We only spent a weekend together."

"No, not crazy at all. I believe true love happens like that, suddenly, devastatingly."

I pay close attention to Josh. "You sound like you speak from personal experience."

"Not my personal experience. My parents. Their story is not so different than yours. They met when they were in Spain on a month-long trip to learn the language. They said it was love at first sight. The funny thing is they lived their entire lives only a few blocks from each other. They even went to the same high school. But they had to travel across the ocean to find each other and fall in love."

"That's a beautiful story, Josh. You should turn it into a movie."

"Maybe I will. Although, I have no desire to make sappy movies a la Nicholas Sparks."

"Shut up. I love *The Notebook*."

He chuckles. "Sure. You love Ryan Gosling in *The Notebook*."

"Whatever. It was a beautiful love story. How about you? Any special lady in your life?"

Josh frowns and looks away. "Nope. I don't have time for relationships. I want to focus on turning my passion into a career, because nothing can take that away from me."

I mull over his words, thinking inevitably about Alistair. My sadness returns, but also anger.

"You're right. Fuck love. Like Tina Turner said, it's a second-hand emotion, anyway."

21

ALISTAIR

I'm the stupidest motherfucker on the planet. I kissed Chiara, and in my office to boot. Anyone could have walked in, ending my teaching career in a minute and also giving Nadine everything she needs to get what she wants. We're separated, but her lawyer would no doubt twist it around since Chiara is my student. Nadine is not beyond blackmailing me.

I should be more concerned about that, but all I can think about is how Chiara crumbled in my office. I wasn't imagining things. There was more to her reaction than simple ego bruising.

Damn it. I thought she was only after a distraction in Italy. That made sense when she bailed without saying goodbye. I won't lie and say it didn't upset me, but I chalked it up as hurt male pride. What if Italy was more than just careless fun for both of us?

No, I can't entertain those thoughts. I have to cut all strings before things get more complicated. It's obvious I can't be trusted to be alone with her, so I have to get her out of my system for good.

I need to get laid.

I text Enzo and ask what his plans are for the weekend. He's the social butterfly in my tight group of friends and the wingman I need. He replies thirty minutes later saying he's going to a party at the Hills on Friday. I groan. That means a party filled with wannabe celebrities, not exactly my scene anymore. But it's either that or take cold showers every time I picture Chiara naked under me. I reply that I'm game, and then I get ready to tackle another task I had been procrastinating: reading and grading Chiara and Josh's paper.

I'm afraid it won't be good and I'll be forced to give her a low grade. She'll think I'm retaliating if that's the case. Fuck. What a mess.

I get to it, because the work won't get done with me just staring at the screen. As I begin to read, the tension slowly leaves my body. They selected three well-written screenplays and their analysis is good. They could have dove deeper in some areas, but overall, it's a solid B-plus.

As I upload the document with my notes and post the final grade online, I instinctively know Chiara won't be happy about it. I checked her transcripts from Italy. She was at the top of her class.

I can't help the feeling of pride that spreads across my chest. It goes beyond what a teacher should feel toward a pupil. All educators want their students to do well, but my desire to see Chiara succeed goes further than that.

Irritated with the conflicting emotions bouncing inside my head, I put on the meditation track Caio recommended a few months ago. I was skeptical at first, but after a few tries, I realized that listening to it for a few minutes does help me focus afterward.

I don't achieve a Zen state of mind this time because I'm interrupted by Forrester, DuBose's principal. He knocks on my door and pushes it open before I even have the chance to reply. His mop of gray hair appears through the crack, probably to make sure I'm alone before he opens the door all the way and walks in.

"Hi, Alistair, do you have a minute?"

I pull my earphones off and watch my friend warily. It's not like him to make unannounced appearances. The fact that if he had come by twenty minutes earlier, he would have caught me with Chiara twists my guts into knots.

"Yes, sure. What can I do for you?"

Forrester closes the door before taking a seat. His face is more serious than usual. I smell trouble.

"I have a delicate matter to discuss with you."

Ah fuck. Has he somehow found out about Chiara and me? A spike of adrenaline shoots through my veins, but I keep my poker face on.

"I'm listening."

"I hate to say this without proof, but I caught wind of a rumor that one of the DuBose's teachers is having an affair with a student."

I swallow hard but don't say anything. If Forrester asks point blank if I'm involved with Chiara, I won't lie.

He laughs nervously. "You know how kids are on social media. Gossip spreads like wildfire."

"How did you catch wind of this rumor?"

"Through my daughter, Jillian. I overheard a conversation between her and a friend. It was by accident, but it made me extremely concerned. That's why I'm here speaking with you. I don't want to accuse Miss Kensington of improper conduct based on mere gossip."

"Miss Kensington?"

"Yes. Apparently she was caught making out with one of her students at a popular bar downtown. I had my assistant look into it, and there is indeed a picture of someone who looks like her in a passionate embrace with a guy. Here, I had Marianne print this out for me."

Forrester pulls a folded piece of paper from his jacket and slides it over to me. Frowning, I pick up the photo and grind my teeth as I stare at a very dark and grainy picture.

"This could be anyone, Forrester."

"I know. But what if the rumors are true? You know what they say, 'where there's smoke, there's fire.'"

"Are you here seeking my advice?"

"In a way, yes."

"Don't do anything. Pretend you've never heard about the rumors. If you bring Miss Kensington in to ask questions without solid proof, you might lose a very good teacher and possibly get your ass sued as well."

Forrester doesn't balk at my crude remark. We've known each other for a very long time. He flattens his lips and stares at my desk.

"Yes, you're right. Besides, I don't want to sound sexist, but the reality is that a relationship between a female teacher and a male student wouldn't do as much damage to DuBose's reputation as if it had been the other way around. Provided the student is of age, naturally."

His careless comment has me clenching my jaw so hard I'm afraid I'm going to break a tooth.

"Well, I'd better get going." He stands up. "You must have plenty of things to do. I still remember how chaotic it gets when classes start. Thanks for your help, Alistair."

"Any time."

I'm still reeling minutes after Forrester's departure. *Fuck.* If this conversation wasn't a clear sign that I have to get my shit together, I don't know what is.

I need to get out of here, but I still have stuff to do. In my inbox, there's a brand-new message from a coworker with the subject line "Huge favor." Curious, I click on it. Vivian never really asks for favors unless she's in dire need.

Scanning the message quickly, I realize that's the case. Her mother suffered a heart attack this morning, and Vivian flew to Houston to see her. She's wondering if I can cover her biweekly class and help with the project she's leading, the Annual Film Festival. I've always been involved in the past, this year being the only time I didn't volunteer thanks to my messy personal life.

The email came with an attachment, a list of all the students who volunteered to help. Vivian isn't expecting me to say no.

I shake my head. This is what I get for always being the dependable guy.

Naturally, I'm going to say yes, but a sliver of apprehension takes hold of me. I open the document she sent, quickly scan through it, and then curse under my breath.

Chiara is on the list.

22

CHIARA

Last week I signed up to help with the Annual Film Festival organized by the school. Every year they focus on a specific country, and this year is Italy's turn. I couldn't pass it up. My film history teacher, Mrs. Weiland, is spearheading the project.

I'm excited as I head to the kickoff meeting. But the moment I step foot inside the lecture hall, the grin I had on my face wilts to nothing. Instead of finding Mrs. Weiland, Alistair is in her place.

What the hell is he doing here?

He turns around and stops talking. My steps falter, and I clutch the strap of my backpack tighter. Unprepared for this unexpected encounter, I'm not quick enough to put on an indifferent mask. In fact, me standing rooted to the spot is not helping my case either.

"Miss Moretti, please take a seat."

"Am I late? The email Mrs. Weiland sent said four o'clock. It's ten to."

"No, you aren't late."

The corners of his lips pull up in an attempted half smile.

His eyes are soft as he watches me, and my stupid heart rejoices.

I force my legs to move, sitting in the nearest chair, which means front row and much too close to Alistair.

"Hey," Valerie greets me.

Jesus, I was so stunned by Alistair's presence that I didn't even notice I took the seat next to hers.

"Hi."

Alistair looks down at the sheet of paper in his hand and says, "It seems everyone is here. As I was explaining before, Mrs. Weiland had a family emergency and asked me to cover her classes and take over the Annual Film Festival project."

My heart begins to beat faster in panic. Film history is a biweekly class. How am I going to deal with seeing Alistair more than once a week?

He approaches my chair, and I immediately tense up. He frowns slightly, which tells me he noticed. *Cazzo.*

"Here's the list of tasks. Your name is already assigned to them. Would you mind?"

He gives me the stack of papers, again watching me as if I'm on the verge of breaking.

Oh God. Is he feeling guilty?

With a nod, I take the stack from his hand, careful not to brush my fingertips with his. I keep one copy and pass the rest to my neighbor. While the list of tasks is being distributed, I glance quickly at them to see what I have to do. I gasp out loud when I see my name next to interviewing the cast and the director of one of the movies showcased in the festival. That's the best task on the list, in my opinion. Did Alistair do this to redeem himself?

I look up to find him watching me closely.

"Ugh, I can't work on the archives. I'm highly allergic to dust," a guy complains. "Can I do something else?"

Alistair frowns at him before glancing at the list again. After a moment, he says, "You can help with the setup and cleanup during the event."

"Oh great. Labor work. Why can't I be the one interviewing the movie cast?" He turns to me, glowering. "I'm on the school paper, after all."

My spine goes rigid right before I open my mouth to reply, but Alistair beats me to it.

"I'm not responsible for the tasks' assignment, but I stand by what Mrs. Weiland has in place."

The guy looks pissed, but he doesn't argue further. As for me, I'm glad Alistair didn't assign the interview to me. I don't want any favors because his conscience is too heavy.

"We still need someone to handle the archives," he says as he looks around the room.

No one volunteers though. Since I already got the best assignment possible, I raise my hand. "I don't know what it entails, but I'll do it."

The look I get from Alistair is not one of relief. It's pained. Why? I don't get it.

"Are you sure?" he asks.

"Yes, unless you don't think I can handle it." I raise an eyebrow at him.

He stares at me without blinking for a few seconds before he turns and sits on the edge of his desk.

"I'll go over the list and explain each task, but I want to give you a brief overview of the festival first, especially for those who are new here. Every year DuBose organizes the Annual Film Festival, usually focusing on a theme or a country. This year we're showcasing Italy, but not only movies made in Italy. The festival covers it all, from wide popular movies set in Italy to films starring Italian actors or directed by an Italian director."

"Thank God. How boring would it be to just watch movies

in Italian?" the same dude who was complaining about the archives task pipes up.

"Boring for someone closed-minded," I reply, glaring at the idiot.

"I'm not closed-minded. It's hard to understand a movie when I have to read the subtitles."

"Someone here can't multitask." Valerie snickers.

"Okay, enough," Alistair cuts in. "Let's go over the tasks."

He briefly explains each item on the list. I'm still aggravated by the lazy guy's comment, so I don't pay much attention. I also don't want to look at Alistair, because his nearness is making it extremely hard to pretend that he doesn't affect me. I can smell his cologne from my chair, and it's doing my head in.

I'm busy drawing doodles on my paper when Alistair calls my name. It startles me, and I end up dropping my pen. He was standing right in front of my chair, so he bends over to get it. Instead of standing up, he offers me the pen while he's still in his crouch position. In an instant, I become ensnared by his intense blue gaze. I feel a crazy fever taking over me. He's devouring me with his eyes like he did back in Italy.

Hell and damn. Does he want me to turn into a ball of goo in front of everyone?

I grab the pen quickly before I combust on the spot. "Thanks."

My reply seems to wake him up. He stands and turns around, walking in the opposite direction.

"Okay, that was weird," Valerie whispers to me.

I don't comment because how can I? It wasn't weird. It was stupid. Does he want people to know we were involved?

"Uh, Mr. Walsh, weren't you going to explain what Chiara's assignment is? I'm kind of curious," the lazy guy says.

"Right. Chiara, I'll send you the contact detail of Giulio Bertollini's assistant. He's the director of—"

"I know who he is," I cut him off.

Everyone in Italy knows the guy. He's one of the most brilliant movie directors in the country.

"Right. Well, she'll be your main contact person. I'm afraid that's all the information Mrs. Weiland had for you, but if you need my help, you know my door is always open."

My jaw drops of its own accord. I can't believe he said that with a straight face.

"Oh, shoot. What time is it?" Valerie asks.

"Five, I think," I say.

She stands up suddenly. "I have to go. I'm already late for an appointment."

The other volunteers follow her lead. This meeting was only supposed to last half an hour.

Not wanting to be left behind alone with Alistair, I collect my things and head for the door without sparing him a second glance, but I sense his stare burning through me all the same.

23

CHIARA

I sit all the way in the back during film history class, hoping the distance and the students in front of me will create a protective barrier between Alistair and me. Valerie sees me there and takes the chair next to mine.

"Why are you all the way in the back when we have a hotter-than-sin substitute teacher?"

Why does everyone I know keep reminding me how good-looking Alistair is? Like I don't already know.

"I'm hoping to fly under the radar today. I'm super tired."

"Smart. I think you caught his attention yesterday."

My entire body tenses. "Why do you say that?"

"He couldn't keep his eyes off you."

Damn it, Alistair.

I shrug. "Probably because of my argument with that idiot who didn't want the archives assignment."

"Yeah, probably. Mr. Walsh is as serious as it gets. You'd be surprised how many of his female students have tried to seduce him since he started teaching here. He shot them all down."

Red-hot jealousy spreads through my veins like wildfire. I did not need to know that.

Alistair enters the classroom, looking as gorgeous as ever. My heart reacts accordingly, lurching forward at the same time the butterflies in my belly turn radioactive. Conversation ceases, but I notice how every single girl in the room is eating him up with their hungry gazes. It wasn't as bad in writer's room, or maybe I didn't pay attention. Now that Valerie mentioned the obvious, I can't not notice it.

When Alistair's gaze sweeps the room, I try to keep my expression neutral. Maybe it's my imagination or wishful thinking, but I swear his eyes shine brighter when he sees me. I hope it was all in my head. Valerie already noticed his peculiar behavior yesterday; if he keeps throwing heated glances in my direction, our little secret won't stay buried for long.

He starts the lecture, and I force my mind to tune into the knowledge, not the man presenting it to me.

One of the hardest things I've ever had to do in my life.

I'M relieved when I finally make it home after a gruesome day at school. I was tense the entire time, even after Alistair's class. I hate how he has so much power over me and we're not even together.

I take a long shower, hoping the hot jets will relax me, but I can't get him out of my head. And when my soapy fingers brush my clit, I let out a moan as I imagine Alistair's tongue there. I'm turned on as hell, but instead of finding release, I finish the shower abruptly and get out. I will not masturbate while thinking about him.

Dressed in comfy clothes, I lounge on my couch and check my emails, determined to forget him. But it seems fate doesn't want me to extract Alistair from my mind. Sitting at the top of my inbox is an email from him.

For fuck's sake.

The subject line says "Film Festival," and I guess he wants to tell me about the archives task I volunteered for. With a deep breath, I click on it. The message is short and to the point. He's asking me if I can work on my assignment later today. It's not that hard. All I have to do is sort out a shipment of boxes that arrived for the festival. DuBose's storage unit is in the school's basement.

I send a quick message back saying I can be there at the time he specified and then stare at the screen without moving for a good half hour, waiting for a reply that never comes through. With a huff, I close my laptop and force myself off the couch. Glancing at the time on my phone, I realize I'll be horribly late if I don't get moving.

If I'm going to be shuffling boxes and dealing with dusty things, I have to dress for it. I grab the oldest pair of boyfriend jeans I own, pairing them with comfy sneakers and an over-sized flannel shirt. My hair looks like crap today, so I just pull it back in a messy bun. It's not like I'm trying to impress anyone. But before I head out the door, I apply some cherry-flavored lip gloss; Bisnonna always used to say the day she left the house looking like shit, that would be the day she would bump into all her acquaintances.

Not feeling like walking from the residence hall to school, I take the bicycle I bought my first week. The air is cool as I ride my bike as fast as I can, loving the sensation of the wind blowing over my skin, though the trip is short—I'm not even winded or sweaty. I have to do this more often.

At this hour, the atrium in the school building is deserted. It's past six, and most of the students are long gone. I keep walking down the main hallway until I see the sign to the basement.

The air gets cooler with each step I take downstairs. And here I thought I would be hot wearing the flannel shirt. To my right, there's a reception desk, but the receptionist is gone for the day too. Alistair only told me to be here at quarter past six. I figured there would be someone to show me what to do.

"Hello?" I call out.

A door opens down the hallway behind me. I turn and find Alistair there. My stomach bottoms out at the same time a fluttering sensation spreads across my chest.

Dio Santo. Am I supposed to work with him?

"Hi," he says.

"What are you doing here?" I blurt, frozen to the spot.

"The school doesn't allow students in the archives unsupervised."

His expression is serious. I gather he's not happy about this situation either.

I finally force my legs to walk in his direction, not looking at him when he moves out of the way to let me inside the room. When the door closes with a resounding click, a shiver runs down my spine. I'm alone with Alistair again, and my body and mind are waging war with one another.

This place looks more like a library than a storage unit. I glance around, noting the black containers pushed against a wall. Alistair walks around me and drags one of them next to a table. My eyes immediately zero in on the bulging of his biceps, on the expanse of his wide back, and the yearning spreads from my chest to between my legs. My core is throbbing, anticipating something that won't happen.

I close my eyes for a moment. *Focus on the work, Chiara. And remember, you're still mad at him.*

"What exactly am I supposed to do?"

"These came from Italy. We need to sort them out and store them properly until the festival."

I walk over but make sure I'm not standing too close to him. He begins to pull items from the box, laying them on the table. I grab a long cylindrical container, popping the lid open. I'm about to stick my hand inside when Alistair stops me, touching my wrists with the tips of his fingers. The simple contact sends a zing up my limb and turns the low burning in the pit of my stomach into a raging fire. How can his touch be so incendiary?

"Wait, you need to put on these nitrile gloves. You don't want to leave your fingerprints behind."

I don't offer a reply because I've lost the ability to speak, too busy trying to control my erratic heartbeat. I set the cylinder back on the table and put on the gloves. Then with care, I remove the poster from inside. I don't recognize the movie—I'm not a movie buff—but considering the artwork, I'd say it's from the fifties. The thick paper is bright and crisp though.

"This isn't an original, is it?" I ask.

"No. As a matter of fact, none of the materials are originals. Even the movie reels they sent are copies. We should consider ourselves lucky we got them."

I glance at the storage shelves on my left. "What else do we have stored here?"

"Only student work. Most studios don't keep their archives in California but rather send them out of state to high-tech storage facilities."

"This place is pretty clean. I don't know why that idiot was complaining about dust."

Alistair makes a strange noise in the back of his throat. "He wanted your assignment and thought he was entitled to it. There's always a student who's like that."

"Well, he can suck it."

I roll the poster again to put it back in its case.

"I tried to find someone else to be here in my place," he says out of the blue, making my spine go taut.

"It's fine, Alistair. I'm over the shock of finding out the truth about you. I've moved on."

"You have?" The surprise in his voice makes me look at him.

I can't read the emotion shining in his eyes. Is he relieved or upset?

"Of course. You don't have to worry about me making a scene."

He shakes his head and pulls his gaze away. "That wasn't what I was worried about."

I open my mouth to demand he elaborate further but decide not to. Better not to open that can of worms.

"What else is there in that box?" I ask instead.

Alistair pulls out a box with a label that says "*Sogni di fiori e nuvole, regista Giulio Bertollini.*"

"Holy shit. Is that Giulio's newest movie?"

"I believe so."

Alistair opens the box, revealing a reel of film inside.

"Ah, man, it's not digital? I'd love to watch it," I say.

"We have a projector here. If we finish unpacking and storing in the next hour, we could watch it."

I whip my face toward him once more, but he's not looking at me. He's busy taking more items out of the box.

Did he just suggest we watch a movie together? Maybe now that I told him I've moved on, he's no longer concerned about our summer fling. Then why the hell did he kiss me in his office and keep throwing heated glances my way during the volunteers' meeting? He seems pretty unfazed right now while I'm here freaking out.

Get your act together, Chiara. You told him you've moved on. He doesn't have anything to worry about any longer.

The knowledge feels like a dagger twisting in my heart, but I force myself to ignore the pain. It seems I'll be forever fated to live in this state of agony. First pining for Pietro, now Alistair. It makes me doubt my own feelings. Maybe I'm just a glutton for punishment and I only want what I can't have.

The idea that I'm not really in love with Alistair makes it easier for me to carry out the task. My heart is still heavy, but now my brain is in control. Every time there's a lurch in my chest, I start to chant silently, *I'm not in love. I'm not in love.*

Alistair and I keep the conversation to a minimum, and before I know it, all the containers are empty and things are stored. I blow a wisp of hair off my face as I look at the clock mounted on the wall. It's only seven thirty.

"That's it?" I ask.

"Yeah. This was one of the easiest tasks on the list. It's probably why Mrs. Weiland assigned it to Lucas."

"Lucas? Oh, you mean that obnoxious guy."

"Yep. Now he's stuck with something much more taxing." Alistair grins at me while his eyes shine with mischief, melting my heart on the spot. *Damn it!*

I look away so he can't see the yearning in mine. "Well, I'd better get going, then."

"You changed your mind about watching the movie?"

I freeze for a split second before looking at him again. *Shit.* I forgot about it. I really should say no, but the prospect of being one of the first people to watch Giulio's newest movie is too tempting to pass up.

"Are you sure? I mean, would that be okay?"

Alistair's neutral mask slips for a moment when he frowns and flattens his lips. "Yes, Chiara. It would be perfectly fine."

With movie reel in hand, he walks to the back of the room where there are a few chairs in front of a white screen. I take a seat, feeling jittery while Alistair sets up the projector. Fifteen minutes later, he chooses the chair farthest from mine, leaving a gap between us. Not that it does any good. In this confined space, I can't escape his alluring presence. But I *will* push through it. This is the ultimate test.

Once the movie starts, it gets easier to ignore Alistair's presence. I'm sucked into the story right away. That's how good Giulio's movies are. I don't spare a single glance in his direction until we come to a scene that changes everything. It's a love scene, which in Giulio's movies translates into an extremely graphic and erotic sex scene. It's impossible not to get turned on. Now all I can think about is the man in the room with me and how I want him to enact what we're seeing on the screen. I rub my legs together because the constant throbbing in my core is almost too painful.

Alistair groans, a sound I don't think he intended to make. Like a fool, I turn to him and catch him adjusting his pants.

Hell. He's as aroused as I am.

Sensing my stare, he looks at me. His eyes are pained, and his jaw is clenched tight. My breathing turns shallow, and I know if I stay here, I'll end up doing something very foolish like throwing myself at him.

"Chiara, I—" he starts, but I can't bear to hear the end of his sentence.

I jump out of my chair and say, "I have to go."

Like a scared little mouse, I run out of the room before Alistair can stop me.

24

CHIARA

Through some snooping—aka asking one of the ladies in the administration department—I learned Alistair isn't teaching any other class at DuBose besides writer's room and film history. He also doesn't come to school on Thursdays. That made my day more bearable, but come Friday, I chicken out and skip his class. I couldn't face him after that charged moment we shared in the school's basement. I need more time to recover from that.

I do show up for creative writing in second period though. We have to write a short scene, and to my dismay, I wrote a very smutty one. I didn't realize what I was doing until Robbie looks over my shoulder and giggles.

"I never knew you had such a filthy imagination, Chiara."

"What?" I look at him.

He taps my laptop screen. "This scene is hot."

Heat rushes to my cheeks, and in a panic, I delete the whole thing.

"Damn, why did you do that? It was really good."

"I don't know what I was thinking. I can't submit that. Mrs. Fallon will think I'm a perv."

Robbie glances at the front of the room, where our teacher is busy writing something on the whiteboard.

"Nah, I think she'll appreciate it. Maybe it will give her some ideas to use with her husband later tonight." Robbie wiggles his eyebrows up and down.

I hit his arm. "Shhh. You have such a dirty mind."

"Not as dirty as yours."

I cover my face with my hand. "You're never going to stop teasing me about that, are you?"

"Never. So, what, or better yet, *who* inspired that scene?"

"Nobody," I say through clenched teeth.

"Right. I'll pretend I believe you."

The class finally comes to an end, and mercifully, Mrs. Fallon doesn't ask us to submit our scenes at the end of it. She says we can keep working on them during the weekend.

Robbie laces his arm with mine and says, "Come on. I'm famished."

On the way to the cafeteria, I notice there are more students heading there than usual.

"What's going on?" I ask.

"Oh, I think the students in the drama program are planning something. Harold heavily hinted yesterday that we should eat in the cafeteria today."

There's a sense of excitement in the air, and I get caught up in it. Something is definitely going to happen. Instead of veering toward the food buffet, Robbie aims for a table, scoring a spot for us with the glee club students. Introductions are made quickly before he asks if anything has happened yet.

"Nope. But it will soon," a guy with a mop of dark curly hair says.

"Robbie, I thought you were hun—"

A commotion in the crowd cuts me off, and like everyone else at the table, I turn in the direction of the noise. The throng of people parts to make room for the dozen guys dressed up as knights. Half of them carry flags with different insignias, and the other half have a sword in one of their hands and a toy horse between their legs.

"What the hell?" I say.

"Behold, fair people of DuBose Kingdom," says a tall blond guy as he walks to the middle of the circle that has quickly formed. "We're the brave knights of the six glittering courts, and today we'll duel in the name of the House Cup."

A loud noise erupts all around us as students begin shouting and banging their food trays against the tables. The blond guy waits until the noise level goes down to speak again. "But before we begin, each of us needs a blessing and a token from a fair maiden."

I roll my eyes when I hear the loud, high-pitched screams of some girls. *Come on, people.*

"I guess since I'm already talking, I'll start."

The guy makes a show of looking at the crowd surrounding him as he rubs his chin. When his eyes land on me, he pauses.

Oh hell to the no.

He strides in my direction until he drops in front of me like an idiot. "What's your name, oh fair maiden?"

Instead of answering him, I narrow my eyes and say, "You haven't earned the right to know my name."

A collective gasp echoes in the vast room, followed by laughter.

"Ouch, we got a fierce one here, folks. I sure know how to pick them," he says.

"Pick them? What are we, flowers ready for the plucking? I don't think so, buddy." I glare at him for real.

Sensing I'm serious, he brings his body to the same level as mine and whispers in my ear, "I don't mean anything by it. This is just for show."

I feel bad now. Maybe I was projecting my frustration with Alistair on this guy. This seems to be just harmless fun after all.

"All right. Carry on. I won't bite your head off."

Relief crosses his face, and he smiles. He returns to his position kneeling at my feet and grabs my hand. "If you allow me, fair maiden, I'll win this tournament and earn the honor to know thy name."

"I'll give you my permission, oh brave golden knight."

He raises an eyebrow and whispers, "Golden knight?"

I shrug and his smile widens, revealing perfect straight teeth. He's kind of cute, actually.

"May I ask for a token to bring me luck?" he asks out loud.

"Sure." I give him the hairband I had around my wrist. "Here. Good luck."

He brings it to his lips, kissing it before putting it on his own wrist. The crowd cheers as he stands and returns to his place in line. The same theatrics follow with the other knights until they all find their maidens and get their tokens.

Then the silly tournament begins. They look like children, dueling with their fake swords and wooden horses. But the crowd is into it, cheering and screaming as if they were watching a real live duel.

"Are those guys all in the drama program?" I ask Robbie.

"Some, yeah, but not all of them."

The tournament comes to the final duel, and I'm not surprised that my knight is one of the last guys standing there. He looks in my direction and winks. To my surprise, I laugh because this situation just became too ridiculous for me to take it seriously. Besides, it's okay to let myself have some fun.

He charges his opponent with a loud roar, hitting him on his shoulder. The guy trips and ends up falling on his ass. The crowd cheers once, the noise much louder than before. Robbie jumps from his seat, dragging me with him.

"He won! Your knight won."

"Okay, okay," I say, not understanding his enthusiasm.

My knight walks over to collect his prize.

"My lady. May I now have your name, please?"

"It's Chiara."

He puts his hand over his chest. "The brightest of them all. I knew you were special, my lady."

Apparently we're not putting on enough of a show because the crowd begins to chant, "Kiss, kiss, kiss."

Shit. I didn't sign up for this.

Robbie is the only one not chanting, and he seems a little annoyed about the situation.

"We don't need to kiss, you know?" the golden knight says, but his eyes are hopeful.

In that precise moment, the image of Alistair pops into my head and how much I'm still hurting because of him. A reckless idea takes root, and before I can overthink it, I go for it. I stand up, stepping closer to my knight. I have to look up since he's so much taller than me.

"What the hell? We can't disappoint them. Just one kiss."

His lips curl into a crooked grin. He grabs my face between his hands and brings his mouth to mine. It's innocent, just a brush of lips, but the crowd goes wild.

I thought kissing another guy would make me feel better, but it has the opposite effect. It just makes my chest tighter. There's no extracting Alistair from my heart anytime soon.

25

CHIARA

I could have never foreseen that my chaste kiss with the golden knight—Phillip—would be such a big deal. Since I didn't go out last weekend again, preferring to watch sappy movies on Netflix rather than partying with Robbie, I only get the full effect of my actions Monday morning while I walk to Alistair's class. Whispers calling me "fair maiden" follow me, and people are staring a lot.

When I enter the classroom, the few students there turn to me and start to clap.

"Ugh, what the hell is going on?" I ask.

The guy nearest to me answers, "You broke the curse."

"What curse?"

"Peter is being dramatic. There's no curse, just a very long stretch without any wins for our football team," someone else replies.

"Yup." Peter bobs his head up and down. "But that changed last Saturday. Your kiss must have special powers, because our QB was on fire."

"Who?" I look from Peter to the other girl who spoke.

"Phillip Harrison, our quarterback."

Understanding finally dawns on me. "Ah, and you think that silly kiss has something to do with it?"

"Yes!" they both answer.

Josh comes into the room, tapping my shoulder as he walks by. "Good job, Chiara. You saved the school's honor."

I follow him, grumbling. "Not you too."

Chuckling, Josh takes his seat, and I do the same. "Do people really believe I'm somehow responsible for this miraculous win?"

"Oh yeah. Most definitely." He nods.

"Ugh!"

"Oh, and there's more. Your magical kiss was featured front and center in yesterday's online issue of the school's paper. You're famous now. People are probably planning your wedding to Phillip."

"Fucking great," I mumble, wondering if Alistair has seen that picture too. If he did, does he think Phillip is the reason I said I've moved on?

For fuck's sake. Why am I distressed about that?

"Don't worry about it. The story will die out soon. I mean, unless you two are actually dating."

I roll my eyes and scoff. "I already told you. I've retired from dating."

"Come on, Chiara. Because of one bad guy? There's more fish in the sea, you know?"

I look at Josh. He's staring straight ahead, so I can't tell if he's referring to himself. I hope not.

I pull out my phone and send Robbie a quick text message. How come he didn't say anything earlier when we had class together? Actually, no one made a fuss. Maybe this breaking the curse story didn't start until later.

ME: Thanks for the heads-up.

Two minutes later, he replies.

ROBBIE: Ah, shit. I totally forgot to warn you. My bad.

"My bad"? What kind of apology is that?

I'm about to send a sassy response back when Alistair walks in. He barely looks at the class, and his "Good morning" sounds more like a grumble than anything else.

"I hope everybody got enough rest last weekend because things are about to get hard in this class."

"Harder than it already was?" Peter asks a little too loudly.

Alistair glances at the poor guy, glaring. "You think the past three weeks have been hard? That was me going easy on you."

I've never seen this side of Alistair before. He sounds so angry. What happened to him last weekend? He can't be mad because I kissed Phillip. No way. Even though it would be nice for my bruised ego if he was jealous.

"Today, you're going to work on a script for a pilot TV show, and I'm splitting the class in groups. The assignment is that a major network is looking for a new high drama series for their prime-time slot. I know just one hour isn't enough to write a script. I'm not delusional. You have a week to complete it and prepare the pitch to present to me next week."

"That sounds kind of fun," I say.

"Sure, but a week to do all that?" Josh shakes his head. "Insanity."

Alistair begins to divide the class into groups. When he calls my name, he doesn't look in my direction but keeps his gaze glued to the sheet of paper in his hand. I'm not surprised that I'm not in the same group as Josh, but I groan silently when I discover I'm in Peter's group. I hope he doesn't want to keep talking about how my kiss broke the team's curse.

He smiles when I take a seat next to his, then asks if I'm going to next week's game.

"I don't like football."

"Shhh. Don't say it out loud. You'll bring the curse back."

I sense someone approach right before Alistair asks the group if we have any questions.

"No question from me," Peter replies, and the other group members say the same.

"Miss Moretti?" Alistair turns to me.

"Nope. All good for me too."

I feel his gaze on my face, so I'm forced to turn to him. His expression remains impartial, but his eyes seem to blaze with an unfathomed energy. It's like he wants to enter my mind, read all my thoughts. Slowly but surely, he reels me in with his intense gaze, and all coherent thoughts escape my brain. *Damn it.*

"Okay then." He knocks on the back of my chair before moving along to check on another group.

I don't realize I'm staring at him until one of the girls in my group sighs.

"Man, that's a hot piece of ass, don't you think? I'd totally go for him if I thought I had a chance in hell."

"He's our teacher," I retort.

"So?" She raises an eyebrow.

Jealousy rears its ugly head, but it's not like I can show how mad I am.

"I don't think he's all that," I reply instead.

"Well, I'm sure you don't considering you've got the QB."

I almost tell her that I don't have anyone, but it seems to me her statement made Alistair tense all of a sudden. So I don't correct her erroneous assumption, even knowing it's a pretty stupid move on my part.

My phone vibrates in the next moment, indicating a new text message. I don't recognize the number, but after reading the content, I figure out who it's from.

PHILLIP: So, I guess you're my lucky charm.

ME: How did you get my number?

PHILLIP: Robbie. You're not mad, are you?

Of course, it had to be him. I *am* annoyed.

ME: I'd have preferred if you'd asked me for it.

PHILLIP: Shit. You're right. I just wanted to ask if you'd like to come to my next game.

I groan. *I swear to God, I'm never making impulsive decisions again. Ever!*

ME: I don't like football. Sorry.

The three dots on my screen tell me Phillip is typing a reply, but I never get to see the text because my phone is yanked from my hands.

"Hey!"

"You're here to work, Miss Moretti, not text your boyfriend. Now get to it."

My cheeks heat as embarrassment mixes with indignation. I can't believe Alistair did that.

"What about my phone?"

"You'll get it back once class is over."

Sure, it's rude to text during class, but it's not like he was talking. Taking my phone feels rather extreme. The startled look on my companions' faces tells me they're just as shocked as me. Needlessly to say, no one jokes around while working on the assignment. They don't want to deal with Alistair's bad mood.

I'm too angry to concentrate on anything and end up being a deadweight.

When the class is finally over, the anger is gone. I carelessly started this silly game, but it's done nothing but leave me hollow inside. I collect my stuff as fast as I can, and when I approach his desk, he doesn't look at me.

"Can I have my phone back, please?"

He slides the device across the desk, finally looking up. "Next time I catch you texting during my class, I'll fail you in a heartbeat. Is that clear, Miss Moretti?"

I swallow hard. "That's a bit extreme, don't you think?"

"I don't have time for students who are using school to party on their parents' dime."

I wince, feeling Alistair's rebuff as if it were a physical blow. That's exactly what my mother thinks I'm doing, which couldn't be further from the truth. I haven't partied at all.

My eyes prickle as my vision turns blurry.

"I'm not a party girl," I say through clenched teeth.

"Prove it."

"No, Mr. Walsh. I don't have to prove jack to you. Yes, it was wrong to text during your class. It won't happen again. But if I party or not, it's none of your concern. Only my grades are, and they speak for themselves." I grab my phone and run out of the classroom.

I'm fuming as I stride down the hallway. Robbie sees me and steps in my way.

"What happened?"

"Nothing."

"It doesn't look like nothing. Do you want to go somewhere and talk?"

I shake my head. I wish I could confide in Robbie, but this secret is not only mine, and despite being furious with Alistair, I can't put his career in jeopardy.

"No. I'll be fine. I'll see you tomorrow, okay?"

I rush out of the building, keeping the fast pace until I reach my apartment. When I walk through the door, I'm winded, and sweat dots my forehead. A spike of pain flares on my right side, but it subsides after a moment. It must be a cramp for practically running a block.

I collapse on the couch. I only plan to rest for a bit, but once my eyes close, oblivion takes over.

26

ALISTAIR

So far, this semester has been a complete disaster. I thought I could put whatever it is I'm feeling for Chiara on the back burner and treat her like a regular student. I thought I was succeeding until I put on that damn Italian movie. Fuck, when that sex scene came on, it changed everything. The sexual tension in the room rose to alarming levels. It was a good thing Chiara left, because I had been close to breaking my rules again.

Then I saw that damn picture of Chiara kissing the school's quarterback, and I completely lost my mind. Riding the jealousy wave, I couldn't keep my temper in check in class, and the result was me acting like a caveman. I didn't have to take away her phone; a warning would have sufficed.

Tonight, I'm giving dating another try. Since I'm not looking for a serious relationship, it doesn't matter that my divorce isn't finalized yet. With Chiara it was different. I knew the closer I got to her, the more I would want her.

This time, I used a different app, making sure I didn't type any of Chiara's attributes in the filters. My date is a redheaded businesswoman from Canada. I've always gotten along with

Canadians, so I figured why the hell not? The plus side is that she looks nothing like Chiara or my ex-wife.

The date is going well. The conversation is flowing smoothly, and Sarine, my date, has even made me laugh a few times. I'm at ease, but so far, the intelligent woman opposite me hasn't made me feel anything else. I could take her back to my place and fuck her—something Sarine already hinted she's more than willing to do—but sleeping with her just for the sake of cleansing my palate feels wrong.

"So, I have a confession to make." She looks at me from under her eyelashes. A lopsided smile unfurls on her lips.

"I'm listening."

"This is the first time I used the app to score a date. My sister is the one who set my account up as a joke."

"I believe that's a normal occurrence." Or people just use that excuse to pretend they aren't desperate.

"Right, but that's not the confession. I only agreed to this date because I recognized you."

"Oh?"

And that's when I know the evening will go downhill faster than a speeding car without brakes. There's nothing that can put me in a fouler mood than when people want to bring up my celebrity past. It was a breath of fresh air that Chiara had no clue who I was. And even now that she knows about my past, she hasn't brought it up.

"We watched *The Lockharts* religiously at my house when I was a kid. Of course, my favorite character was yours. You were my first crush."

My reaction is to clench my jaw hard. I don't know what to say. I never do in these situations. This isn't the first time someone's told me I was their first crush, but it's the first time a date has mentioned it.

Sarine notices my hard stare and drops her gaze to her plate. "I'm sorry. You must hear that all the time."

"I do."

I could have tried to make her feel better, but I'm honestly not in the mood to appease anyone. It's not Sarine's fault I get annoyed easily when someone mentions my ten-year stint on the family-oriented TV show. Nor is it her fault that talking about it inevitably brings Jamie to the forefront of my mind, and with that, the guilt.

"I want to know all about it. What was it like on the set?"

How about great until I lost my best friend?

Grinding my teeth, I draw our waiter's attention. I'll need something stronger than wine to make it through dinner.

"It was work. So, you only have one sister?"

"Oh come on, Alistair. You can elaborate more than that. Did everyone in the cast get along?"

"Yes."

"Do you still keep in touch with them?"

"No."

My monosyllabic answers don't seem to clue her in that I don't want to talk about my glory days.

"What happened to Jamie Lewis was so sad. I'll never understand why he did it."

Fuck me. She had to go there.

When the waiter finally approaches our table, instead of asking for another drink, I hand him my credit card.

Sarine's jaw drops as a glint of surprise shines in her eyes.

"Is there something wrong, sir?" The waiter eyes my barely eaten dinner.

"No, nothing's wrong with the food."

I don't elaborate further, letting the guy draw whatever conclusion he wants. Sarine's glint of surprise vanishes. She's now glaring at me.

"Are you going to bail on me? I thought dinner was going great."

I drop my napkin on top of my sixty-dollar uneaten steak

and stand up. "It was nice to meet you, Sarine. Enjoy the rest of your evening."

I head after the waiter because waiting for him to bring my card back while sitting at the table with Sarine is unnecessary torture. I catch her entering a cab when I walk out of the restaurant. If the story she told me about her sister setting up her account on the dating app is true, I'm sure she's on the phone with her right now. In the back of my mind, I know what I did was a douche move, but I'm too fucking busy battling old demons to care.

I should drive straight home, but instead I go to the last place on earth I should be.

The Brandywine Hall building looms in front of me. Parked across the street from it, I make a mental list of all the reasons I shouldn't be here. I ignore all of them as I get out of my car.

It's my luck—or demise—that someone is walking out and I'm able to slip into the building. I have no idea what apartment number Chiara's is, but that mystery is quickly solved by looking at the names on the mailboxes.

I forgo the elevator in favor of the stairs, taking them two at a time. There's a reason for my urgency—if I take too long, my sanity will return, and right now, I don't want to have common sense.

Once in front of her apartment, I ring the doorbell. When I don't hear anything, I knock instead, hard.

"I'm coming!" she says from somewhere inside.

The door opens, and the sight of her robs me of air. Her hair is disheveled, and her cheeks are flushed. I wonder for a second if I interrupted her with someone. Jealousy surges through me, suddenly and violently.

"Alistair. What are you doing here?" Her voice comes out as a breathless whisper.

"I think we need to talk. May I come in?"

Her eyes widen slightly, but she does open the door all the

way and allows me in. I just take a couple of steps before I turn around. Chiara is standing in front of the closed door, frozen like a statue, watching me with wary eyes. A myriad of emotions clashes inside my chest. Longing, regret, anger. But the feeling that stands out the most is something I never thought I would feel again. I can't believe it took me this long to realize the truth.

"Why are you here, Alistair?"

"I went on a date tonight," I blurt like a moron.

She winces. "And you just came here to rub it in?"

I pass a hand over my face. "No, I came here because I'm done pretending that our weekend in Italy was meaningless."

Leaning against the door, she closes her eyes and presses a hand over her forehead. It's then that I notice she doesn't look well.

"Chiara, are you okay?"

"No. I feel... faint."

No sooner does she say it than she stumbles forward.

"Chiara!" I reach her with a giant stride, catching her in my arms before she hits the floor.

With her head pressed against my chest, I can tell she's burning up. I lift her in my arms, noticing how she feels like deadweight. She's passed out.

I cup her cheek. "Goldi, wake up."

Her eyelids flutter, but she only opens them halfway. "Alistair, I don't feel good."

"Of course you don't, sweetheart. You have a fever. Do you have painkillers?"

She closes her eyes again and nods.

"Where are they, Goldi?"

"In the cabinet above the sink in my bathroom."

I don't need directions to find her bedroom and adjacent bathroom. I lay Chiara on her bed first and then go in search of the medicine.

God, what would have happened if I hadn't decided to act recklessly and come see her tonight?

There's a water bottle on her nightstand already. I help her swallow the pills and then try to get her as comfortable as possible.

"Alistair?" she croaks.

"Yes, honey?"

"Please don't leave me. I don't want to be alone tonight."

I kiss the top of her head. "Nothing could pry me away from you, Goldi. Now sleep. You need to rest."

"Okay."

I don't move from my spot by the edge of her bed until Chiara's breathing becomes even. Once I'm sure she's asleep, I head back in the living room to grab some pillows and then return to her bedroom to make a makeshift bed for myself on the floor. I could take the couch, but that would be too far from her; I don't want her to wake up in the middle of the night and think I've left.

I stare at the ceiling, but sleep eludes me. It's not only worry about Chiara that's keeping me wide awake. I'm thinking about my life and what I truly want out of it. Being reminded about Jamie today brought things into perspective for me.

I knew what I felt for Chiara was bigger, more powerful than anything I had experienced before, but fear made me push her away.

Not anymore.

27

ALISTAIR

The sound of soft feet near my head wakes me. My vision is blurry, and it takes me a moment to remember where I am. Then I see her face, hovering over mine like a golden angel.

I lean on my elbows. "Chiara, you shouldn't be out of bed."

"You spent the night... on the floor."

I rub my eyes, trying to get rid of the last vestiges of sleepy fog. "Yeah. I was afraid you'd need me during the night."

"You should have taken the couch."

"How are you feeling?" I reach for her forehead to check her temperature, but she leans back and away from my hand.

"I feel fine."

She's leery of me. Perhaps she doesn't remember much of last night. Not that I had the chance to tell her why I came.

I sit up and touch her arm before she can move farther back. "You scared me, Goldi."

Her delicate eyebrows furrow. "Why? It was just a fever."

"You passed out. It wasn't simply just a fever. If anything had happened to you...."

"What? Why do you care?"

"God, Chiara, I've been a mess since you left me alone in that hotel room in Italy. I haven't been able to get you out of my head."

"You haven't?" Her reply is like a soft breeze.

"No, Goldilocks. I haven't."

I loop my arm around her tiny waist and bring her onto my lap. Her plump lips are inches from mine now. She doesn't flinch or try to move; instead, she keeps her bright blue eyes glued to mine. I slide my fingers into her hair, curling them around a golden lock, and shorten the distance between us so I can taste her sweet mouth.

When our tongues clash, the simmering fire in the pit of my stomach becomes a blaze so intense it's almost impossible to restrain myself. I bring her body flush against mine, deepening the kiss. She melts against my frame, waking everything male in me.

Chiara pulls back too soon and stares at me with hooded eyes and flushed cheeks. "Alistair, what does this mean? What about your job?"

"I don't care about my job, or my ongoing divorce. I had an epiphany last night, sweetheart. I know it sounds crazy, and I have way too much baggage, but I need you in my life, Chiara. I need you."

"As a convenient booty call?"

Frowning, I tuck a loose strand of hair behind her ear. "Never. You're not a booty call. You never were."

Chiara drops her gaze and shudders. Pinching her chin between my thumb and forefinger, I bring her face up. Tears have formed in her eyes, turning the blue in them even brighter.

"Goldilocks, why are you crying?"

"Because I'm so in love with you, I can't stand it. I'm afraid that if this turns out to be just a meaningless affair to you, I'll shatter to pieces."

Her confession sucks the air out of my lungs. "You're in love with me?"

She covers her face with her hands. "*Cazzo!* I can't believe I just blurted that out. I'm such a mess."

I pull her into a tight hug, kissing the top of her head. "I'm a mess too, Goldi."

I want to confess that I've fallen for her as well, but the words get lodged in my throat. I've only said the L-word to two people in my entire life: my first crush when I was thirteen and Nadine. I'm afraid the word has lost its meaning to me. Or I'm just too fucking afraid to blurt it out and curse us.

I kiss her again, harder and deeper. I want to brand her, or maybe I just want to show her how much she means to me.

Without breaking our kiss, I get up with her still in my arms and then set her at the edge of the mattress. I take a step back and drink her in to make sure she's well enough for what I have in mind.

"Where are you going?"

"I need a moment to take in the sight of you."

She finger-combs her hair. "I must look hideous."

"Impossible. You're the most beautiful woman I've ever seen, Chiara."

She twists her face into a grimace. "Your ex-wife is gorgeous."

I wish she hadn't brought up that snake.

"Goldilocks, let me make something very clear to you. Nadine is nothing to me. You're a thousand times smarter—" I kiss her nose., "—sexier—" I kiss her neck. "—and prettier than her. Plus, you taste fucking delicious." I claim her mouth like a starved man.

She leans back too soon and speaks against my lips. "Really?"

I take her hand and place it over my chest. "Do you feel this,

Chiara? See how my heart is beating at a hundred miles an hour for you?"

She stares at my chest for a couple of beats before looking into my eyes. Without a word, she pulls her T-shirt off, revealing her glorious breasts. My mouth goes dry as I glance at them, the nipples already hard.

"Touch me, Alistair."

Like a puppet without control, I obey her command. My hands cover her breasts, kneading them softly. Chiara throws her head back and lets out a moan. *Fuck.* If she keeps making sounds like that, I'm going to come in my pants.

I kiss the hollow of her throat before trailing my tongue down her collarbone until I reach her hard nipple. I suck the nub into my mouth while playing with the other with my hand. She digs her fingers into my hair, pulling at the short strands.

Letting go of her scrumptious tit, I drop to my knees, placing my hands on each side of her hips. There's a sharp intake of breath on her part right before she whispers my name, filled with raw need.

Looking up, I say, "I hope you're ready for this, Goldi, because this wolf is fucking hungry."

***

CHIARA

Is this real life? Is Alistair really here in my room, ready to devour me, or am I suffering from a fever-induced hallucination?

If this is a figment of my imagination, I don't want to return to reality.

Alistair slowly rolls my underwear down my legs without looking away from my face. My cheeks are blazing, and anticipation has made my breathing shallow. His focus switches to my pussy, and I swear my clit throbs in response. He leans closer, his warm breath fanning over my exposed skin right before he kisses the junction between my leg and pubic bone.

"Alistair, please...."

"What is it, Goldi?" He moves closer to where I so desperately need him to be with another soft kiss.

"Stop torturing me."

With a chuckle, he nudges my legs wider, and I watch him with a lust-infused gaze. Alistair's eyes connect with mine right before he licks my bundle of nerves in one long, delicious sweep of his tongue.

"*Dio Santo!*" I let my head fall back because Alistair just sent me dangerously close to the edge already.

With a groan, he starts his merciless torture. His hands are on my hips, keeping me in place, while his tongue pushes me into oblivion. My head becomes light, and the room starts to spin. Alistair alternates between licking and sucking me, making it impossible to slow down the orgasm that's fast approaching. I bite my lower lip, hoping the pain will distract me. It does the opposite.

With my fingers in his short hair, I call his name from the top of my lungs while my body shatters into a million pieces. Instead of slowing down, he eats my pussy with more gusto, frying every nerve in my body.

When I collapse back on the bed, I'm as light as a feather. It's only when I feel the mattress dip on my side that I peel my eyes open. Alistair is lying next to me with his head propped on his fist while his free hand makes lazy circles over my belly.

"Hi." I smile.

His lips curl in a crooked grin. "Hi."

I roll onto my side and touch his cheek. "I can't believe you're here."

He kisses my open palm before replying, "I'm here, Goldi."

Pulling my hand free, I run my fingers down his torso until I find the edge of his pants. The fabric is taut, stretched to accommodate his bulging erection. "I think someone wants to come out and play."

I make quick work of the button and fly, making Alistair hiss in the process. When I curl my fingers around his shaft, he cups the back of my head and pulls me closer for a long, hard kiss. Loving the feel of his cock in my hand, I match the tempo of our tongues with my pumping motion. Alistair growls right before he rolls on top of me, forcing me to stop my fun.

"Hey! I wasn't done."

"Goldi, as much as I love your hand, I need to be inside your sweet pussy."

He thrusts his hips forward, and the tip of his cock teases my entrance. But he won't slide all the way in, driving me insane.

He does it again, penetrating a little farther but still not buried deep inside like I want—no, *need* him to be.

"Alistair, what are you doing?"

"Fuck. You feel so good, Goldi. But we need a condom."

"There are some in my nightstand drawer."

He's gone in a flash.

As he stands next to my bed to look for protection, I take my time to stare at him. My heart is so full it feels like it's going to explode. He got rid of his pants and boxers, but his button-down shirt is still blocking the wonderful view of his abs.

I throw a pillow in his direction.

"You're taking too long."

His eyes narrow to slits, turning predatory in an instant. With the foil packet now in his hand, he rips the packaging and rolls the condom over his rock-hard erection without taking his eyes off me.

"You need to strip too." I point at his shirt.

I've never seen a guy get rid of clothing so fast. He only released the first two buttons before grabbing the back of his shirt to pull it over his head. He's between my legs in the next second, caging me in with his strong arms.

"You have no idea how many times I dreamed about you, Goldi."

He silences my reply with a kiss, and then he's inside me, filling me completely. I raise my knees to welcome the fullness of him better.

Mamma mia. I had forgotten how good Alistair's cock feels.

We don't stop kissing as he hammers into me, going deeper and deeper. He kisses me like he fucks me, with feverish passion. I'm transported back to our dreamlike weekend in Tuscany, and it feels as if no time has passed.

I moan against his lips as the pressure builds below. His movements become faster, harder until everything ceases to exist and I'm flying through another earth-shattering orgasm. He lets go of my lips to hide his face in the crook of my neck, grunting as he's consumed by his own pleasure.

Minutes go by before I return to my body and become aware of my surroundings once more. Alistair rolls off me, but he keeps me tucked tight in his arms. Resting my head against his chest, I close my eyes and savor the moment.

"Can we just stay in this room forever and never leave?" I ask.

"I'm okay with that." He chuckles.

We don't speak for a moment. Eventually, the post-orgasm bliss ebbs away, allowing my annoying brain to interfere. Alistair didn't confess his feelings for me. He said he needed me, but that's not the same as loving someone. Was I an idiot for blurting out the truth like that? What if he thinks I'm a needy girl?

"Hey, what's wrong?" he asks.

"Nothing."

"You got tense suddenly. Don't tell me it's nothing, Goldi."

I sigh loudly. "Fine. I started to think about the practical side of things."

"I don't want to give you up. But I can't resign in the middle of the semester. That wouldn't be fair to my students or the school."

"I don't want you to resign on my account. You're a good teacher, Alistair."

"On the other hand, I can't not have you, Chiara. I tried to stay away from you, and it almost drove me insane."

I pull back, leaning on my elbows so I can look at his face. "We could keep seeing each other in secret."

He furrows his eyebrows. "I hate to put you in that position. You're not a dirty affair I should have to hide."

"I know, but unfortunately, while you're my teacher, I *am* a dirty secret." I grin slyly. "We'll be like Romeo and Juliet."

"Goldi, their love story ended tragically."

I kiss his nose. "But ours won't. Now, I'm hungry. Do you want to eat something?"

Alistair looks at his watch. "I should get going. It's already six. The longer I stay, the harder it will be to leave your apartment without anyone seeing me."

It's hard to keep the disappointment from showing on my face. With a tight smile, I say, "Okay. I guess I'll see you in class, Mr. Walsh."

His eyes narrow, turning smoldering in a second. "You have no idea how hard it will be to see you in school and pretend you're nothing but a student."

His admission turns the butterflies in my stomach wilder than they were already.

"But I thought you were an actor."

"Sure, but I never claimed to be a good one."

28

CHIARA

My heart is hammering inside my chest as I wait for Alistair to walk into film history class. I feel much better than I did last night. The fever I had must have been triggered by emotional distress. Or maybe Alistair's dick has healing powers.

I kept my seat at the back of the room to make it easier for both of us. Valerie, the only student in this class I know, hasn't shown up yet.

My phone pings, announcing a text message. I glance down and fight to keep the goofy smile off my face. It's from Alistair.

ALISTAIR: I'm about to walk in. I hope you have your game face on.

ME: It depends. What are you wearing?

ALISTAIR: The usual.

ME: Cazzo. That's going to be a problem.

ALISTAIR: Goldilocks...

ME: It's okay, I'm all the way in the back. Just don't look in my direction.

Robbie drops into the chair next to mine while I'm distracted, scaring the crap out of me.

"Shit."

I fumble my phone and end up dropping it to the floor. Robbie makes a motion to reach for it, but I push him off with a jerky movement.

"I got it."

"Gee. What's gotten into you?"

"Too many espressos. What are you doing here?"

"When I heard Mr. Walsh was the substitute teacher for Mrs. Weiland, I had to sign up. Luckily, there was still room."

Shit. This is not good at all. Hiding my relationship with Alistair will be much harder with Robbie around. He already noticed my interest in him; he'll be able to put things together in no time if I'm not careful.

"I can't believe they let you change your schedule after the semester started."

He gives me a devious smile. "Both my mothers are on the school board. They have sway. Oh, by the way, it's my mom's birthday this Saturday—the Brazilian one—and you're invited to the party. Both are *über* excited to meet you. I'll text you the details later."

I open my mouth to reply, but Alistair's booming voice announces the beginning of class. A shiver runs down my spine, and heat pools between my legs. Squirming in my seat, I try and fail miserably to control my reaction to his voice. The vivid image of him naked in my room comes to the forefront of my mind, and a little moan escapes my lips.

"Chiara, are you okay?" Robbie asks.

My cheeks burst into flames. "Yes, I'm fine."

Fuck. I'd better get my act together.

It turns out I can't concentrate at all during class, and when Alistair asks me a question, I make a complete fool of myself and answer, "Present," instead. People laugh. Usually I wouldn't mind it so much, but I hate that it happened in his class. I sink in my seat, trying to make myself even smaller than I already am.

Why couldn't he pretend I'm invisible?

Once the two-hour class is finally over, I can't wait to get the hell out of there. On my way to the door, I avoid looking in Alistair's direction. But five minutes later, he texts me asking if I can drop by his office. He must have memorized my schedule to know I have study hall after this class.

"I have time before my next class. Do you want to grab a drink at the cafeteria?" Robbie asks.

"Uh, rain check on that? I need to use the restroom."

"I can wait."

Come on, Robbie. Why are you being such a pain today?

"It's a number two situation," I reply through clenched teeth.

It's a lie, but my embarrassment is real. My face is hot, meaning it must be redder than a tomato.

Robbie's eyebrows arch. "Oh. Then go. I'll catch up with you later."

I hurry to the restroom and hide inside a stall until I'm alone. Then I apply a damp paper towel to my cheeks to try to get rid of the redness. The few minutes alone with my thoughts only work against me though. My asshole brain starts to conjure up the worst possible scenarios to why Alistair wants to see me. Maybe he changed his mind. After the way I reacted in his class, he probably realized I'm a liability he doesn't need.

Depressed, I head to his office, trying my best to look innocent. There's nothing wrong with a student going to see her teacher in his office. I hope my face isn't showing the mess of emotions that's making my heart beat faster when I knock on his door.

"Come in," Alistair says.

He's not at his desk but standing in front of a bookshelf,

looking for something. He turns once I close the door with a soft click.

"You wanted to see me, Mr. Walsh?"

He raises an eyebrow and smirks at me. "Is it terrible that I love when you call me that?"

Okay, he's definitely not breaking up with me, not with the way his eyes are devouring every inch of my body.

His gaze makes me feel powerful and beautiful, and I'm taken over by recklessness. I don't know why Alistair wanted to see me, but I do know what I want to do *to* him now that I'm here.

Looking over my shoulder, I find the door's dead bolt. *Perfect.* I lock it before moving closer.

His eyes narrow.

"Hmm, it depends," I say.

"On what?"

"On whether you're planning to do something about it." I stop in front of him, as close as I can get without our bodies actually touching.

I'm teasing, but I don't expect him to take the bait, not here in his office anyway.

To my surprise, he pushes me against the bookshelf and kisses me with a passion that I'm beginning to realize only Alistair can summon. I'm taken over by lust-induced madness when I maniacally work his fly. He seems to be caught on the same crazy train. His hands find their way under my skirt before he lifts me off the floor. I wrap my legs around his hips, and before I know it, my panties are pushed out of the way and he's inside me.

Holy shit, this is the hottest thing I've ever done.

His mouth devours mine without mercy while his thrusts become more relentless. The bookshelf starts to shake behind me, and a few books fall to the floor. Neither of us cares.

To avoid crying out when the most intense orgasm hits me,

I bite his shoulder. Alistair comes soon after amid his muffled grunts of pleasure.

Another minute goes by before I unlatch myself from him. The reality of what we did hits me hard when the evidence of Alistair's release drips down my legs.

Fuck. We totally forgot a condom.

Clarity returns to his eyes, and guilt sneaks in them as well. "Chiara, I'm so sorry. I didn't mean—"

I place a finger over his lips. "Shhh. It's okay. I'm on the pill and one-hundred-percent healthy."

He touches my face affectionately. "It's not only that. I didn't ask you to come here so I could ravish you. I just wanted to ask if you were okay. You spaced out in my class today."

"That's only because I was remembering your visit yesterday."

"Oh." He sounds genuinely surprised.

Shoving my insecurities aside, I say, "I think we need to talk, don't you?"

He walks to his desk, returning a second later with a Kleenex in hand. "Yes, we do."

I make a grab for the tissue, but Alistair drops to his knees and does the job for me. When his hand brushes near my sex, I pry the tissue from his grasp; if he touches the sensitive spot now, I might come again.

"Are we a couple?" I blurt before I lose my nerve.

Alistair smiles as he unfurls from his crouch. "Yes, Goldi. We are." A wave of relief rushes through my chest until he continues, "But we can't be out in the open. Not until this semester is over."

I try to hide my disappointment by looking down. "I know. That means coming to my apartment is probably too risky since a lot of DuBose students live there."

"Yes, I'd say so."

"How are we going to see each other, then?"

"You can come to my place if we're careful." He rubs my lips with his thumb.

I grin. "Hmm, a covert operation. I like the sound of that."

"I wish it didn't have to be this way. I hate seeing other guys coming on to you."

"Oh, are you referring to Phillip? That was just a silly act. It meant nothing."

Relief is evident in his expression. He captures my face between his hands and places a soft kiss on my lips. "Good."

"What about you, Alistair? Who does your heart belong to?" I sound pathetic and desperate asking the question, but I have to know.

There's only a brief pause before he replies, "It's yours, Goldilocks. Mangled and bruised, but it's all yours."

29

CHIARA

After our impromptu hookup in Alistair's office on Wednesday, we didn't dare take any more risks. We were both busy during the rest of the week, which meant I didn't get my booty fix. Friday, I was supposed to go over to his place, but he had to cancel it last minute on account of having dinner with his lawyer. And today, I have Robbie's mom's birthday party.

I'm about to order an Uber when Valerie texts me asking if I want a ride.

She arrives thirty minutes later, driving a freaking yellow Ferrari. My jaw is still hanging when I slide into the supple leather seat.

"Nice car."

"Thanks. It was a gift from my sugar daddy."

I give her an incredulous look. "What?"

She laughs. "Relax. I'm just kidding. My father gave it to me for my eighteenth birthday. He tries to compensate for missing every important milestone in my life with lavish and expensive gifts."

"I'm sorry."

"Don't be. I haven't spent that much time with the man to miss him, and I get to reap the benefits of his guilty conscience. It's a win-win situation for me."

Hardly. But I keep my opinion to myself.

I grew up around wealth. My family is well-to-do, but here in LA, it's all about wealth excess. No one in my private school back in Italy drove a Ferrari. Although if they did, they'd flaunt it, unlike Valerie. I couldn't tell her family came from money by the way she acts in school. She's super laid back and doesn't flash designer accessories—something I'm guilty of.

When we arrive at Robbie's house in Beverly Hills, the party is already going at full speed. From outside the gates, we can hear a live band playing a song I don't recognize but makes my bones want to dance.

"Have you ever met Robbie's parents?" I ask Valerie.

"Oh yeah. A few times. Monica Santos is the birthday girl. She owns a real estate business that caters to all the A-listers in the city. Tessa Donavan is an executive for a TV network."

"Talk about power couple." I eye the small box I got from Cartier, a suggestion from Robbie when I asked. "I hope she likes my gift."

"Oh, I'm sure."

I see a few people from school as I follow Valerie deeper into the party. Phillip, Harold, and even Josh are here. We don't stop to chat until we find the hosts though. Finally, we spot Robbie in the living room, wearing a velvet peacock-blue suit and equally bright pink button-down shirt.

"Chiara! You're here. Finally." He engulfs me in a hug.

"Hello to you too, jerkface." Valerie scowls.

He waves her off. "Pff, you practically live here." With his arm over my shoulders, he turns me around. "Mom and Mom, this is Chiara Moretti, the new transplant from Italy."

Two gorgeous women stare at me. One has luscious dark hair that cascades down her back and a deep tan that's accentuated by her skintight white dress, emphasizing her luscious curves. The second is fair and freckled and has red hair that matches Robbie's tone. She's wearing a less revealing dark green dress and seems more reserved than her wife. I can easily guess who is from Brazil, but I don't want to assume and end up sounding like an ass.

The brunette hugs me enthusiastically. Definitely the Brazilian.

She takes a step back. "Welcome. I'm Monica, and this is my wife, Tessa."

"Nice to meet you. Here, this is for you." I offer Monica the small box. "Happy birthday."

"Oh, thank you, sweetie."

Robbie hooks his arm with mine. "All right. Introductions were made. I'm going to show Chiara around now."

He steers me away from his mothers faster than a speeding train, surprising me.

"Where's the fire?" I ask.

"I had to get away from them. They were getting on my nerves."

"About what?"

"Stuff." He waves his hand dismissively. "Let's find the rest of the DuBose gang."

"We saw Phillip, Harold, and Josh earlier," Valerie pipes up, trailing behind us.

A raven-haired girl steps in our way with a bright smile on her face. Robbie has to stop suddenly to avoid barreling into her.

"Hi, Robbie," she says in an overly sweet tone.

"Hey, Jillian. What's up?"

There's no mistaking the coldness in his voice. She's our age, but I haven't seen her at DuBose.

"Not much. I just got here." She glances at me and Valerie.

"I see you invited some people from school. I'm raging mad that you didn't invite me."

She says it with a grin on her face, but her eyes are shining with annoyance.

God. Who the hell is this chick?

"You're here, aren't you?"

She pouts. "Yeah, I came with Dad."

He shrugs. "I figured I didn't need to bother inviting you since Principal Forrester was on the guest list."

Her phony smile wilts, and then she turns to me. "You're the new student from Italy, right?"

"Yep. That's me."

"Good job catching the eye of our QB. I could have sworn he was gay because I've never seen him with anyone. I mean, with any girl."

What the hell is she implying? If Phillip is gay, so what? I just met this girl, and I already don't like her.

Robbie scoffs. "Really, Jillian? You've been at this party for five seconds and you're already talking shit. And you wonder why I didn't invite you. Come on, Chiara. Let's continue the tour."

He walks around her, taking me with him.

"That was so rude, Robbie," Jillian complains behind us.

"So, that's the principal's daughter?" I ask after we're out of earshot.

"Yep. The biggest gossipy bitch in school. I hate her."

"I just met her and I'm with you on that."

"No one really likes her, not even her friends. They stay close out of fear. The bitch has destroyed more lives with her forked tongue than Daenerys Targaryen with her dragon."

We finally find the guys, who greet us with overexaggerated cheers. They look drunk already, even Josh. And here I thought he was so serious and responsible.

With a goofy smile, he hugs me. "Chiara, glad you made it."

I hug him back while looking wide-eyed at Robbie over Josh's shoulder. He gives me a boyish shrug and then whispers something in Phillip's ear. The guy throws his head back and laughs. Josh is still glued to me, so I have to push him back to break free. He staggers, and I notice his eyes are bloodshot. Is he drunk or high? Or maybe both? After getting judged by him when I accidentally ate Harold's brownie, I'm annoyed to see him in this state.

"Ooh, look who's here, Chiara," Robbie says, looking over my head. "Our favorite teacher."

My chest becomes tight suddenly. *No, Alistair can't possibly be here.*

I turn around slowly, and sure as shit, there he is, across the swimming pool talking to Robbie's parents.

"I didn't know he was friends with your mothers," I say.

"Oh yeah, through my uncle Caio, my mother's younger brother. He and Alistair are tight, went to college together."

"Small world," I mumble.

"LA is a village. Come on, let me get you something to drink."

I should pry my gaze from Alistair. If I stare at him too long, I'll give away that I'm hot for teacher. But knowing I should and doing it are completely different things.

As if sensing my stare, Alistair turns to me and, in a plot twist, curls his lips into a crooked grin. I didn't tell him I'd be here tonight, but he probably guessed since I'm friends with Robbie. Why the hell didn't he tell me he was coming too so I'd be prepared?

"Chiara? What are you staring at?" Valerie asks me.

I shake my head. "Nothing."

Robbie snorts. "Yeah, right. I think Chiara has a major crush on Mr. Walsh."

Heat creeps up my cheeks. "I do not! You're the one who's always drooling over the man."

Phillip steps closer and throws his arm over my shoulders. "Of course she's not crushing on old Mr. Walsh when she has me, her golden knight, by her side."

My instinct is to push Phillip away, but I don't. It's in my best interest to get Robbie off my case. I do, however, roll my eyes.

"You're just saying that because I broke the curse," I say.

"That was just a perk."

Robbie is the one who comes between us and pries me away from Phillip. "Get off her, you goon. You're wrinkling her pretty dress."

"Hey, no I'm not. Tell him, oh fair maiden."

I laugh at their antics, immediately feeling less nervous about Alistair's presence here. If I just hang out with my friends, there's zero chance I'll mess up and reveal my secret.

Robbie hands me a caipirinha—a typical Brazilian cocktail that's super strong. I take one sip, and it immediately goes to my head.

"Whoa. What are you trying to do to me, Robbie?" I ask, then take another large sip.

This stuff is good.

"What?" He widens his eyes innocently as he laughs. But suddenly his amusement vanishes. He squints and curses, "Son of a bitch. What is she doing here?"

I turn around to follow his gaze. It takes me a moment to find the person he's staring at. When I do, my blood runs cold.

Nadine Perez, Alistair's ex-wife, is here.

30

ALISTAIR

Enzo would kill me if he knew I came to Monica's birthday party knowing Chiara would be here. To be fair, I wasn't completely sure, and that's what I'm going to say when he calls to bite my head off. I could have given Monica an excuse to bail, even though I'd already said I'd come, but I couldn't resist seeing Chiara at a social event even though I have to stay away from her.

Idiot that I am, I didn't count on succumbing to jealous rage from witnessing Chiara have fun with her male classmates. Josh Flannigan and Phillip Harrison are getting too close to her for my liking.

"Earth to Alistair." Caio snaps his fingers in front of my face. "Where the hell have you been?"

"What?" I bark.

"I've been talking to myself for the past minute."

I shake my head. "Sorry. I spaced out for a moment."

"Divorce shit?"

"Yeah. What's new?" I take a sip of my drink to mask the lie.

His spine goes taut suddenly as his eyes narrow. "Things are about to get worse. Fucking Nadine is here."

I almost choke on my beer. "What?"

I look over my shoulder and see the viper in the arms of an older guy I don't recognize.

"I can't believe she had the balls to show up here," Caio says, his voice tight with anger.

"I can. It fits her MO."

I drain the rest of my beer and wish I could drink something stronger, but that'd be a mistake considering Chiara is also at this party. I have to keep my head straight to avoid a disaster.

Tessa, Caio's sister-in-law, walks over. "I'm sorry, Alistair. We didn't invite Nadine. I didn't even know Greggory knew her."

"Don't worry."

I notice Nadine and her date are coming our way. I stay put, even though my desire is to keep my distance from her venom. There's no chance in hell I'd give her the satisfaction of leaving the party because of her.

Greggory exchanges pleasantries with Tessa and Monica while Nadine smiles triumphantly at me. I don't know what she's so smug about. Fucking an old fart to stay afloat? Hardly an accomplishment.

Greggory turns to me. "Alistair Walsh, I hope you don't mind that I'm escorting Nadine tonight."

I snicker. "Mind? Not at all."

"Alistair is not the type to show his emotions, Greg dear. He may look as calm as a cucumber, but he could be simmering with anger."

"This is not my calm mask, Nadine. It's my indifferent look."

I walk away before she can twist my words around and truly make me mad. Manipulation is her game, but she can't play it alone.

On my way to the restroom, I stop a waiter carrying a tray of shots and grab one. I mistakenly thought it was tequila, realizing too late it's cachaça, a Brazilian spirit that burns ten times hotter down my throat. I should have known.

Chiara suddenly crosses in my line of vision, veering toward the restroom I had been going to a moment ago. I quicken my steps and reach her before she can disappear through the door.

"Chiara," I call out.

She stops and glances over her shoulder. I was expecting a neutral expression, not the fury burning in her eyes.

"Mr. Walsh. I didn't expect to see you here," she replies coldly.

"I RSVPed a while ago."

"Sure." She turns away to continue on her path to the restroom.

I should let her go. She's angry at me, and now is not the time to fix things, especially with Nadine here. But I'm an idiot, and also, I can't stand to see Chiara mad. So I reach over and grab her arm.

She pulls free from my grasp with a jerk and glares. "Don't touch me."

"You're drunk."

"So? Are you going to play the mature adult and burst my bubble?"

I pass a hand over my face in an attempt to rein in my temper. I can't have an argument with a student in front of all these people. It'd be like waving a flag that we're together.

"No. I'm leaving. Have fun, Miss Moretti."

***

CHIARA

My heart sinks as I watch Alistair walk away. I can't believe I let jealousy and insecurity take control like that just because his ex-wife showed up at the party—with another man, I might add. I'm an imbecile.

Tomorrow, I can blame my behavior on the two caipirinhas I had. Right now, I just want to hide in a bathroom and cry.

Someone touches my shoulder, and stupid me thinks it's Alistair who came back.

"Are you okay, Chiara?" Robbie asks, and I'm not quick enough to hide my disappointment.

"Yeah, I'm fine."

"You don't seem fine. Did you expect someone else?"

"What? No."

He hooks his arm with mine and begins to steer me up the stairs. "We need to talk."

"Where are we going?"

"I promised you a tour, and I never delivered. I want to show you my room."

I think nothing of it until I'm inside his bedroom and find Phillip lounging on Robbie's bed like he belongs there.

"Hey, babe. What took you so—" His eyes widen when he sees me standing next to Robbie.

"What's going on?" I ask.

Phillip sits up straighter and looks from me to Robbie in a panic. "Yeah, I'd like to know as well."

"I'm gonna tell her," Robbie replies.

Phillip jumps from the bed as if he'd been electrocuted. "Tell her what?"

"That we're together."

Dio Santo. I didn't expect that.

Phillip laughs nervously. "In your dreams, buddy. Don't believe a word he says, Chiara. Robbie is a jokester."

"I can't keep this secret anymore, Phillip. I love you, and I want to be able to tell the world that."

Phillip's eyes widen, shining with anguish.

Shit. So Jillian's insinuations were true.

"I don't care if you're gay, Phillip," I say.

He whips his face to mine, frowning now. "You may not care, but society does. Do you think I have a chance in hell of playing football at college level if people knew I was gay? No one would recruit me."

Robbie pulls his hair back and begins to pace. "It's not fair."

"Babe, we've talked about this."

"Uh, maybe I shouldn't be here," I chime in.

"Yeah, I don't think you should," Phillip retorts.

"No, I brought Chiara here because she's the only one who would understand our situation and maybe help us."

"What do you mean?" I ask, feeling leery now.

With a glint in his eyes, he says, "I know about you and Mr. Walsh."

What the hell! I feel the blood drain from my face.

"Mr. Walsh and me?" I laugh nervously. "Are you for real?"

"You don't need to lie, Chiara. I heard you in his office. It was pretty clear to me what you were doing in there."

Oh God. I want a hole to open in the floor and swallow me whole. My cheeks are burning up from mortification.

"You were eavesdropping?" I grit out. "I can't believe this."

"I didn't mean to."

"Oh no. You *did* mean to do it. You followed me and then stood outside Alistair's office."

"Robbie, why did you do that, babe?" Phillip asks.

"Because I had a suspicion, and I wanted to be sure. Can't you see? Chiara is having an illicit affair with a teacher. And we can't disclose we're together either. We can be each other's alibis."

I curl my hands into fists, trying my best to not yell obscenities at him.

"You want me to fake date your boyfriend. Is that your plan?" I ask.

"Yeah. You can't deny it's a brilliant idea," Robbie replies.

I shake my head, disgusted. "I can't be here."

"Chiara, where are you going?" Phillip asks.

I don't answer as I walk out of Robbie's room, then sprint down the hallway and the stairs. I try to find Valerie to tell her I'm leaving, but there are too many people, and I can't see her anywhere.

Phillip calls my name from somewhere behind me. I don't slow down. He doesn't catch up with me until I'm outside.

"Chiara, wait." Grabbing my arm, he turns me around.

"Let go of me, Phillip."

"I know you're mad at Robbie, but please don't do anything harsh."

"Who do you take me for? I'm not going to blabber. Now let me go."

Suddenly Alistair is there, yanking Phillip away from me by the back of his shirt. "You heard her."

Phillip staggers back, looking as white as a ghost. "Mr. Walsh. It's not what it looks like."

Alistair ignores Phillip to look at my arm, then at my face. "Are you okay? Did he hurt you?"

His eyes are shining with barely contained rage. If I say one wrong thing, he'll unleash that on poor Phillip.

"I'm fine," I insist. "I just want to go home."

"I'll take you."

I shouldn't accept Alistair's offer, but staying another minute here is not an option either.

"Okay."

Phillip throws me a pleading glance before he heads back inside.

I meant what I said. I'd never reveal his secret to anyone, no matter how angry I am at Robbie.

But will Robbie grant me the same courtesy?

31

ALISTAIR

I should have left the party like I said I would and not lingered in the hopes of talking to Chiara again. I don't know what I'm doing here, acting like a fucking teenager. But I can't help myself. Every time I'm with her, I unravel.

No matter what happens, she'll be the ruin of me. I know that deep in my bones. And yet here I am, jumping off the edge gladly.

I'm in the middle of a casual conversation with acquaintances when I catch Chiara dashing through the party, followed by Phillip. She seems upset about something. I excuse myself and follow them, not thinking clearly about what I intend to do once I catch up.

Forrester spots me as I'm closing in on Phillip and waves me over. If I stop to speak to him now, it might be too late to investigate what happened to Chiara. I show him my phone and signal that I need to make a call.

When I finally step outside, the scene I witness makes my blood boil. Phillip is holding Chiara by her arm, ignoring her when she asks him to let her go.

What the actual fuck?

I'm on the son of a bitch in an instant, yanking him back by the collar of his shirt.

"You heard her," I almost snarl like an enraged beast.

"Mr. Walsh. It's not what it looks like," he stammers.

I ignore him as I stare at the red mark his fingers left on her arm, then at her face. She looks frightened, but of me or the imbecile behind me?

"Are you okay? Did he hurt you?" I ask.

"I'm fine. I just want to go home." She hugs her middle, looking even smaller than she is.

"I'll take you."

There's no question about it. I don't care about the risks or consequences. I can't let Chiara go home alone. If she says no, I'll have to insist, beg if needed.

"Okay," she whispers.

Damn it. What the hell happened between her and Phillip to put her in this state?

I try not to let my imagination run wild. I don't need more reason to be furious at him.

We walk in silence to my car, and when I open the door for her, she doesn't glance at me. Once I'm behind the steering wheel, I can't hold my tongue any longer.

"Tell me the truth, Goldi. Did Phillip hurt you?"

"No. He really didn't."

I rub my face, a vain attempt to regain some control.

"Explain to me what I saw, then."

She crosses her arms and stares out the window. "There's nothing to explain. Are you going to drive, or are you waiting for your ex-wife to catch us here and ruin your life?"

With a push of a button, my car roars to life. It works to hide the noise of my teeth grinding together. Only when Monica and Tessa's mansion disappears from my rearview mirror do I speak again.

"I didn't know Nadine would be at the party."

"Did you know I'd be there though?"

"I guessed."

"You guessed?" Her voice rises an octave. "Why didn't you tell me? I wasn't prepared to see you there."

"I don't know, Goldi. Maybe I didn't want you to not go on my account. Maybe I just fucking missed you, okay?"

"I missed you too."

With a groan, I throw my head back, hitting the headrest with a soft thud. "I hate this."

My confession feels immature, like a teenager throwing a tantrum. I'm a grown-ass man. I should be handling this situation better than I am.

"Hate what?"

"Not being able to take you to a party. Having to watch you flirt with guys who are your age and much better suited for you."

"God. You make it sound like you're an ancient man. You're only eight years older than me. Besides, I wasn't flirting with anyone."

I glance at her again, finding her looking out the window.

"I'm sorry." I touch her arm, drawing her attention back to me.

A pitiful smile pulls at her lips. "I hate this situation too, especially when I see you in front of your ex-wife."

Fuck. I can't drive when all I want to do is take Chiara in my arms. I pull into a business complex parking lot and stop the car.

"What are you doing?" she asks.

"You have no reason to be jealous, Goldi. I only have eyes for you." I lean over and unbuckle her seat belt, then pinch her chin between my thumb and forefinger. "Come here."

Chiara doesn't offer resistance. I kiss her tenderly, loving the taste of her tongue. I cup the back of her head so she can't move away when my soft kiss becomes something else.

I loop my arms around her waist, and with ease, I help her cross to my side so she can sit on my lap. A sense of déjà vu hits me. The first time we kissed was also inside a car. I vividly remember how turned on she made me, how hot and smooth her sweet pussy was under my fingers. I want to make her come again, just like that.

My hands disappear underneath her skirt, traveling up her thighs until they reach her hips. The difference tonight is that she's wearing tights, which unfortunately makes access to her core a little more difficult. I cup her sex just the same, applying pressure to her clit through the layers of fabric.

Chiara hisses against my mouth before whispering my name softly. My cock twitches, more than ready for action. *Down, boy. It's all about Chiara right now.* I slowly circle her bundle of nerves with my thumb while I keep kissing her like there's no tomorrow. She bites my lower lip right before her entire body trembles and she says, "Yes," several times in a row.

I pull my hands from under her skirt to crush her against my chest. She rests her head on my shoulder and lets out a contented sigh.

"Was that your way to say you were sorry for not telling me you'd be at the party?" she asks.

"Yes." I kiss the side of her head before I continue. "Do you want to come to my place?"

If she says no, I don't think a cold shower will suffice.

"To spend the night?" She leans back to peer at my face.

"Yes, of course."

"I don't have anything with me."

"I have a spare toothbrush, and you can wear one of my T-shirts to sleep in. Or nothing if you prefer," I tease.

She leans forward and kisses me again, making my desire escalate to a new height. I'm tempted to move the action to the back of my truck and fuck Chiara there. That's how badly she's messing with my head. I'm breaking all the rules for her.

"Okay, then. Let's go," she whispers against my lips but makes no attempt to get off my lap.

"Goldi, I can't drive with you on top of me."

"You can't?" She kisses my neck. "That's too bad."

"I never knew you to be so cruel. I'm dying here."

"Okay, okay." She finally slides back to her seat, putting the seat belt on without taking her eyes off me.

With a new sense of urgency, I peel out of the parking lot faster than lightning.

"How long until we get to your house?" she asks.

"At this hour, probably around twenty minutes."

"Good." She unbuckles her seat belt and bends over, leaning over my crotch.

"Goldi, what are you doing?"

"I'm trying to prove I'm not cruel. I don't want you to wait that long to get some well-deserved release."

She makes quick work of my fly, releasing my cock in the next second. Her apt fingers curl around my shaft right before she swipes her tongue over the sensitive head. A hiss escapes my lips, and I'm forced to grip the steering wheel tighter to keep the truck in its lane.

Chiara doesn't waste time teasing—thank fuck. She brings my entire length into her warm mouth until my cock hits the back of her throat. She repeats the motion, holding the base with one hand and applying just the right amount of pressure. My balls become tighter; it won't take long for her to send me over the edge.

I place one hand on her back because I need to touch her. I'm glad my windows are tinted when I stop at a red light right next to a police cruiser. I don't glance in their direction, just keep staring straight ahead. The light mercifully turns green, and the cruiser veers to the right. I come in the next second, letting out a guttural sound as Chiara swallows my hot release.

I forget to drive, and the light turns red again. Yes, I'm definitely lucky the cops are gone.

"Holy fuck. You're a magician, Goldi," I say once I catch my breath.

"So I'm no longer cruel?"

I glance at her, catching her wiping the corner of her mouth. A sexier sight I've never seen. "No, you're not cruel, but you have a wicked mouth."

She rewards me with a lazy smile, and my semihard cock starts to come to life again.

Jesus, I need to get home ASAP.

32

CHIARA

I don't know if it's the clandestine nature of my relationship with Alistair or the man himself that brings out the naughtiest side of me. I've never blown a guy in a moving car before. I never had the desire to do so, but with him, I want to try everything.

After a twenty-minute ride, Alistair parks in front of a luxurious condo. Now that I know about his past, I no longer wonder how he can afford certain things.

He cuts the engine before twisting his body to retrieve something from the back seat. A hoodie.

"Here, put this on before you get out of the car."

"You're really that worried? It's the middle of the night. No one will see me."

"I can't be too careful, Goldi. I'm going through a nasty divorce. I wouldn't put it past Nadine to have hired a PI to dig up dirt on me."

It hits me then how much Alistair is risking to be with me. The notion brings conflicting feelings into my heart. He can lose his career, his reputation.

I put the hoodie on, swallowed up immediately by the

excess of fabric. Once I pull the hood over my head, you can't see my face at all. Well, *I* can barely see, that's for sure.

Satisfied that there's not a chance in hell I can be identified, we both get out of the car. He motions for me to walk ahead of him, as if he's afraid I'll get attacked. I've never dated a guy who wanted to protect me so fiercely, and it feels nice. I think he'd have turned Phillip into mush if he had indeed hurt me.

Alistair's home is a mix of modern and rough, just like him. The exposed brick fireplace works well with the contemporary fixtures and the few pieces of decoration. The L-shaped couch is plush and inviting in a deep brown color. I take in the open living space with a quick glance, noticing the absence of something vital to me.

"You don't own a TV?" I ask.

"I don't have cable."

"So, you're not the typical American guy who watches *Sunday Night Football*?"

Alistair smirks. "I don't hate football, but I usually prefer to watch it at a sports bar."

"What about movies?"

He grabs a remote control from the end table, and with the push of a button, a home theater screen descends from the ceiling.

"Okay, it's official. I'm never leaving your house."

Alistair laughs. "I'm more than okay with that, but I'm afraid that if you're here—" He hugs me from behind and kisses my neck. "—we wouldn't have much time for movies."

I lean against him, loving the feel of his virile body against mine. He keeps placing soft kisses on my neck as his right hand disappears through the elastic band of my skirt. He cups my breast with his other hand, making me moan like a kitten. When his fingers find their way to my core, my legs turn to jelly.

"I love how wet you get for me, Goldi."

I reach back, trying to touch his erection as well. I manage, but through his pants, I doubt he can feel much.

With a growl, Alistair pushes me against the back of the couch, pulling my skirt up and my tights and panties down. I don't mind the roughness. I love it. His cock teases at my entrance, and I try to move closer.

With one arm still wrapped around my chest, he whispers in my ear, "I want to take you hard, Goldi. Is that okay?"

"Yes." I arch my back, wanting—no, needing more contact.

He rams into me, and I cry out. He pauses immediately. "Chiara?"

"Why did you stop?"

"I thought I hurt you."

"You're hurting me right now with all this talking."

He chuckles against my ear before thrusting his hips against mine, harder than before. With every pump, he sends me higher and higher, and I know it's the same for him. He bites my shoulder, and that sends me right over the edge. I cry as loud as I can, not worrying for once about neighbors or school staff overhearing us.

"Chiara, fuck!" Alistair says right before he climaxes as well.

I clench my internal walls, milking his orgasm and mine. With a final thrust, he shudders against my neck. My heart feels like it's about to explode with the way it's hammering inside my chest. When he pulls out, I feel empty.

"Don't move. I'll be right back," he says.

I twist my neck to see where he's going. "You do realize this is a very awkward position, right?"

He returns a second later with a washcloth in his hand. "I find it a very appealing position."

Like he did before in his office, Alistair cleans the mess he left behind. I moan when he wipes my clit. I'm still so sensitive there. He moves the cloth away, down my legs, but I want him to go back to my bundle of nerves. I grab his wrist and bring his hand to my pussy again.

"I'm still dirty there."

"Oh yeah?"

He rubs the cloth over my clit again, and I open my legs wider to grant him better access. I must look ridiculous with my ass up in the air like this, but with Alistair, I don't feel ashamed. His hand moves away, and I open my mouth to complain, but it dies in my throat when his warm tongue replaces the cloth.

Madonna santa. This feels so good.

Alistair said I was a magician back in the car, but he's the one with the magical tongue. He licks and sucks, drinking my juices with gusto as he goes. It doesn't take long for me to come again. By the time he's done, I can't so much as move a muscle. I'm boneless as I sink against the couch, content to fall asleep just like this.

"Goldi, are you still with me?"

"Yeah, give me a minute. I'm trying to recover."

I hear him unfurl from his crouch, but I don't move. I let out a soft yelp when he lifts me up and carries me across the room. That's the only sound I make before I wrap my arms around his neck and snuggle against his chest.

If this is a dream, I don't want to wake up.

33

CHIARA

A loud buzzing noise wakes me from a perfect sleep. I sink farther into the mattress, pulling the covers over my head. Behind me, Alistair growls, wrapping his arm over my belly, infusing my body with heat when his naked body is flush with mine. He presses his erection against my back, reminding me of the constant throbbing between my legs. I melt into him but keep my eyes closed.

The irritating noise comes again, and I finally realize it's the doorbell.

"For fuck's sake." He pushes the cover off him with a jerky movement and gets out of bed.

I look over my shoulder and get an eyeful of his naked glory. My mouth waters at the sight of his wide back, corded with muscles, and his yummy ass.

I can't believe this man is all mine.

"What time is it?" I ask, my voice still rough from sleep—or from all the screaming I did last night.

"Too early. Go back to sleep, Goldi. I'll be right back." Alistair puts a pair of loose pants on before walking out of the room.

Not completely awake yet, I close my eyes, trying to go back to sleep, but without his warm body behind me, the bed no longer feels that welcoming. Plus, whoever was at his door on a Sunday morning is now in the house, speaking loudly.

Curiosity makes me fully awake.

I throw my legs to the side of the bed and get up. Goose bumps break out all over my body as the cold air hits my skin. *Where the hell are my clothes?* Alistair was the one who undressed me last night. Heat rushes to my cheeks as the memory comes to the forefront of my mind.

A moment later, I find them neatly folded on the chair in the corner.

Alistair's muffled voice reaches me through the door, but I can't make out what he's saying. I can hear the annoyance in his tone though.

I put my clothes on, not bothering to look at my reflection in the mirror to see if I'm presentable or not. I have no intention of showing my face to whoever is downstairs.

Opening the door slowly, I stick my head out. The voices are a little clearer now but still hard to hear. I tiptoe down the hall-way, stopping just at the top of the stairs. The conversation ceases for a moment, replaced by the loud banging of cupboards being opened and shut.

"Where the hell do you keep your coffee, Alistair?"

"I don't think you need any more stimulants."

"I'm fine. This is just my post-workout burst of energy."

"And you want to add coffee to that?"

"I have a full day of work today, and I've run out of coffee. I know you have the good stuff here."

"Does my house look like a fucking Starbucks to you?"

"You know I can't stand that shit."

Alistair groans before telling the visitor where the coffee is.

Who is this guy, and why is Alistair putting up with him?

Curiouser and curiouser.

"You still haven't told me why you're here," Alistair says.

"Nadine's lawyer is pushing the joint account issue, but I think I've found a way to fight that. It'll drag out the process though."

My heart stops beating for a second. So the man downstairs is Alistair's lawyer. I shouldn't be eavesdropping, but my feet are glued to the floor.

Bad, bad Chiara.

"About that. I've decided to give Nadine the money and be done with it."

"Son of a bitch. Tell me you're joking."

"I want that woman out of my life for good, Enzo. She's not asking for an unreasonable amount."

"That's what I said from the beginning, but you were dead set on pursuing the case. Does your change of heart have anything to do with the student you screwed in Italy?"

I wince at the crude manner in which Enzo talks about me. At the same time, my heart starts to beat faster, anticipating Alistair's answer.

"No," he answers quickly, and disappointment washes over me. "I saw Nadine last night at Monica's party and realized she'll never leave me alone until she gets what she wants. I want that viper out of my life for good."

"Hallelujah. You're finally listening to me."

"I wasn't thinking clearly. Rage and thirst for revenge clouded my judgment. I'm ready to move on. I don't want to waste my time dragging out the divorce process just out of spite. It's not like I was still in love with Nadine when she cheated on me."

Enzo sighs. "Sometimes ego drives us to make bad decisions. I can start working on the settlement papers if that's what you want."

"Yes, that's what I want."

I bite my lower lip to keep from shouting out of happiness.

Alistair is finally getting a divorce. He'll be free, which is one less thing for us to worry about.

Deciding I've heard enough, I begin to retreat when I feel a strange sensation on the top of my foot. I look down and find a huge tarantula crawling on me. I scream from the top of my lungs as I jump back, kicking my leg to dislodge the giant arachnid.

Alistair comes running up the stairs the next moment, his eyes round with worry. "What happened?"

I point a shaking finger at the eight-legged critter scurrying away. "That."

"Oh, fuck. Mildred, how did you get out of your container?"

"You own that thing?"

He bends over and lets the spider crawl on his hand. "Yeah. Don't worry. Tarantulas are harmless."

I take a few steps back. I hate spiders.

"For fuck's sake, Alistair. Is that the girl?" Enzo asks from the bottom of the stairs, his hard expression showing how pissed off he is.

Alistair doesn't glance in his direction, just keeps staring at me with an apology in his eyes when he replies, "Yes."

The guy walks back to the kitchen, cursing loudly. Alistair takes a step toward me, but I raise my hand. "Don't move any closer with that thing in your hand."

"Are you afraid of Mildred, Goldi?"

A shiver runs down my spine, and I hug my middle. "Terrified."

He chuckles. "Okay. I'll put her back in her cage. I must not have shut the latch properly yesterday."

He disappears into another room, returning a moment later. "Shall we?" He points down the stairs.

"Is it wise? I think your lawyer is about to bite your head off."

"Enzo? Nah. He's only ruthless in court."

I follow Alistair downstairs, still feeling unsure of myself. Enzo is in the kitchen, leaning against the counter with a mug of freshly brewed coffee in his hand. His eyes narrow when he looks at me, and I want to run back to the bedroom.

"When did this happen?" he asks.

"Does it matter?" Alistair throws his arm over my shoulders and kisses the top of my head.

Enzo's eyes seem to shine with understanding. He takes another sip of coffee. "You're getting good at bullshitting me, Alistair."

"I don't follow," he says.

"When I asked you earlier if your decision to settle with Nadine had anything to do with your student, you said no. Now I know that's not true."

Heat rushes to my cheeks, and I drop my gaze. I don't dare to hope Enzo is speaking the truth.

"Well, now you know," Alistair replies.

"I need coffee," I blurt, trying to divert the conversation away from me.

Acting as if the house is his, Enzo grabs another cup and fills it up for me. I step away from Alistair's embrace, feeling exposed as I do so, but I don't want to give the impression that I'm a scared mouse, even though I'm quivering inside.

"Thanks." I grab the cup, bringing it immediately to my lips to partially hide my face. The most wonderful flavor hits my tongue. I've only tasted such divine coffee in Italy. "This is amazing."

Enzo shrugs. "It must be the Italian touch. I'm very good at making coffee."

"You're Italian?"

He chuckles. "Didn't the name Enzo clue you in? Second-generation Italian-American."

I switch to Italian, and Enzo replies. We only exchange a few words before Alistair puts a stop to it.

"Okay, enough with the secret code language."

I giggle, and Enzo rolls his eyes. Alistair was right, he isn't that intimidating.

He drinks the last sip of his coffee, then puts the cup back on the counter. "Well, thank you for a very entertaining morning, Alistair. I'll start the paperwork as soon as I get home. And please, for the love of God, be careful. We don't want Nadine finding out about you two before she signs the papers."

Enzo turns to me, extending his hand. "Nice to meet you...."

"The name is Chiara," I say.

"Nice to meet you, Chiara."

We shake hands, and then Enzo claps Alistair's shoulder before heading out.

After the lawyer is gone, Alistair pulls me to him and kisses me tenderly. I melt like butter in his arms. This man has so much power over me; it's a little scary. The kiss doesn't last long, and when Alistair pulls back, he says, "I'm sorry."

"For what?"

"For Enzo. No one needs to be exposed to him early in the morning."

I smirk. "You should be apologizing about the spider."

"I'm sorry about that too."

"I have to apologize as well."

He furrows his brows. "For what?"

I lower my gaze. "For eavesdropping on your conversation."

He places his finger under my chin and lifts my face to his. "That was very naughty of you. I think I have to punish you for that."

I should laugh, but instead I ask, "Did you really mean what you said? Does your decision to settle with your ex-wife have anything to do with me?"

"In part, yes. Does that scare you?"

I'm scared, yes, but not about that. I'm afraid one day Alistair will get tired of me. I don't share any of my insecurities with him though. Instead, I say, "No. It makes me happy."

"Good. I want to make you happy, Goldi."

"I love you, Alistair," I say despite the deep-rooted fear that I'm not good enough for him.

I kiss him again, not wanting to hear the sound of his silence. He hasn't said he loves me, even though he's done many things that show he cares about me.

He tangles his fingers in my hair, keeping me in place while his tongue mingles with mine in a slow, sexy dance. I'm so ready to go back to his room, and the bulge pressing against my belly tells me he is too.

Alistair pulls back and stares into my eyes. "I love you too, Chiara."

My breath catches while my heart takes off in a mad race. "You do?"

"Yes. You have no idea."

He crushes his lips against mine, melting my anxiety away.

34

CHIARA

I spent the entire weekend with Alistair, which was amazing. In consequence, I can't walk properly today. The first-period teacher is not in the classroom yet, but Robbie is. I purposely tried not to think about our fight while I was with Alistair, but now it's all coming back to me. Our gazes lock, and even with the distance, I can read the remorse in his eyes.

I'm still mad at him, but I choose to be the bigger person and pull out the chair next to his.

"Hi, Chiara. I've called and left you several messages," he says.

"I know."

"I'm so fucking sorry about that whole mess. Please say you forgive me."

"What you did was shitty, Robbie. You could have asked me instead of spying. You know how embarrassing that was?"

"True. I could have asked, but can you honestly say you'd tell me the truth? Besides, anyone walking by could have heard you. It's not like you guys were being quiet."

Hell, I thought we were.

"Shhh." I glance around, afraid others are listening to our conversation, but the classroom isn't full yet, and the students present aren't near us.

"Sorry. I know what I did was bad, but I did you guys a favor. I'd totally cover for you if needed."

Cazzo. We were careless that day.

"All right. I forgive you. Can we please stop talking about it, please?"

"Sure. Have you thought about—"

"I'm not going to cover for you," I grit out.

"I understand. Phillip wasn't sold on the idea either." Robbie shrugs, looking defeated. "He's sorry for manhandling you."

"He didn't manhandle me."

"Well, apparently Mr. Walsh thought otherwise. When Phillip came back, he was as white as a sheet of paper."

"Yeah, Alistair wasn't happy. But it's all good."

Valerie drops in the seat in front of us, forcing our conversation to a stop.

"Morning, bitches. What's up?"

"Not much," Robbie replies.

Valerie looks at me. "Were you feeling okay on Sunday?"

Her question makes me tense because for a moment, I forget that I texted her with an excuse to leave the party early on Saturday.

"Yeah," I reply when my brain catches up.

"I could have taken you home, you know."

"I didn't want to be a pain. You were having fun. It's not your fault that I can't handle more than one caipirinha."

Valerie snickers. "You're not the only one who couldn't handle his alcohol. Josh was pitiful. I've never seen him that wasted."

The teacher enters the classroom, and we have to put a pin

on our conversation. I want to ask about Josh, but that will have to wait until later.

As the day progresses, I begin to relax. I was worried that someone had seen me leave the party with Alistair. I told Robbie we were cool, but it will take a while for the annoyance to completely go away. We manage to fall back into the easy rapport we had when we first met though.

But when we bump into Phillip on our way to the cafeteria, things become awkward again, and the reason for our fight comes back to the forefront of my mind. Phillip looks more sorrowful than Robbie did. Poor guy. It sucks that they can't be together, and it also breaks my heart.

"Hey, Chiara. How are you?" Phillips asks, staring at me with a dejected puppy look in his eyes.

"I'm good. And you?"

"Good."

A moment of uncomfortable silence follows.

"Oh, for fuck's sake. Can we just go back to last week when all secrets were still secrets?" Robbi asks, exasperated.

"Oh, and what secrets would those be, Robbie?" Jillian asks from behind us.

Crap.

"Get lost, Jillian," Robbie retorts.

"If you don't want people to know about your depraved ways, you shouldn't have hookups during a party, Robbie." She smiles maliciously while glancing at Phillip.

Robbie rolls his eyes. "Oh, honey. Do you think I care about what people say about my sex life?"

"Maybe you don't, but I'm sure Phillip does." She raises an eyebrow.

Shit. Did she see Phillip go in Robbie's room last Saturday?

I don't want her venomous tongue to hurt my friends. I step closer to Phillip, looping my arm around his waist.

"I hardly think making out with my boyfriend in a private room is depraved."

Jillian's eyes go rounder. "You're dating Phillip?"

He smiles at me as if I was the object of his affection. "Yep. She captured my heart at first sight."

To seal the deal, I cup his cheek, rise on my tiptoes, and place a soft kiss on his lips.

There. That should be enough to stop this bitch from spreading more gossip.

I'm smiling when I look at her again, but it's an effort to keep it up when I see Alistair standing in the hallway, glaring at me.

ALISTAIR

It takes every ounce of self-control I have not to stride across the hallway and punch that punk in the face. Jealousy is a dangerous beast, and I can't claim to be its master. So I do the best I can in this situation—I turn around and walk away.

I'm seething when I finally enter my office and close the door. Behind my desk, I rest my head in my hands and take deep breaths. That's what I get for falling for my student. God, I'm such an idiot.

I should have never restarted things with Chiara. But hell, resisting her was impossible. She got under my skin, left a brand on my heart. I've never wanted anyone like I want her. She puts my sex drive on steroids. I'm constantly semihard when she's around, which is a fucking problem when I'm her teacher.

I can't head to my next class in this state, that's for sure.

I turn on my laptop, hoping email checking will distract me.

A knock on my door makes me grind my teeth. I hope she isn't foolish enough to come see me.

"Who is it?"

"It's Phillip, Mr. Walsh. May I come in?"

I curl my hands into fists. *What is this asshole doing here?*

Damn it. I'm really losing it. Here I am cursing at a student because he likes someone he thinks is available.

"Yeah, sure."

He looks nervous as he steps inside and closes the door. I avoid eye contact because the urge to punch his face is still there, simmering just below my skin.

"How can I help you, Mr. Harrison?"

"I want to explain what you saw just now."

That gets my attention. "What do you mean?"

"There's nothing going on between Chiara and me. She's just pretending to be my girlfriend to help me out."

There's a loud roar in my ears. I want to yell obscenities, but I have to keep a level head here.

"I don't understand how that's my concern."

"Sir, I know about you and Chiara."

Damn everything to hell.

"Excuse me?"

Phillip raises his hands, palms facing me. "You don't have to worry, Mr. Walsh. Robbie and I won't say a word. I swear."

"Robbie knows about this?" I grit out, gripping the edge of my desk.

"Yeah, but you see, we have a secret too. I'm with Robbie. He's...." Phillip glances down, rubbing his neck. "He's my boyfriend."

Like a balloon deflating, the jealousy whooshes out of me, though not the annoyance. Chiara didn't tell me any of this.

"I see. Not that it matters, but I met Chiara before she was a student here. You do understand that if this secret leaks, it will tarnish her reputation, don't you?"

My statement seems to surprise him. "What about your reputation? Aren't you worried about that?"

"Not as much as I should be."

CHIARA DIDN'T SHOW up for writer's room class. I'm sure Phillip told her about our conversation. I thought not having her there to distract me was a good thing, but it turns out, she doesn't need to be present to take over my thoughts.

I'm in the middle of working on next week's lecture when Enzo calls me. I've been waiting to hear from him about the Nadine mess.

"Hey, man. Please tell me you have good news," I say.

"It depends on what you call good news. Nadine's lawyer finally called back. It seems your ex-wife is not as keen to be rid of you as you are to be rid of her."

"What do you mean? What does she want now?"

"Nothing that will cost you more money, unless you count the five-star meal in a fancy restaurant."

"Can you please get to the fucking point?" I pinch the bridge of my nose.

"She wants to have dinner with you first before she signs anything."

"No chance in hell. I can't sit through an entire dinner with her."

"I know it sucks, okay? But do you want her to sign the papers or not? It's just dinner."

I can already imagine Chiara's reaction when I tell her I'm going to have dinner with my ex. She's going to fucking hate it, especially now after the whole Phillip incident.

"Fine. Set it up. I want to get this over with as quickly as possible."

"Any day of the week good for you?"

"Yep. Make sure you pick the loudest, most family-oriented restaurant you can find. Nadine always hated those."

"Do I sound like a fucking secretary?"

"Bite me. Just do it, Enzo."

Grumbling, he ends the call.

I stare at my computer screen for minutes after, still pissed that Nadine is forcing me to have dinner with her. That snake is up to something; I know it deep in my bones. I rub my face, frustrated that I let my ego dictate my actions for far too long. If I hadn't been so stubborn, I could be free of the woman by now. Clenching my jaw, I force myself to focus on my screen.

A text message from Chiara flashes on my phone.

CHIARA: I'm sorry I missed your class. I didn't want to make things harder in case you're still mad.

ME: You shouldn't have missed class on my account.

God, that sounded too harsh. She doesn't reply right away, and it makes me feel like an asshole.

ME: I'm afraid that infraction requires punishment.

CHIARA: What kind of punishment?

ME: The kind that will make you scream my name.

CHIARA: Tonight?

I'm about to reply when I get a text from Enzo saying Nadine wants to have dinner tonight. The goofy grin I had vanishes in an instant. *Fuck.* I did tell Enzo I wanted to handle Nadine as soon as possible. I didn't think she'd give an answer so soon.

ME: I can't tonight. I have to deal with divorce stuff. Tomorrow, I promise.

CHIARA: Okay.

ME: I'll call you later. I love you, Goldi.

CHIARA: I love you too, Big Bad Wolf.

Guilt makes my chest heavy. Technically, I didn't lie, but I shouldn't have omitted that I'm meeting Nadine tonight.

I try to dissuade the bad feeling by listing all the reasons it's better if I tell Chiara after the fact and when I have Nadine's signature on the divorce papers. It's a meaningless dinner. She doesn't need to worry about it, especially when there are still unresolved issues between us.

35

ALISTAIR

I have to give Enzo props. The restaurant he picked is a fucking zoo. With kids running around and screaming, I don't think anyone can have a proper conversation here, which is exactly what I wanted. Yet Nadine managed to snag a table in an isolated part of the restaurant that offers us some privacy. I grind my teeth when the hostess walks me to her. I should have gotten here first.

Nadine smiles broadly, showing all her veneered teeth when she sees me. I get a whiff of her heavy perfume before I even get to the table. She doesn't stand to greet me but rather leans forward a little to show off her cleavage. She's playing the seductress role tonight. She's definitely up to something.

"What did you do? Bathe in perfume before coming here?" I scowl.

"It's your favorite fragrance. You used to love it."

I pick up the menu, ignoring her offended expression. "No, I used to pretend I liked it. It gave me headaches."

"You're so grumpy today. You need to relax, babe."

"Don't call me that," I snap.

"Fine. I'm here, trying to be civil, and all you're giving me in return are barbs."

I put the menu down and glower at her. "Let's cut the bull-shit. What do you want, Nadine? I've agreed to give you half the amount of what the vineyard is worth even though you're not entitled to any of it."

She reaches across the table and covers my hand. I pull away with a jerky movement. Her touch makes my skin crawl.

"Are we really doing this, Alistair? We used to be so in love. What happened?"

"What happened? Let's see. How about you fucked my friend behind my back? Does that ring a bell?"

Her face twists into a grimace. "That was just me lashing out. You had lost interest in our marriage way before that."

"You're right. My fault in this mess was not asking for a divorce when I should have. But I'm willing to rectify it now."

"I don't want a divorce. I thought you were being petty to punish me but that, in the end, we could still save our marriage."

I laugh without humor. "That's fucking rich. It's over, Nadine. I don't love you. I haven't loved you in a very long time. Let's end this now and move on with our lives."

She narrows her eyes, flattening her lips too. "You seem in an awful hurry to sign the papers now. What changed, Alistair? It's another woman, isn't it? You've got a girlfriend and you want to be free again."

Nadine is not the only actor at this table. The difference is I was always better than her. My expression reveals nothing.

"Do you think I can only let you go if I have a replacement? Don't flatter yourself, darling. I just want you out of my life for good. I can't stand the sight of your face."

The waiter comes to take our order, but I tell him we're not staying.

"Is there something wrong?" he asks.

"No. I just lost my appetite. I'm leaving. I don't know about her."

"I'm not having dinner by myself!" she shrieks.

If looks could kill, I'd be dead already.

I push my chair back to stand, and Nadine follows suit. Ignoring her, I head out of the restaurant and give my ticket to the valet guy.

"Alistair, look at me."

The idiot that I am, I do so. I don't expect Nadine to grab my face between her hands and kiss me on the lips. I push her off as fast as I can, but not fast enough to avoid the paparazzi flashes.

"You set me up!" I wipe my lips, knowing for sure I have a red smear on them.

She doesn't seem one bit fazed by my reaction. "You're not getting rid of me as easily as you think, babe. Not when I'm about to sign a contract for a reality TV show. I need drama, and our rocky relationship will provide plenty of that."

I want to shake her, scream at her, but I do none of those things. I won't be played again.

The valet guy comes with my car, and I grab the keys so fast, I forget to tip the man. Two minutes into my drive, I receive a text from Chiara. It's only a bunch of kiss-face emojis.

Fuck me, I didn't even factor her into all this mess. How long until she sees those damn pictures online?

I call her, and it goes straight to voice mail. *Goddamn it.* Anger and frustration mix, making a vein throb on my forehead.

Without a choice, I drive to Chiara's apartment. Once again, I'm not using my best judgment here. The parking lot in front of her building is full, so I circle around and park my truck a block away. As if an omen that things are about to turn to shit, heavy rain starts to fall in big fat drops. I grab the hoodie I always keep in my car and put it on. It still carries Chiara's sweet scent from when I loaned it to her the other day. Pulling the hood over my head, I brave the weather. I get drenched within seconds.

Walking fast with my head down, I reach the front of her building in less than a minute. Of course, tonight I won't be so lucky to catch someone leaving the building so I can enter quickly. I try the door just in case, finding it locked. I call Chiara again and get the same thing, voice mail.

My teeth start to chatter as I look for her name on the intercom system. I have to squint to read the small letters. Finally, I locate the damn button with her name next to it. I press the buzzer several times without an answer.

Shit. Chiara isn't home.

Where the hell could she be?

"Can I help you?" a guy asks.

I turn, getting hit by a bright light on my face. I have to raise my arm to protect my eyes.

"Yeah, can you lower your goddamn flashlight?"

The light stays in place, but the voice gets harder. "Are you a resident at Brandywine Hall?"

Fuck me. I forgot this area was patrolled by a private security company paid in part by DuBose. There have been some break-ins lately, so they've been more vigilant about strangers in the area.

"No, I'm a teacher at DuBose High School. Just lower your light, please. You're going to blind me." I take a step in his direction.

"Don't move."

This is fucking ridiculous. I don't have time for this bullshit. "I'm leaving."

"You're not going anywhere until I see some identification."

I ignore the guy and keep walking. The last thing I expect is for him to grab the sleeve of my hoodie and yank. Caught by surprise, I lose my balance and fall backward, the middle of my spine hitting the edge of the concrete step. Sharp pain shoots up my back.

"Fuck!"

"I told you not to move, punk!" He jams his knee into my chest, still holding that ridiculous flashlight over my face.

I shove him off me with ease, and he lands on his knees with the grace of a giraffe on stilts. I manage to get back on my feet before he comes at me again, ramming his body against mine. He tries to knock me down, but I've been practicing martial arts for years; he doesn't stand a chance.

The sound of a police siren in the distance distracts me, leaving me wide open to receive a punch to my jaw. My head snaps back with the impact, and blood fills my mouth.

The next several minutes happen in a blur. Cops are yelling, the security guy is yelling, and suddenly I'm shoved against the pavement with my head pressed against the cold ground while my hands are cuffed behind my back.

A sense of déjà vu hits me hard. Forrester was there to bail me out the first time I got arrested. Is he going to do the same this time?

36

ALISTAIR

I'm lucky to get a cell to myself tonight. A stark difference from the first time I was arrested for reckless driving when I was younger. Back then, they stuck me in a cell with ten other guys, thugs who wanted to murder me on sight. If I hadn't been recognized by a fan, one of the biggest guys in there, I would have had my ass kicked.

Resting my elbows on my knees, I keep my head down as I replay tonight's events. If Nadine gets a whiff of this, she'll have a field day. I can't believe I let her get to me like that. I'm such a moron. The fact that I couldn't talk with Chiara makes me even more frustrated.

I must have been locked up for about an hour when the sound of a metal door opening snaps me to attention. Enzo walks into the detention area, followed by Forrester.

Fuck. Why did he call him?

I level my lawyer with a glare as I clench my jaw.

"Don't look at me like that. I didn't call your boss," Enzo says.

"I was notified by the security company," Forrester explains.

"What in the world were you doing trying to break into student housing, Alistair?"

"I.... Nothing."

Forrester narrows his eyes, knowing I'm lying. Shit, I should know better. Before he became the principal at DuBose, he was a renowned therapist—*my* therapist. The guy knows me better than my parents do.

"No one is pressing charges, and we're brushing this off as a misunderstanding," Forrester continues.

"Thank you." I lower my gaze, shame making me unable to look my friend in the eye.

A police officer unlocks my cell and then leads me to a different part of the building where I can collect my personal belongings. Forrester stays behind, but Enzo tags along. It doesn't take long for him to speak his mind.

"What kind of stupid bullshit was that?"

"I don't want to talk about it."

"Fine. Don't. But don't come crying when Nadine wipes your bank account clean and Forrester fires your ass."

I scoff. "I'm not in the mood for Italian dramatics, Enzo."

"What were you doing in front of you-know-who's building? Are you out of your goddamn mind?"

Ignoring Enzo, I check that all my belongings are accounted for before signing the paperwork the clerk presented me.

"Nadine set me up. She had paparazzi waiting for us outside the restaurant. She kissed me in front of them."

"That's ridiculous. What is she trying to accomplish by doing that?"

"She's trying to score a contract for a reality TV show, and she needs drama."

Enzo makes an annoyed sound in the back of his throat. "Let me guess. She won't sign the divorce papers now because of that."

"You got it. That's why I was where I was. I needed to talk to Chiara, to explain to her that those images aren't what they seem. But her phone was switched off."

We walk to the front of the police station. Forrester is waiting for me there, so any criticism Enzo might still have about my behavior dies in his throat. My boss rises from his seat, his hard gaze transporting me back to when I was younger. *Shit*. It feels like I'm about to receive a tongue-lashing.

"Since all is well, I'm heading out. I'll call you tomorrow, Alistair." Enzo walks out of the precinct before I can stop him.

I was hoping to score a ride with him back to my truck.

Forrester must have read my mind, because he says, "Come on. I'll give you a lift."

Resigned that I won't escape getting stuck with him in a moving vehicle, I follow him outside. The rain has mercifully stopped, but my clothes are still damp from before. I bring the lapels of my jacket closer together, but it does nothing against the chill seeping through my clothes.

Forrester turns on the heater as soon as the engine is on, and less than a minute later, I'm nice and toasty on the outside. On the inside, it's a different story.

"I'm sorry about tonight."

"I'd believe that if you were being honest with me."

"Shit, Forrester. Nadine and the divorce are getting to me. That's why I wanted a year off."

He sighs loudly. He's probably feeling guilty now. It's not the complete truth, but it's not a lie either.

"I shouldn't have asked you to come back. I know. Listen, if you need to talk like old times, my door is always open."

I chuckle. "You want to be my therapist again? You might need to fire me after our first session."

Forrester laughs at my joke. If he only knew it's not a laughing matter.

"Good point. I can refer you to someone else. I'd hate for you to feel like your life is unraveling again. I don't want to see you derail."

"That's the last thing I want. You know that."

He doesn't speak for a moment. He's wearing his therapist hat, even though this isn't a session. Old habits are hard to break, I guess.

"Listen, I want you to take time off. Go visit your parents in the vineyard. If you leave me your lesson plan for the week, I can cover for you."

I whip my head to face him. "Are you serious?"

"Dead serious. You're one of the best teachers I have. I won't lose you on account of a mental breakdown."

I open and shut my mouth. Here I am, hiding a truth that can devastate my friend's institution, and he's going out of his way to help me.

I feel like a fucking prick.

"I don't know what to say."

"There's only one thing you can say. It's 'Yes, boss, I'm taking a break.'"

Shaking my head, I look out the window, noticing we're already back on Chiara's street. A moment later, Forrester parks next to my truck. Before I can open the door, he turns to me.

"I mean it, Alistair. I don't want to see your face next week. I expect your lesson plan by the end of the day tomorrow."

"Okay, I hear ya. Anything else?"

"Yes, bring me a couple of bottles of wine from the vineyard, will you?"

I smirk. "Now the truth arises. No worries, Forrester. I'll bring you a case."

I hop into my truck but take my time turning the engine on. Instead, I call Chiara again. It's past two in the morning, but I still get her voice mail.

When I finally put the truck in Drive, it takes a Herculean effort to drive away from her building. I'll have to suck it up and wait until tomorrow.

37

CHIARA

I blink my eyes open, and a sharp pain shoots up my forehead. There's a weird taste in my mouth, a mixture of tequila and tortilla chips. It takes me a moment to get my bearings. I'm on a couch, but it's not mine.

Loud snoring coming from the king-size bed to my right snaps my memories into place. I remember where I am now. I came to Robbie's house after school. I was upset about the whole deal with Alistair, so instead of moping in my apartment alone, I agreed to come over for a *The Big Bang Theory* marathon.

Phillip, Valerie, and Harold were also here. I see two people on Robbie's bed though.

Oh God. That must be Phillip.

I get up and tiptoe to Robbie's side of the bed.

"Hey, Robbie, wake up." I shake his shoulder, which only makes him turn on his side and hide his face under a pillow.

Phillip moans in his sleep and slings his arm over his face. He's shirtless, but I hope he's not naked under the covers.

"Fine. Be like that. It's not like we have a quiz in half an hour."

Phillip rolls over suddenly, falling off the bed. He sits up tense and wide-eyed.

"Shit! What time is it?"

"Quarter to seven."

He jumps up, and I'm relieved to see he's wearing boxer shorts at least. But when he turns, mortification fills me. *Hello, morning wood.* I look away as heat rushes to my cheeks.

"*Dio Santo.* Cover yourself, please."

Robbie sits up, rubbing his eyes. "What's going on? Why are you two being so noisy?"

"I'm going to be late for practice." Phillip dashes to the bathroom and closes the door.

I spot the tequila bottles on Robbie's desk, plus the leftovers of our dinner, and get queasy.

"How much did we drink last night?"

"Judging by the pounding in my head, I'd say too much." He reaches for his phone on the nightstand and frowns. "Valerie texted me. She said we need to check *ET Online.*"

"Why?"

Robbie lifts his gaze, meeting mine. "Something to do with Alistair."

The floor seems to vanish beneath my feet. "Oh my God. What?"

"She didn't say. And before you ask, she doesn't know that you and Mr. Walsh are an item."

Frantically, I begin to search for my purse. My phone is in it.

"Ah hell," Robbie blurts.

"What? What is it?" I grab his phone, too nervous to care about manners.

Then I wish I hadn't been so abrupt and let Robbie prepare me for the image on his screen.

Alistair and Nadine kissing.

"What the hell!" I say.

"Don't jump to conclusions, sweetie. Not everything is as it seems in this town."

"How is that viper shoving her tongue down Alistair's throat not what it seems?" I shriek.

"If you look closely at his expression, he doesn't seem into it. Maybe she jumped him."

I return his phone, not wanting to look at the picture for another second. My eyes are already tearing up anyway.

"I can't believe this," I say.

A moment later, Robbie touches my lower back. "Don't cry, Chiara."

"I'm not crying," I reply through a choke. "You must think I'm an idiot, huh?"

"Why would I think that?"

I shake my head. "I don't know. Maybe because a relationship between a teacher and a student never ends well."

"I'm sure there's an explanation. Check your phone. Maybe he called."

"Help me find my purse."

A minute later, I'm looking at the black screen of my phone. It died sometime last night. Robbie has a different phone than mine, so I can't use his charger, which means I won't know for sure if Alistair tried to contact me until I get back home.

For now, I have to deal with the heartache that won't go away.

ALISTAIR

I'm in front of Chiara's apartment first thing in the morning. Apparently, I haven't learned my lesson. I stay in my truck though, waiting for her to appear. She has to go to school. I didn't try calling her again because by now, she must have seen the pictures of Nadine kissing me. It's all over the internet, which surprises me, to be honest, as I'm no longer a hot commodity in Hollywood, and Nadine was never a star.

The ping of an incoming text makes me look down at my phone.

ENZO: You'd better not be stalking your girlfriend.

I groan and toss the phone aside. *Fuck off, Enzo.*

Movement ahead catches my attention. I recognize Phillip's truck. Then the surprise comes. Chiara climbs out of the vehicle wearing yesterday's clothes.

Fuck me. Did she spend the night with him?

I'm out of the truck before I can put my thoughts in order, blind jealousy coursing through my veins.

Phillip drives off before I finish crossing the street. It's for the best. In my current mood, I could have very well committed another insane act.

Chiara freezes by the curb when she sees me coming over. There's an initial shock on her part, right before her gaze turns murderous.

"What are you doing here?"

"I came to talk to you."

She crosses her arms and glowers harder. "I'm not sure I'm interested in what you have to say."

I glance at the front of the building, knowing it's only a matter of time until a student from DuBose walks out and catches us having a heated argument.

"Can we please go somewhere so we can talk?"

"Fine."

I maintain a safe distance from her as we walk over to my truck. It's bad enough that we're once again going somewhere together in my vehicle, but I can't leave all our unresolved issues alone to fester and become worse.

Inside the car, the silence feels like a third passenger. It's heavy, uncomfortable, almost tangible. I don't break it, not while I'm parked in front of Chiara's apartment in broad daylight. I drive off, putting the pedal to the metal.

"Where are you taking me? I have class in an hour," she says.

"Nowhere specifically. I'll bring you back in time." I sigh, preparing myself. "Listen, about the picture you must have seen already. That was a setup."

She scoffs. "Convenient excuse."

"It's the truth. Nadine is trying to get on a reality TV show, and she thinks dragging the divorce out will give her a better shot at it. She had the paparazzi waiting for us outside the restaurant and jumped me."

"You could have pushed her off."

"I did, in the next second. I tried calling you last night. I didn't want you to find out via the tabloids, but your phone was switched off."

"Yeah, it died at Robbie's."

"Oh, you spent the night at Robbie's, then."

"Yeah. You saw Phillip drop me off, didn't you?"

"I did."

She sighs heavily. "Alistair, there's nothing going on between Phillip and me. What you saw yesterday was me trying to help a friend. Jillian suspects that Phillip is gay, and he's not ready to come out yet."

"I'm sorry, Chiara. I'm a hot-blooded male. I'm not going to be happy to see you kiss another guy, even if it's just pretense."

"It's the same for me."

I reach over and grab her hand, needing the contact to ground me and to let Chiara know she doesn't have anything to worry about. I'm glad she doesn't pull away.

"I hate feeling like this," she whispers so low, I almost can't hear it.

"Me too, Goldi. Me too." I pause, struggling to put my next confession into words. "There's something I have to tell you."

She turns to me. "What is it?"

"I was arrested last night."

"What? Why?"

"I went to your apartment, and, well, a neighborhood security patrol thought I was trying to break into the building. Long story short, I got arrested, and Forrester had to come bail me out."

She gasps. "DuBose's principal?"

"Yeah."

"Alistair, I don't know what to say. Are you in trouble? I mean, with the school?"

"No, Forrester and I go way back. He used to be my therapist when I was younger. I don't think I ever told you that. Anyway, I almost caved last night and told him about us."

Her sharp intake of breath makes me peel my gaze from the road for a brief second.

"You did? What stopped you?"

"I didn't want to disappoint him. He helped me out more than I can ever repay him."

"You still have to tell me that story."

"I will, Goldi. I promise. Actually, Forrester is making me take the next week off. I'm going to my parents' vineyard. I know you have school and all, but I'd love if you could come, maybe only for the weekend."

"You want to introduce me to your parents?" Her voice rises an octave.

"Yes, sweetheart. I do."

"Do you think they'll like me?"

"They're going to fall in love with you just like I did."

I glance at her again, finding her smiling from ear to ear. The shadow of doubt I saw earlier is gone. I want to stop the car and kiss her, but we're in the middle of the highway. I take the first exit and return to her neighborhood, dropping her off in front of her building.

She unbuckles her seat belt and turns to me. "These windows are super dark, right? No one can see us from the outside?"

"Yep." I grin.

She launches herself at me, covering my lips with hers. I let her invade my mouth with her sweet tongue as I wrap my arms around her tiny waist. I want to erase every moment of doubt and jealousy by branding Chiara with my kiss. Immediately, a red-hot fever takes over me, and my cock is straining against my pants. I'm dying for some release, but all I can do right now is kiss her like there's no tomorrow.

She pulls back first, out of breath. Lust is running rampant inside my truck. I'm one second away from driving off and taking her back to my place.

"Goldi, if you don't leave now, I'm afraid you'll miss all your classes today."

"All right. You make it so damn hard though." She combs her curls with her fingers, then pulls the passenger mirror down. "Okay, not too bad."

"Do you want to stay at my place tonight?"

She frowns. "I wish I could, but I have to study for an exam."

I can't help the disappointment. It's easy to forget that Chiara and I are at different stages in our lives.

"No problem. I'll be thinking about you."

"You know, you could call me later if you're feeling lonely." She smiles at me with a glint of mischief in her gaze. I don't miss the hint.

"Are you proposing phone sex, Goldi?"

Her grin wilts a fraction as she averts her gaze. "Maybe. I've never done it before."

I pinch her chin, bringing her face to mine. "You shouldn't

have mentioned it. Now I won't be able to think about anything else besides our call later."

Leaning toward me, she plants a quick kiss on my lips. "Until later, then."

She's out of the car in a flash, leaving me hornier than I was before.

38

CHIARA

Five Days Later

Betetween school and sneaking around to see Alistair, the days flew by. Now, we're on our way to his parents' vineyard. I don't get the jitters until he announces we're about five minutes away from the property. The knot of anxiety becomes tighter in my stomach, and my hands turn clammy. Looking out the window to appreciate the view does nothing to ease my worries.

What if his parents hate me? What if they think I'm too young for their son?

A charming country farmhouse appears straight ahead. The driveway is lined with tall oak trees and beautiful land-scaping. It's a place that belongs on a postcard or a Pinterest inspiration board.

Alistair parks in front of the house and turns to me. "Ready?"

"No. What are their names again?"

"You've asked me a dozen times already. Duncan and Molly. You got this."

"I know. I'm sorry. I've never met the parents before."

He chuckles as he unbuckles his seat belt, then leans across the gap and kisses me. For the first time since meeting him, I don't melt right away. I'm too nervous to let myself properly enjoy the kiss.

Alistair moves away, frowning a little.

"Don't worry, Goldi. It's going to be okay."

He gets out of the car, and I do the same, but I stay rooted to the spot while Alistair grabs our duffel bags from the trunk and walks around the car toward me. He laces his hand with mine and tugs me toward the house. My heart is beating so fast, it's a miracle he can't hear it.

The front door opens before we step onto the porch. A tall man with gray hair fills the frame. He has a full trimmed beard, unlike Alistair, who prefers a scruff. However, it's impossible to not see the resemblance.

"Hey, Dad." He hugs the man.

"Alistair, you arrived just in time for lunch." He turns to me, smiling. "And this must be the lovely Chiara I've heard so much about."

Shit. What could Alistair have possibly told his parents? Do they know I'm his student?

There's a twinkle of mischief in his dad's eyes, and I can't figure out why. I glance at Alistair with a question in my gaze.

"Dad's being sarcastic. I only told them about you a couple days ago."

"Oh, that makes me feel so much better," I joke.

Duncan grins. "It's okay, honey. Alistair can be a little stingy about sharing information."

"Nonsense! I tell you everything," Alistair rebuffs.

His father rolls his eyes. "It's amazing how you can say that with a straight face."

"Well, he's an actor," I chime in, earning a glare from Alistair.

"Whose side are you on?" he asks.

"Oh, I like her." Duncan winks at me. "Come in already. I'm hungry."

Duncan heads inside, but I hesitate until Alistair places a hand on my lower back and pushes me forward. With slow steps, I cross the threshold, taking my time to look at everything. An open living space greets us. The décor is rustic but also homey. I can tell a lot of work was put into picking every piece. It's lovely.

Alistair drops our duffel bags next to the massive brown leather couch and continues down a wide hallway. The delicious smell of food tells me that's where the kitchen is. His mother, a petite woman with a red bob, turns as she hears us. She's wearing an apron that says "Kiss the chef" and holding a wooden spoon in her hand.

"Ah, just in time. Lunch is ready," she says.

"Dad told us. What did you cook, Mom? It smells delicious." Alistair places a kiss on her cheek, then proceeds to peer at the pan on the stove.

I remain at the kitchen entrance, unsure of what to do. All my insecurities decide to come to the surface, and I have to control my urge to fidget nervously.

"I figured I'd dust off my old recipe book and make something Italian for Chiara." She looks at me, smiling. "Come here, sweetie. Don't be shy."

I do as she says, not expecting her to hug me. I reciprocate, looking a little startled at Alistair. He just grins at me.

"Oh, my. You're more petite than I am. I hope you're being gentle with this one." She turns to Alistair, and embarrassment makes my cheeks burn.

Is she implying what I think she's implying?

"Mom! Come on, don't start."

Yes, yes she is. I want to die.

Alistair circles around Molly and grabs my hand, dragging me away from the kitchen.

"Where do you think you're going? Food is ready," she calls after us.

"I'm going to take our stuff to the guest house and wash up," he replies.

"Forget it, Molly. I think we're eating alone," Duncan grumbles.

I bite my tongue, waiting until we're outside the main house to turn on Alistair. I hit his arm, not hard enough to do any damage though.

"You should have warned me about your parents."

"What? That they have no filter?"

"Yes!"

Alistair chuckles. "What would be the fun in that?"

"I hate you."

We stop in front of a small house that looks like a miniature of the main structure. He pushes the door open, and the first thing I see inside is the king-size bed. Before I can make any comment, he spins me around and crushes his mouth to mine. He runs his hands down my arms and then rests them on my hips, bringing me even closer to him.

Reluctantly, I pull back. "Alistair, your parents are waiting for us. We're being rude."

"Sorry, I couldn't resist."

"You're acting like a horny teenager going away with his girlfriend for the first time."

"I feel like a horny teenager. That's the effect you have on me, Goldi."

"You'd better behave or there won't be any sexy time tonight."

"Fine. I'll behave. Just one more kiss before we go?"

I should say no because his kisses are like a drug, but I can't resist when he looks at me as if I'm the sexiest woman alive.

ALISTAIR

I don't remember ever feeling this complete in my life before, not even when I was married to Nadine. I watch Chiara talk with my parents—finally more relaxed after a couple of glasses of wine—and I think, *This is it. She's the one for me.* I don't know how I can be so certain—I thought the same before with Nadine—but it's somehow different with Chiara.

My parents seem to like her; they ask questions, they tease her—something they'd never done with Nadine. And Chiara takes it all in stride. She does get flustered on occasion, but eventually she starts to tease my parents in return. I worried she wouldn't be able to handle their bluntness and dry humor, but she's giving it as good as she's getting.

After lunch, I take Chiara on a tour of the vineyard. It's not the biggest one in the area, only a few acres, but I'm still proud of it and of what my parents have accomplished.

"This is lovely, Alistair."

"I fell in love with this property as soon as I came here for the first time. It doesn't compare to the vineyards in Italy, but it's very special to me."

"Have you ever considered retiring from teaching and working full time here?"

"Yes, many times. When I first started to look in the area, that was exactly my plan, but Na—well, she was completely against the idea. Then the separation happened."

"Before I decided to come to LA to study at DuBose, I briefly considered taking sommelier classes and studying more about the wine business. But the appeal to study far away from my family won out. Plus, I've always been fascinated by the film industry."

"You had no idea who I was, did you?" I ask, not that it would matter if she did.

"No. Your show didn't air in Italy. Plus, you look so different now. Is that why you're never clean-shaven? To avoid recognition?"

"In part. Nadine wanted me to remain recognizable for her own benefit, and it grated on my nerves. I don't like talking about my past celebrity life."

"Because of your friend Jamie?"

I nod.

Chiara stops in front of me, rising on the tips of her toes to kiss me. "Let's talk about something else, then."

I'm glad she doesn't push to know more, unlike many people I know. Her attitude makes me want to share everything with her, even my darkest parts.

"No. I don't want to keep secrets from you. If you have questions, ask away."

She shakes her head. "I don't have specific questions. I just want you to know I'm here if you need to talk."

"Do you know why I feel so in debt to Forrester? Why I can't walk away from my position at DuBose in the middle of the school year?"

"Because you're friends?"

"That too, but most importantly because he saved my life. After Jamie died, I was in a very dark place. Hanging out with the wrong crowd, drinking too much, doing drugs. I almost killed my mother when I got us into a car wreck. I was stupid drunk that day."

Her eyes water. "Oh, Alistair. I'm so sorry."

"Yeah, me too. The guilt still eats at me. I was lucky enough to get a lenient judge who sentenced me to community service and mandatory therapy. Forrester was my therapist, and he helped me more than he knows. I went to rehab, got clean, and walked away from showbiz."

She cups my cheek. "I'm so grateful you were able to find yourself again."

"I don't think I have, not yet. But I know I can with you by my side."

Her breath catches. She's staring at me like a deer caught in headlights, making me think that maybe she wasn't ready for that truth.

"I'm sorry. Too mushy?" I add quickly.

"No, not at all. I like corny love declarations."

"Oh, so I'm corny now, huh?" I bring her flush to my body.

She rests her face against my chest and inhales deeply. "Yes, very much so."

Desire is quickly spreading through my body, but I have to ignore my hardening cock for a while longer. There's one more thing I want to do before I bring Chiara back to the guest house.

Taking a step back, I pull a little wrapped box from my jacket pocket.

Chiara focuses on the gift before she lifts her eyes to mine. "What's that?"

"Something I got for you back in Italy and never had the chance to give you."

With eager hands, she takes the package from me. I hold my breath as I watch her expression change from curiosity to utter shock.

"You got me the bracelet like Bisnonna's." She looks at me with bright eyes.

I nod. "Do you like it?"

She throws herself in my arms, wrapping her hands behind my neck and kissing me hard. I match her passion beat by beat until my erection is straining painfully against my jeans.

Breathlessly, she pulls back and says, "I love it. Thank you."

"You're welcome, Goldi."

"You know what? I'm feeling a little tired." She smiles shyly at me.

I brush my lips against hers. "Me too. I think a nap sounds good right about now."

39

CHIARA

Duncan and Molly have gone to bed already, and it's just Alistair and me on the back porch. Us and the stars. The air is chilly, but Alistair said starting a fire is too dangerous this time of the year. I'm snuggled up against him though, and a warm blanket covers us. Plus, the mulled wine is helping keep us toasty.

I look around and sigh. "No wonder you fell in love with this place. It's lovely and so peaceful."

"Yeah. I'm surprised you enjoy the quiet though. I thought you were a city girl."

"I am, but lately, I'm enjoying places not blemished by noise and pollution more and more. I guess I'm getting old."

Alistair chuckles, a low rumble that shakes his chest. "You're only eighteen."

I glance up, peering at his profile. "Does our age difference bother you?"

Looking down, he smiles. "Not at all, Goldi."

"I'm afraid you'll eventually get tired of me. Don't you ever think about the future? What's going to happen to us?"

"I do, my love. All the time."

Heaviness presses on my chest, making me regret opening my big mouth and ruining the moment.

With his fingertips, he touches the space between my eyebrows. "What's up with this frown?"

"I love you so much. I'm afraid this will be over soon." I drop my gaze to his chest. "You must think I'm an immature, silly girl."

He places his index finger under my chin and brings my face up again. "I don't think that at all. You act more mature than many adults I know. That's why it was such a shock to see you in my class at DuBose."

"How old did you think I was?"

"Twenty-one, at least. Your confidence was such a turn-on. I think I fell for you the moment you offered me that ride."

His confession makes me feel a thousand times better. I smile against his chest.

"You don't think I also worry this is nothing but a dream? I've never loved anyone as fiercely as I love you, Goldi," he continues.

My heart soars. I look up again.

"Really?"

"Yeah. And it terrifies me. I lost my best friend, and I almost lost my mother. I don't think I can handle losing you too."

The pain etched on Alistair's face breaks my heart. I caress his scruffy cheek while I grasp for what to say. Nothing seems adequate. I can promise I'll never leave him, but I can't cheat death.

"Tell me about Jamie."

Alistair releases a heavy breath and looks out in the distance. "Show business is tough, more so when you're young. I loved acting, don't get me wrong, but the pressure of growing up in front of millions wasn't easy. Jamie and I bonded early on during the show, and we helped each other out when things got tough. He knew things not even my parents or Forrester did."

He threads his fingers through his short hair, taking a deep breath.

"When he killed himself, it came as a shock to me. I was his best friend, and I never knew he was suicidal. I blamed myself for not seeing the signs, for not being there when he needed me the most. My way of coping was not good, as I said already."

"Alistair, surely you know it wasn't your fault."

"Yeah, now I do."

I brush my thumb over his lips, desperately needing to see that sadness gone from his eyes.

Desire sparks in his gaze. He grabs my wrist and then shortens the distance between our mouths. The kiss is soft at first, but like always, they never stay innocent for long, and before I know it, I'm lying on my back and he's on top of me.

"Alistair, won't your parents see us?"

"After all that wine, they're sound asleep."

He trails open kisses down my collarbone while he runs his hands down my arms. I'm wearing a thick sweater and jeans. I didn't expect a make-out session outside his parents' house.

Alistair scooches back, lifting my sweater and the T-shirt up, revealing my stomach and bra in the process. Instead of trying to cover myself, I arch my back, offering my breasts to him. He cups them with his large hands and licks my cleavage, sending a shot of pleasure down my spine.

He pushes my bra up, freeing my girls. The cold air makes my nipples turn hard in an instant, and when he sucks one of them into his hot mouth, I let out a moan. It's going to be extra hard to keep the volume down.

Alistair switches his attention to my other breast while he cups my sex over my jeans. As much as I wish there were no barriers between us, the friction of his hand over the fabric feels amazing.

"Oh my God. You're killing me, Alistair."

He presses his thumb over my clit, making a circular

motion. *Dio Santo*. My entire body is caught in an electric current. I couldn't stop the orgasm from coming so suddenly even if I tried.

I cover my face with the blanket to muffle my cries as I come swiftly. That was record time. I'm still riding the wave of pleasure when he lifts me in his arms.

"Where are we going?"

"I need a bed for what I plan to do with you."

He strides across the backyard and reaches our little piece of heaven in a few seconds. Kicking the door closed, Alistair seals his lips with mine, and together we fall onto the bed. We're acting in a frenzy, our hands working furiously to rid the other's clothes.

Finally completely naked, Alistair lies on his back with me on top. I rub my aching core against his cock, but he has other ideas. He grabs me by the hips and pulls me farther up until I'm practically sitting on his face.

"Alistair, what are you doing?"

"I want to feast on your sweet pussy, Goldi." His warm breath fans over my sensitive skin, and pleasure makes my toes curl.

"I have a better idea."

I turn around, leaning forward until his erection is within reach. Grabbing his cock at the base, I bring his entire length into my mouth at the same time he strokes my clit with his tongue. I almost forget what I'm doing for a moment, but his grunts spur me on, so I try my best to concentrate on the task at hand. I love the saltiness on his skin, how with each stroke he gets larger in my mouth. When he begins to pump his hips up and down, I know he's close to his release. And so am I.

He grunts against my pussy right before his hot seed fills my mouth. I climax not long after, fighting to keep myself from collapsing too soon.

After I finish drinking everything Alistair has to give me, my muscles finally give out. I fall to the side and don't move for several beats, more than happy to lie next to the man I love in this awkward position. I only open my eyes when I feel the mattress move. Alistair switches position in bed, and he's now lying by my side, face-to-face.

"That was amazing." He kisses my nose.

"I've never done that before."

"You've never had a sixty-nine?"

"Nope. Before I met you, I was pretty much a virgin."

He grabs my ass, bringing me closer to his body. "What else have you never done before?"

"I think it's easier for me to list what I *have* done. I'm pretty vanilla when it comes to sex."

"It's my favorite flavor."

He kisses me again before rolling on top of me. His cock is hard and ready to go.

"Boy, you recover fast."

"It's you, Goldi. It's all you."

He thrusts forward, sliding in with ease.

It seems we aren't getting any sleep tonight.

ALISTAIR

The acrid smell of smoke wakes me from a very peaceful sleep. I blink my eyes open, feeling disoriented for a couple of seconds. The room is shrouded in darkness, and there's no visible smoke around. So where the hell is the smell coming from?

I freeze. *Fuck.* Throwing my legs to the side of the bed, I get up.

"Alistair, what's the matter?" Chiara asks in a sleepy voice.

"Something isn't right."

Not bothering to put clothes on, I head out. Instead of being greeted by a midnight blue sky, an orange horizon has my undivided attention.

Wildfire.

Lord have mercy.

I run back inside the house, turning on the lights. "Chiara! Get up, get up."

She sits up in bed, looking startled. "What happened?"

"The valley is on fire. We have to leave. It's not safe here."

She blinks a couple of times, unmoving, before she jumps out of bed. I put last night's clothes on as fast as I can, forgetting my socks as I shove my feet into my boots. I look at Chiara, relieved when I see she dressed just as fast. I take her hand and together we run to the main house. I burst through the back door, calling out to my parents. Dad and Mom emerge down the corridor, wearing their pj's.

"Alistair? What's all that ruckus?"

"Wildfire is coming our way. We have to leave."

It sickens me to witness the sorrowful glance my parents trade. The vineyard is everything they have, their dream. They only allow themselves that single exchange before spurring into action. While they get ready, I fill a duffel bag with supplies —food, medicine, and any item that might be necessary during an evacuation.

"What can I do?" Chiara asks.

"We need nonperishable food and water, lots of water," I reply.

"We just bought a case yesterday," Dad says as he comes into the kitchen.

"Where is Mom?"

"She's packing clothes and other irreplaceable items."

"I'll go check if she needs help," Chiara says before disappearing down the corridor.

Dad turns on the TV, and what we see on the news channel

makes my heart twist in agony. The entire Sonoma region is in danger.

"Why weren't you alerted?" I ask.

"I forgot to sign up for it."

"Dad—"

"Now is not the time for sermons, son. Come on, let's get the trucks loaded."

Half an hour later, we're on the road. The streets are already filled with smoke, and visibility is almost nil. When we get to town, flames have already claimed some of the buildings. Deputies from the Sonoma sheriff's office are helping people evacuate. I see a family running on foot and don't think twice as I stop the truck ahead of them.

"Get in the car!" I shout.

The father ushers his wife and son into my truck, saying a million thank-yous once they're inside.

"This is so awful. We had no warning," the woman says.

Chiara offers them water and gasps. "You're hurt."

The traffic is moving at a crawl, so I chance a look back at the woman. Indeed, there's a nasty burn on her forearm. "We need to take you to the hospital."

"They're probably evacuating the nearest ones."

I hold the steering wheel tighter as frustration simmers in my gut. We finally begin to move faster again as we exit the residential area. On the outskirts of town, I spot a couple of news vans and ambulances parked on the side of the road, so I stop the car. A deputy tries to get us to move on, but I explain we have someone who needs medical attention.

Both Chiara and I get out of the car to help the family. It's not only the mother who's badly injured, but also the kid. The woman collapses in her husband's arms, and finally the deputy understands the gravity of the situation. I pick up the kid and take him to the paramedics.

I watch for a few minutes while they take care of the family

I was lucky enough to spot in the middle of the road. If I hadn't seen them, they probably wouldn't have made it. Chiara is next to me, crying, and I throw my arm around her shoulders and kiss the top of her head. She looks up, her eyes wide and filled with tears. Soot blemishes her cheeks. I try to wipe it off with my thumb, only to make it worse.

"Alistair, we need to get moving, son." My father's head is sticking out of his car, a look of urgency on his face.

"Come on, let's get out of here," I say.

40

CHIARA

When we got back to LA Saturday afternoon, I asked Alistair to drop me off at home; I didn't want to be an extra burden on him while he tried to deal with the aftermath of the fire that most likely destroyed his parents' vineyard. He protested like I thought he would, but he didn't fight too much.

Throughout the day, Alistair and I exchanged several messages, but we didn't talk until late Sunday night. The worst had been confirmed. The fire had reached the vineyard and probably torched it to the ground. I cried in silence, not wanting to let Alistair know how devastated I was for him and his family. His voice sounded hollow, and I wanted nothing more than to comfort him.

I didn't sleep for shit last night, so it's no surprise this morning that I look like a raccoon, and no amount of concealer can hide the dark circles under my eyes. I put on my sunglasses and head to class, knowing Alistair won't be at school today. I arrive to class one minute before it starts, finding the room already full.

Everyone's gaze turns in my direction, and the previously silent area gets filled with low murmurs. *What the hell is going on? Did I forget to put my skirt on?* I look down, finding everything in place.

I take one step forward before I'm yanked back and pulled out of the classroom by Robbie and Phillip.

"What the hell? Why did you do that?"

"I'm saving you from a mortifying situation," Robbie replies. "Come on. We need to go."

With his hand firmly clasping mine, he keeps walking until we're out of the building. It's only then that I dig my heels into the ground and pull free from his hold.

"For fuck's sake, Robbie. What the hell is going on? You're freaking me out."

He takes a deep breath and looks at his shoes. "Chiara, I don't know how to say this."

"You're making me nervous, Robbie."

"You and Mr. Walsh made the front page of the *LA Times*," Phillip pipes up.

My stomach bottoms out even though I don't know what he means. "What are you talking about?"

"There's a picture of you and Mr. Walsh in a candid moment. The newspaper liked your picture so much, they decided to post it. Right now, it just says two of Sonoma's fire victims comfort each other, but both of you are recognizable. It won't take long for people to connect the dots."

I close my eyes and pinch the bridge of my nose. "I believe that already happened. Everyone was staring at me in class. Hell, Alistair! I need to warn him."

"I'm pretty sure he already knows," Robbie says.

I shake my head. "If he did, he would have called me."

No sooner do I say those words than my phone rings. With a shaking hand, I dig for the device in my purse. It's him.

"Hello?"

"Chiara, I'm glad you're not in class yet."

"I know about our picture," I blurt out.

"I'm so, so sorry. I'll fix this. I promise."

If I didn't already love this man, I would have fallen in love with him right now. He's dealing with so many problems already, and the outing of our relationship will only make his life even more complicated. But here he is, worrying about me.

"I'll be fine. I'm with Robbie and Phillip. They saved me from school today."

"Good. You shouldn't be alone. Go home. I'll call you when I know the extent of the damage."

"Okay."

"Everything will be fine, Goldi. I promise. I love you."

"I love you too."

He ends the call, but I remain frozen, staring at my phone for a couple of beats.

"What did he say?" Phillip asks.

"He told me to go home and wait to hear from him."

"I don't think you should go back to your apartment," Robbie replies. "It's only a matter of time before the media finds out you're his student. And you know Nadine will create a circus."

"What am I supposed to do, then?"

"Come home with me. You can lie low for a while there and stay as long as you need."

"Okay. I appreciate that."

"I'll go back to school," Phillip states. "You need someone to report on the gossip."

"Oh, Phillip. They're going to think you were cheated on."

He gives me a lopsided grin. "Hey, that's okay. I'll get all the pity from the girls."

Robbie crosses his arms. "Yeah, that's peachy. I don't like it at all."

Phillip's amused expression vanishes. "I'm sorry, Robbie, but what can we do?"

"I guess nothing." He links his arm with mine. "Come on, girl. Let's get you out of here."

Before we can reach Robbie's car in the school's parking lot, we're intercepted by a cameraman and the last person I ever wanted to meet—Nadine, Alistair's ex.

She points at me. "There she is, the little Italian whore who thought she could steal my husband."

What the hell!

"Hey, what do you think you're doing?" Robbie shouts at the cameraman who's practically in my face.

"Get out of my way!" I push him off.

"Not so fast." Nadine blocks my path. "Do you think you can fuck my husband and not expect any type of retribution from me? I don't think so."

"Oh, but cheating on your husband with his friend is okay? If I'm a whore, what the hell are you?"

The slap to the face comes fast, and I'm unable to protect myself. My ears ring and my eyes water. Fuck, I had forgotten how much one of those hurt.

"Are you out of your goddamn mind?" Robbie yells. "Chiara, are you okay?" He positions himself in front of me, protecting me from another assault.

"I'm fine," I say.

No, I'm not fine. I'm far from it. But I won't give Nadine the satisfaction of seeing me cry.

"You'd better get your ass out of here before I call the police," Robbie tells Nadine.

"With pleasure. I've already delivered my message."

I watch the viper walk away with cameraman in tow. Does that mean she got the contract for her reality TV show?

I touch my sore face, and once the anger recedes, it leaves

me devastated and hollow. The confrontation with Nadine reminded me too much of my relationship with my mother.

"Come on, let's get you out of here," Robbie says.

I nod, wanting nothing more than to hide away from the world.

41

ALISTAIR

I've been listening to Enzo shout in my living room for the past hour since I got off the phone with Chiara. He called me as soon as he saw our picture on the front of the *LA Times*, but yelling at me over the phone wasn't enough. He had to come knocking. Now he's furious because I've been recognized already, and the story running in all celebrity gossip outlets is reporting that Alistair Walsh, former child TV star, is having an affair with a student. People seem pretty hung up on the fact that I'm still legally married. Nadine must be loving all this.

"I can't believe you were that careless, Alistair. I just can't believe it. You were so close to being free of that snake." Enzo continues pacing back and forth in my kitchen.

"Do you think I was worried about being caught in that moment?"

"Fuck," Enzo curses.

"You should call Forrester," my father says.

He's right; I should call him before he comes knocking at my door too.

I head to my office to make the call in privacy. I don't need

Enzo breathing down my neck while I talk to Forrester. Too fucking bad he doesn't answer his cell phone, so I call his office, getting his assistant.

"He's locked in a meeting at the moment," she says, "but he wants you to come by his office as soon as possible."

"Of course. I'll be there in an hour."

When I announce that I'm headed to DuBose, Enzo asks if that's a wise idea. I tell him Forrester wants to see me in person.

"Maybe I should come with you as your lawyer."

"I don't think that'll be necessary. I didn't break any laws."

I walk out before he can start another argument. There's no sign of paparazzi outside my door, and for that I'm both relieved and surprised. I can't believe Nadine didn't send her vulture friends to harass me.

As I drive to DuBose, I can't help but think that I'd been right all along. Chiara will be responsible for my downfall, but I don't regret a single moment of it. If given the chance to do it all over again, I would.

I have to steel myself as I walk from my car to Forrester's office. I get looks; I hear whispers. They all remind me of the time I lived in the limelight. I should be used to it by now, but scrutiny by strangers is not something anyone ever gets accustomed to.

When I arrive at his office, his assistant asks me to take a seat. Forrester isn't done with his meeting yet. The reproachable glance she aims my way doesn't escape my notice.

I have to wait for another half hour before she tells me I can come in. Since I didn't see anyone come out of Forrester's office, I can only assume he was on a call.

He doesn't say a word as I walk in and sit across from him. Instead, he stares at me with his indecipherable gaze, the one he used on me when I was his patient. Only I'm no longer eighteen, and I have no time for this type of intimidation tactic.

"Stop staring at me like that. Let's cut to the chase. Am I fired?"

"You're not even going to apologize for this whole mess? I vouched for you when I brought you to DuBose despite your past record. And that's how you repay me?"

"You make it sound like I did it on purpose."

"You're sleeping with one of your students! I hardly think you did that by accident."

"I met Chiara in Italy, before she became my student. And for the record, I tried to fight it."

"Until your dick won the battle." He twists his face into a scowl.

"It isn't like that. I love her."

My confession seems to dilute a bit of Forrester's anger, but he continues to glare. "That doesn't change the fact that she's eighteen and your student."

"Fire me, then."

"Oh, I will, but I'm afraid I must expel Miss Moretti as well."

"What? Why? She's done nothing wrong."

Forrester raises an eyebrow. "Really? You don't consider sleeping with her teacher as something reproachable? All the grades she's earned in your classes will be questioned now."

"I didn't give Chiara any special treatment. She earned her marks by her own merit."

"Even so, she broke the student code of conduct. It's out of my hands. The board demanded your head and hers."

"That's such bullshit!" I stand up, not willing to sit here and listen to Forrester destroy Chiara's academic reputation.

"Shouting and cursing won't get you anywhere. You should have thought about the consequences before you gave in to your urges. I expected more from you."

That last reproach feels like a punch to my gut. I also expected more from myself.

"I'll collect my belongings and be off the premises within the hour."

"Wait, you need to be escorted by security."

I turn, leveling him with a glare. "Are you fucking kidding me?"

"I'm sorry, Alistair. Those are the rules. I can't keep covering for you."

Fuming, I leave his office but wait for the babysitter in the waiting area. I'm not sure what Forrester thinks I'll do, but he sent two guys to escort me. Fucking great. I feel like a criminal.

My walk of shame draws as much attention as I thought it would. At least I'm the one facing it, not Chiara.

God, she's going to be devastated when she learns they're expelling her.

I pack my things as fast as I can, at least the personal belongings I can carry with me. The books and other bigger stuff will have to be packed by someone else and shipped to me later. It feels bittersweet to hand over my staff ID and the keys to my office. I did enjoy teaching here.

The vineyard is also gone.

What the fuck am I going to do with my life now?

42

CHIARA

fter the encounter with Nadine, I changed my mind about going to Robbie's place. I need to be home, surrounded by familiar things, so I can break down in peace. Robbie wanted to come up to my apartment with me, but I told him I needed to be alone.

My cheek still stings from Nadine's slap, but it's my ego that's more bruised. I should have reacted, scratched her face, done something. But no, I just cowered, just like I did every time Mom was cruel to me.

I take the stairs, not wanting to risk getting stuck with anyone in the elevator. When I reach the landing, I find someone standing in front of my door.

"Max! What are you doing here?"

God, did he already know about what happened that fast? I never told him Alistair was my teacher. He's going to be so mad I hid it from him.

He glances at me, and I can tell he's had a rough day, or maybe night.

"Chibi, you're finally home."

He hugs me, and I'm at a loss for why.

"Max, did something happen? Why didn't you call me?"

"I couldn't tell you over the phone. It's about your father."

My blood runs cold in an instant, and I fear the worst.

"He's been arrested," Max continues.

I blink a couple of times as my brain tries to grapple with the news. My heart rejoices that he's not dead, but in the next beat, it twists painfully in my chest again.

"What do you mean? Why?"

"He's been accused of money laundering and fraud."

I shake my head, my body automatically denying the accusations. "My father is not a criminal."

"Chibi, calm down. I'm sure it's a misunderstanding. I just learned about it last night and caught the first flight out of New York to get you. I didn't want you to travel to Italy alone."

"I didn't even know you were in New York."

"I booked a photo shoot last minute. I wanted to pay you a surprise visit after, and that's why I didn't tell you."

My immediate response should be to say, "Yes, let's book the first flight out to Milan," but I hesitate.

What about Alistair?

"I-I can't come to Italy."

"Chiara, your father is in jail facing serious charges. I'm sure he'd like to have you there."

"I have school, Max. I can't simply leave at the drop of a hat." My phone rings then. It's from the principal's office. "I have to take this."

With my heart stuck in my throat, I say, "Hello?"

"Is this Miss Chiara Moretti?" a woman asks.

"Yes, this is she."

"This is Principal's Forrester's assistant. He'd like to schedule a meeting with you today."

I glance at Max, who's watching me with a question in his gaze. I appreciate him coming all the way to tell me the bad news in person, but I'm not free to simply go as I please.

Guilt gnaws at my insides. Despite his faults, Dad always tried to do his best for me. If it weren't for his support, I wouldn't be here.

"Can I ask what this is about?"

"I'm not at liberty to discuss it over the phone."

"Chiara, come on," Max urges me. "If we hurry, we can catch the noon flight."

Maybe me leaving the country for a few days will be the best thing I could do right now. Hopefully the scandal will be forgotten when I return.

"I can't meet with Principal Forrester today. I have a family emergency, and I have to fly to Italy in a few hours."

"Oh, I'm sorry to hear that. Hold a moment, please." The line goes silent before I can tell her I can't hold.

Shit. I bet the principal wants to talk about Alistair.

"Miss Moretti," his assistant says, coming back on the line, "Principal Forrester would like to schedule a meeting online at your earliest convenience. I'll email you the details."

"All right. Sounds good."

Better than me going back to school while the gossip mill is still churning furiously. Meeting with the principal via computer will hopefully be less humiliating.

I turn to Max. "I need to pack."

As soon as I'm in the apartment, I call Alistair. He doesn't answer. I try to leave a voice message, but his inbox is full. *Cazzo.* I send him a text instead, asking him to call me back as soon as he can.

I pack only essentials since I still have a ton of clothes back home. By the time Max and I leave my apartment, Alistair hasn't called back yet.

What can he possibly be doing?

ALISTAIR

After getting my stuff, I head straight to Enzo's office. There's gotta be a way to fight Chiara's expulsion. His office is downtown in one of the fanciest high-rises the city has. The place is as opulent as the man. Modern sophistication with a hint of arrogance.

The receptionist recognizes me, so all she does is greet me with a bright smile. I head to his office without waiting to be announced. One of the founding partners of this prominent law firm, he has the coveted corner office with sweeping views of LA.

He's on the phone, yelling at some unfortunate soul, when I walk in. Swiveling in his chair, he nods at me, then proceeds to yell some more.

I walk to the window, trying to distract my mind with the view. It's useless. I pat my pocket, looking for my phone, then realize I forgot it in my truck.

Enzo hangs up the phone and looks at me. "I didn't expect to see you soon, Ali-boy."

"Don't call me that." I glare at the man.

He whistles. "What's with all the pent-up aggression? Maybe you should stop by at Ginga on your way home."

"I need your help with something."

"More than what I'm already doing? Pretty soon, hiring my services is what's going to make you go bankrupt."

"No shit. It's about Chiara. Forrester fired me, as I knew he would, but he also said Chiara will be expelled."

"Ah, and let me guess. You want to fight that."

"Damn straight I do. I was the one in the wrong, not her. It's unfair to penalize her."

"Have you discussed this with Chiara? Do you know if that's what she wants?"

"I don't follow."

"Have you stopped to consider that maybe Chiara doesn't want to stay at DuBose after the scandal?"

"That's beside the point. They have no right to penalize her for something I did. I was the authority figure. I'm the one who has to suffer the consequences. If she decides she doesn't want to return, that's fine, but at least she should have the option."

"Okay, okay. Monica and Tessa are on the school board. Talk to them. If they pressure Forrester, he'll listen to them. Money and power talk."

I rub my face. "Fuck, I can't believe I didn't think of that."

Enzo shakes his head, then pulls a bottle of the finest whiskey and two glasses from the cabinet behind his desk. "I swear to God, Alistair, when it comes to this girl, you're as clueless as a fifteen-year-old, acne-faced virgin."

"That's fucking ironic considering I'm eight years older than her."

"And should naturally be wiser?" Enzo raises an eyebrow.

I take a large sip of the whiskey. "Yep."

"Well, you sure like your love life dramatic. I can't believe Nadine brought the hounds after Chiara."

I narrow my eyes. "What the fuck are you talking about?"

"Ah, shit. You don't know? Nadine showed up on campus with a cameraman. She threw insults at your girlfriend and then ended the show with a slap on the face."

"She did what? That, that.... I'm gonna kill her."

I make a move to burst out of Enzo's office, but he grabs my arm, stopping me. I didn't even see him jump off his chair.

"Calm the fuck down. That's exactly what Nadine wants. Don't worry. Caio's nephew was with Chiara, so it's not like she didn't have support."

Fuck, and I left my damn phone in my car. I need to call her to make sure she's okay.

"Anyway, I know it sucks that Chiara got to experience the Tasmanian-devil Nadine, but it'll only serve your cause."

"Can you please just get to the point? I need to go check on Chiara."

"Nadine posted the video of her slapping Chiara. That's an assault charge right there. I've already downloaded the video in case Nadine's lawyer tells her to pull it down. I can use it as leverage to make her sign the damn divorce papers."

"Great. You get on with that."

I walk out, not waiting for Enzo's reply. If I could fly out the window to get to my car faster, I would.

When I finally reach my car and grab my phone, I see I have a missed call from Chiara and a text message. She asks me to call her back as soon as possible. When I get her voice message, I feel like throwing the fucking phone against my windshield.

Damn it. I'm unraveling, and I don't know how to stop it.

43

CHIARA

Max and I barely make it to the airport in time to catch our flight. I check my phone several times to see if Alistair called, but so far, nothing. It's not until my bag with my phone inside is going through the X-ray machine that I hear it ring.

Fucking great.

As soon as I have access to my stuff again, I reach for my phone. In my desperation to see if I missed a call from him, I fumble the device, letting it drop to the floor. The screen shatters, which wouldn't be so problematic if the phone wasn't also dead.

I killed my phone. You've got to be kidding me.

And the worst part is I don't know Alistair's phone number by heart.

"Shit, Chibi. How did you manage that?" Max asks.

"Shut up. How am I going to tell Alistair I'm headed to Milan?"

"Wait. What? Alistair, as in the dude you brought to Paola's wedding?"

Ah hell.

"Yes, him. We've reconnected, and, well, we're together now."

I don't want to tell Max the whole story in the middle of the airport. There will be plenty of time during the long flight.

"Wow, small world."

"Yeah."

"Hmm, can't you message him on Facebook?"

"He doesn't have an account."

"Okay. Email, then. You *do* have his email, right?"

Yeah, I do, but only his work email and most likely Alistair has been sacked.

God, what a nightmare.

"I'll message Robbie and Phillip on Facebook and ask them to find Alistair for me."

"You know I have no clue who those two are, right?"

"Yeah, sorry. They're friends from school. God, Max. There's so much I have to tell you."

He nods. "It seems like it."

He lends me his phone, and I quickly log into Facebook and send the guys a message. One of them is bound to find Alistair.

"Do you think the charges against Dad are real, Max?" I ask.

"I don't know. I always liked Uncle Giovanni. He's so different than my piece-of-shit father."

"Dad's innocent. I know he is," I say with more conviction than I feel.

In fact, I'm terrified that he's done illicit things. Besides Max, Dad is the only one in the family who has my back, who believes in me.

"Your mother wants you to stay at the penthouse," he says.

"Why?"

"To use you as a punching bag, most likely." I wince at Max's words because he's not wrong. "I told her you're staying with me."

"Thank you."

"You don't need to thank me, Chibi. We underdogs have to look out for one another. You were there for me when I had to deal with my father. We may not be siblings, but you're my sister of the heart." He throws his arm around my shoulders and kisses my head.

"Yes, you do annoy me like a big brother." I elbow his side playfully.

Max tries his best to distract me with his crazy stories and silly jokes. It works for a little bit, until something he says reminds me of Alistair or my dad.

Once we're on the plane, he offers me a sleeping pill. I usually hate those, but today, I don't refuse. If I stay awake during the flight, I'll go insane. I need to get some rest because I know it will be hell when we land.

ALISTAIR

Since the cat is out of the bag, I go back to Chiara's apartment, not caring who sees me there. I buzz her intercom, but after the fifth attempt without an answer, I get the hint that she's not home. I call her phone again, but now it goes to voice mail.

I don't linger in front of her building because, with my luck, I wouldn't put it past someone to call the cops on me.

I'm about to get into my truck when I see a familiar car approach. Phillip parks behind me and rolls his window down. I look past him, more precisely at the passenger seat, finding it empty.

"Phillip."

"Hi, Mr. Walsh. You're probably looking for Chiara, right?"

"Yes. She won't answer her phone."

"She busted it. Anyway, since you're not on any social media network, she asked me to give you a message."

"I'm listening."

"She had an emergency back home. She's probably on a plane to Italy right now."

"What kind of emergency?"

"She didn't say, only that her cousin is with her."

I rub my face, frustrated as hell with the way my life is derailing. "Did she give you Max's phone number?"

"Yes. Hold on." Phillip turns to his side, then sticks out his hand with a folded piece of paper pinched between his fingers. "Here."

"Thanks."

"I'm sorry about your job. Everyone I know really enjoyed having you as their teacher."

"Thanks, Phillip. I'll miss DuBose for sure."

"What are you going to do now?" he asks.

"Figure out how to fix my life."

"You really should go after Chiara. After what your ex-wife did to her, she's probably feeling like shit."

"Nadine will get what's coming to her," I state matter-of-factly. "As for going after Chiara, I have to tie up some loose ends here first."

Phillip narrows his eyes at me. It seems my answer wasn't what he wanted to hear. I wish I could just drop everything and go after Chiara, but I can't leave my parents alone to deal with the aftermath of the fire, and I also have to make sure Nadine doesn't have another nasty surprise waiting for me.

44

CHIARA

I knew my mother wouldn't leave me alone just because I'm staying with Max. She only gives me a few hours of peace before she starts to hound me, blowing up the new cell phone I bought in Italy like the world is about to end.

The insecure and terrified little girl who still lives inside me wants to answer her call, but I fight the urge. My mother can go fuck herself. I'm done trying to make her like me. So the first thing I do is call my father's lawyer. I want to visit Dad. To my dismay, he tells me Dad doesn't want to see any visitors.

I'm already crying before I even end the call.

"What's the matter, Chibi?" Max asks.

"Dad doesn't want me to visit."

He sits next to me on the couch and throws his arm around my shoulders. "Can you blame him? This is the lowest moment of his life. He doesn't want you to see him like that."

I hastily wipe my tears dry. "You're right, but it doesn't make things easier."

"Here, maybe this will make you feel better." He offers me his cell phone.

"What is it?"

"Your boyfriend left you a voice message."

"And you listened to it?" I shriek.

Guilt takes over his face. "I'm sorry. I didn't recognize the number. I didn't know it was from him."

I give him the stink eye as I grab the phone from his hand. When Alistair's voice comes through, my heart tightens. I miss him so damn much already. I wish he was here with me. He tells me to call him back as soon as I'm able, no matter the time.

I'm ready to do that when the annoying sound of the intercom buzzer interrupts. Max heads to the kitchen to answer it while I head to the bathroom to wash my face. When I return to the living room, he's sporting a grimace.

"Who was that?"

"Your mother. She's on her way up."

"I don't want to talk to her."

"I know, Chibi, but I couldn't just not buzz her in. She would keep pestering us. You knew you wouldn't be able to avoid her, so you might as well get this over with. I'll head to my room to give you some privacy."

I want to ask Max to stay, but that wouldn't be a smart move. If my mother doesn't like me, she hates him with a passion. It has always been this way since we were kids.

No sooner has Max disappeared into his room than the doorbell rings. I take a deep breath, steeling myself for this unpleasant encounter before I open the door.

As usual, Ofelia Moretti is the example of poise and perfection. Her sharp dark Chanel suit doesn't have a wrinkle that can be seen. I open the door wider and let her in.

She glances around Max's small apartment with a sneer on her face, as if searching for something to criticize.

"I see your cousin has made himself scarce."

"He wanted to give us some privacy. What are you doing here, Mother?"

"I came to get you, of course."

"You've wasted your time, then. I'm not staying with you at the penthouse."

Her eyes widen. "How dare you speak to me like that? Don't you think I've suffered enough?"

"Tell me, Mom. Are you suffering because the love of your life is in jail or because the family name is tainted now?"

"As usual, you're an ungrateful little brat. Let's see how you fare now that the money tree has died. The government seized all our assets. Did you know that? We're lucky the penthouse belongs to my family."

"Yes, the lawyer filled me in. I'll be okay. I can get a job. I'd be more concerned about your situation. What can you do?"

My mother's eyes flash with rage. I'm playing with fire here, but I'm too angry to care about the consequences.

"I'm not going to stay here and listen to you throw insults my way. If you want to stay with your worthless cousin, be my guest."

When she walks to the door, I let out a sigh of relief. Too soon though. I should have known she wouldn't just leave without delivering a killing blow. She looks over her shoulder with hate pouring out of her eyes.

"Paola told me all about your affair with that married teacher. I was right all along. All you wanted was to sleep around. You're a filthy whore and a disgrace to our family."

The insult shouldn't hurt as much, coming from her. It's nothing new. But it does. It feels like I've been sucker punched in the gut.

I wince, unable to hide my reaction from my mother. The worst part is to see her take pleasure from my pain.

She walks out without saying another word.

She doesn't need to. She won this round.

THE NEXT DAY, Max receives a call from our uncle, Paola's father. He paid for Dad's bail, and he's going to be released in the next couple of hours. A wave of relief washes over me, followed by dread. I have to be at the penthouse when Dad arrives, which means I have to deal with my mother.

I never told Max the details of her visit yesterday, but he knew it was bad by the look on my face. I'm still reeling from it, and I almost start to believe that maybe I *am* a filthy whore.

I wasn't in the right frame of mind to speak with Alistair after her visit. I settled with sending him a text message explaining why I had to leave and that I would call him today. I'm a mess, and he'll be able to tell right away if he hears my voice. He's already dealing with so many problems; I don't want to add to the tally.

I get dressed and wear the best outfit I brought with me, a dark gray pantsuit that I bought in case I needed to look professional. It's overkill—Dad has never cared about what I wear—but I don't want to give my mother any more reason to throw insults my way.

Who are you kidding, Chiara? She doesn't need a reason.

By the time Max and I arrive at my parents' luxurious apartment, the entire family is already there. *Fuck, it's the middle of the week. Don't they have jobs?* At least Pietro didn't come with his wife. Paola is sitting next to my mother on the couch, and staring at them side by side, they look more like a mother and daughter duo than Mom and me. A sliver of jealousy spears through my heart, even though by now, I shouldn't feel anything at all.

Will I ever stop wanting that odious woman to love me?

Max leaves me alone for a second to speak with his mother. She used to be one of the most beautiful women in Italy, but years of abuse under the hands of Max's dad took their toll on her. She's overweight and looks ten years older than she really is. Plus, she's now a drunk. As a matter of fact, she's hovering near the dry bar in the living room with a glass of whiskey in her hand.

Poor Max. He doesn't deserve this.

"Is Dad already home?" I ask no one in particular.

"He's in his office with your uncle and the lawyer," Paola's mother answers. "What a scandal. What a blemish to the Moretti name."

And so it starts. I don't have the stomach to hear dear Auntie's lamentations, so I head to the dining room table where food has been served.

I'm busy spreading foie gras on a piece of toast when Paola stops next to me.

"Like father like daughter, I guess."

"Don't start, Paola. I'm not in the mood for your petty games."

Ignoring my comment, she continues. "I'm surprised your boyfriend didn't tag along. Did he get tired of you already?"

"That's none of your business. I'm surprised your husband isn't here. Did *he* get tired of you already?

"Pietro is on a very important business trip. He would be here if he could."

Her defensive tone tells me things aren't as rosy as she wants me to believe. I can't help but push the dagger deeper.

"Right, but not because of you."

"What's that supposed to mean?"

"Oh, I guess I forgot to tell you how Pietro confessed moments before your wedding that he was in love with me and that you were his second choice."

"You lie!"

I shrug. "It doesn't matter. I told him I would never have him, so you don't have to worry about me stealing your perfect husband away."

"It wouldn't be the first time," she grits out. "Isn't your boyfriend married?"

I pop a grape in my mouth. "Not for much longer. And let me tell you, stealing Alistair away from his conniving wife was so much fun."

If I'm going to be labeled a home-wrecker, I might as well have fun with it.

I turn on my heels, putting extra sass in my steps.

Was it mean to tell Paola about Pietro? Absolutely, but I can't find an ounce of regret in me. She more than deserves the pain.

45

CHIARA

I t seems everyone gets to speak with Dad before he calls me into this office. He stands from his chair and walks around his massive desk to hug me.

"Dad, are you okay?"

"I'll be fine, bambina. Don't worry about me."

Pulling back, I stare at his face. His eyes are bloodshot, and he has dark circles under them. I can smell the whiskey and cigar on his breath.

He moves away, returning to his chair. I have no choice but to sit across from him.

"Is it true?" I ask before I lose my nerve.

He smiles tightly at me with sad eyes. "It's complicated, Chiara."

"What's complicated about it? It's a simple question, Dad. Is it true or not?"

"No, of course it's not true." He fills his empty glass with more whiskey and leans back.

He's lying. The certainty makes my heart sink. Part of the respect I have for him dies. I would have preferred if he had been honest with me. Does he think I'll stop loving him because of what he's done?

"Mom is worried about the frozen assets."

"She'll be fine. But I'm afraid you won't be able to continue your studies abroad."

"Why? I thought my tuition and boarding had been paid for already."

Dad shakes his head, and regret fills his eyes. "I'm afraid not. I'm very sorry, Chiara."

I stare at his desk while my brain processes the news. If I'm no longer a student, I can't stay in the US.

Alistair comes to the forefront of my mind. I should be more concerned about my education, but graduating from DuBose seems small compared to losing him.

"I'll be okay, Dad. I can always finish high school in a public school."

"Joe is helping me. So if you need any assistance, don't be shy to ask him. He's your uncle, after all."

The last thing I want is to ask Paola's father for help. I don't care if he's Dad's older brother.

I nod, pretending to agree with him.

"Your mother told me you're staying with Max. What kind of nonsense is that? You should be here."

"I can now that you're back."

"Good. Now go collect your things. I still have lots to talk about with your uncle and the lawyer."

"Okay, Dad. I'll see you later."

I avoid the living room, choosing to hide in my bedroom. Closing the door, I check my emails and see several from Alistair. Guilt sneaks into my heart. I've been avoiding him for too long, and he must be going out of his mind. It's still early in California, so I text him.

He replies right away, asking how I am.

Taking a deep breath, I call him.

"Goldi, thank God you called."

Sitting on my bed, I rest my head in my hand. "Hey, I'm sorry I didn't until now. It's been difficult."

"I read on the news about your father. I'm so sorry, Chiara. I wish I could be there with you."

"Me too. But you have your own problems to deal with."

I should tell Alistair about not coming back to DuBose, but I can't bring myself to give him more bad news over the phone.

"I swear, Goldi, if it weren't for my parents. I'd be there with you."

"I know. How are they holding up?"

"Devastated. We were allowed back in town. It's gone. Everything has been razed to the ground."

"I'm so sorry, Alistair."

"Don't worry about us, sweetheart. We'll be okay. When do you think you'll be back?"

Oh God. I have to tell him I'm only going back to pack my stuff. "I-I don't know. Dad has been released on bail, but everything is still a big question mark."

"And your mother?"

"As awful as always. But I've got Max here. I'll be okay."

"Call me whenever you need me, Goldi. It doesn't matter the time."

"I will. You do the same, okay?"

"Okay. I love you, and I miss you."

"I love you and miss you too."

My eyes fill with tears as I end the call. I don't want to say goodbye to Alistair, but I can't expect him to make a commitment to me so I can stay in the US.

There's a knock on my door before it opens and Max's head pops through the sliver. "There you are. I can't stay here for a minute longer. I'm heading to town to meet some friends. Do you want to join me?"

"Yeah, sure."

I'm not really in the mood to socialize, but staying in this apartment surrounded by family members who hate me would be masochistic to say the least.

ALISTAIR

"Did you talk with Chiara?" my father asks when I come into the kitchen at five in the morning.

"Yes. What are you doing up?"

"I couldn't sleep. How is she holding up?"

"She's having a hard time, I could tell. It kills me that I can't be there with her."

"If you're staying here on our account, don't. Your mother and I will be fine."

"It's not only that, Dad. I want to settle things with Nadine first. She'll always be a hindrance until the divorce is finalized."

"Is your lawyer making progress?"

"Oh yeah. That video Nadine posted turned out to be a big mistake on her part. Anyway, we have a meeting with the insurance company tomorrow. We had a good policy coverage. The insurance money should be enough to start anew."

"Listen, son, about that. Your mother and I have been talking, and we decided we don't want to run a vineyard anymore."

My eyes widen. "But it was your dream."

"Yes, it was. But it was more hard work than we anticipated, and we don't want to start from scratch."

"So what are you going to do?"

"Travel, see the world."

"I confess I'm a little disappointed. I was hoping that now that I don't have a job teaching anymore, I could help you with the business."

"If you want to own a vineyard, what's stopping you?"

I open and shut my mouth, but no sound comes forth. Dad

is right, there's nothing stopping me from forging ahead without my parents. Well, there's Chiara to consider now. She wouldn't want to give up a career in the city to move to wine country with me. She hasn't even gone to college yet.

He pats my shoulder. "You don't have to decide everything right this second, son. Take your time, talk with your girl."

"How did you know I was thinking about her?"

"I wasn't born yesterday. I know that glint in your eyes. I see it every day when I look at my reflection in the mirror. You are head over heels in love with Chiara, just like I'm still in love with your mother. I never saw that spark in your gaze when you were married to Nadine."

I look down and cross my arms. "There are so many obstacles in our way though. It's hard for me to think about the future and see a happily ever after as much as I want to believe it's possible."

"Stop focusing on the problems and focus on the reward. Is she worth it?"

There's no hesitation on my part.

"Fuck yes."

46

CHIARA

I turn the doorknob very quietly, not wanting to make any sound and wake the banshee—aka my mother. It's past two in the morning, but I wouldn't put it past her to be waiting for me in the living room. With my shoes in my hands, I tiptoe toward my room.

The entire house is as quiet as a tomb and dark as well. When I walk by my father's office, I notice light pouring through the crack. I hesitate for a second. Maybe I should go check on him. We hardly had time to talk earlier, and maybe I can offer him some comfort, even if he's not willing to tell me the truth. My hand is on the semi-open door when a gunshot rings in my ears, loud and terrifying.

"Papa!" I burst inside his office, and suddenly time seems to move in slow motion.

Dad's body is on the floor. The only thing visible from where I stand is his prone hand and a gun. I run around the desk, dropping to my knees next to him. Blood is splattered on the carpet.

I hear screaming moments before I'm pushed to the side and my mother takes my place. I'm in too much shock to do anything but stare and cry. Then my mother is shaking me and yelling, but I can't discern her words through the loud roar in my ears.

She shoves me out of her way and stands up. I don't know if she's still in the room or not. All I can do is stare at Dad.

Eventually, more people come, and then the police show up. Someone lifts me from the floor and cradles my face against his chest. At first, I think it's Alistair, but the scent isn't his. Max is the one holding me. He steers me out of Dad's office and back to my room. Then he forces something strong down my throat, making me gag. I cough as the potent liquid turns my veins into fire.

"Chibi, please talk to me."

"I-I was just outside his office when it happened. If I had come home a few minutes earlier, he'd still be alive."

"No, you can't think like that."

I stare at my cousin through blurred vision. "How can I not say that, Max? It's the truth."

A knock on the door interrupts what Max was about to say.

"Who is it?" he asks.

"The police would like to take Chiara's statement," Uncle Joe says.

Max turns to me. "Are you okay to do this now?"

I nod, and Max lets my uncle and the officer come in. He doesn't leave my side, and for that I'm grateful. The officer is kind, and I try to answer his questions to the best of my ability without losing my mind. I think after the initial reaction, I became numb.

The interview doesn't last long, maybe ten minutes, tops. Max walks out of the room with them to get me some tea, and Mom comes in a second later. Her usually perfect hair is disheveled, and without makeup on, she looks much older. Her eyes are red, but even in this tragic moment, she still finds time to stare at me with loathing.

"What do you want?" I ask.

"Are you happy now?"

I don't speak for a couple of seconds. "Happy that my father, the only parent who ever loved me, is dead? How dare you ask me that?"

"What did you say to him earlier? I bet you made him feel so guilty that he decided to put a bullet through his head."

"You're mad."

She throws her head back and laughs. "No, I'm not mad. It doesn't surprise me, considering you're the devil's spawn."

"If you're referring to yourself, then you're right," I seethe.

"Me? You think I'm the devil? I'm talking about *your* father."

I stand up with my hands balled into fists at my sides. "How dare you speak ill of him? He's not even cold yet."

A deranged glint takes over my mother's eyes. "Oh, you stupid girl. Your father is very much alive, rotting in jail where he belongs. You wanted to know why I hate you so much? So here it is. Antonio Pesaro, the bastard who spawned your beloved cousin, is your real father."

Sudden vertigo hits me. I drop to the floor like a sack of potatoes when my legs can no longer hold my weight.

"No, you're lying."

"I wish I was. That scum raped me the night I met your father. When I found out I was pregnant, I let Giovanni believe the baby was his. He proposed on the same day. I knew he wouldn't have done it if it weren't for my pregnancy. That's why I kept you, but there hasn't been a day since that seeing your face doesn't remind me of the worst day of my life."

Tears stream freely down my face. "So that's your revenge? To tell me Dad wasn't my real father on the evening he dies?"

"Yes," she stares at me coldly.

Suddenly, I snap. I get up and push my mother against the wall. "I never asked to be born. All I ever wanted was for you to love me!"

Ofelia Moretti stares at me with dead eyes, as if I'm nothing but an insect. Ugly sobs rack my body. I can't stay under the same roof as her for another second. I run out of the room, veering toward the front door. I grab the first set of car keys I see on the foyer table and disappear down the stairs. Once out on the street, I press on the fob like a maniac until I hear the sound of a car beeping.

I have Max's car keys. Jumping inside the vehicle, I bring the engine to life and peel away from the curb with a loud screech with no destination in mind. I just have to get the hell out of this city.

ALISTAIR

I'm in Enzo's office, listening with rapt attention as he gives me the latest report about Nadine. She's finally agreed to give me the divorce and accepted the settlement. She's not getting a penny from the vineyard. I've already signed the divorce papers, and now we'll just have to wait for her to do the same.

"Also, I spoke with Tessa about Chiara's expulsion," Enzo continues. "She convinced the other parents on the board that expelling her is an extreme and unnecessary measure."

The pressure in my chest eases as relief washes over me. "Thank God. Chiara would have been devastated if she couldn't return to DuBose."

I glance at my phone when I feel it vibrate in my hand. It's Max's number. I'm worried in an instant. He wouldn't be calling me if it wasn't an emergency.

"What happened to Chiara? Is she okay?" I ask without preamble.

"*Cazzo*, no. Her father committed suicide a few hours ago, and now she's gone missing."

I jump out of my chair, body tense like a coiled spring ready to launch. "What do you mean?"

"She had a fight with her mother and bailed. Took my car. I don't know where she went."

"Goddamn it, Max. Find her!"

"I'm trying my best, okay? I know you have shit to take care of in America, but Chiara needs you, man. She needs you." Max's voice gets choked at the end.

"I'll be on the next flight out. Please keep me posted, Max."

"Will do."

I'm about to leave when Enzo stops me. "What happened?"

I run my hand through my hair, feeling useless. "I have to get to Italy."

"Take the company's private jet so you don't have to wait for the next commercial flight out."

I stare at my friend with unblinking eyes. Then I hug him, almost crying like a baby all over his five-thousand-dollar suit.

"Jesus fucking Christ. Enough with this bullshit already." He pulls back. "Go get your passport. The plane will be ready for you at the airport."

"Thanks, man."

47

CHIARA

I shouldn't be surprised that my grief-stricken brain led me to the place where I had one of the best days of my life: Villa Moretti. Despite always associating the house with misery thanks to my cousins' antics, the place is now imprinted with memories of Alistair.

I get out of the car and take a deep breath, inhaling the lemony scent that hangs in the fresh air before veering toward the front door. The key is inside a keypad lockbox we all have the code for.

The heavy door creaks as I push it open, the sound echoing in the empty foyer. Without stopping, I go straight to the back, where the valley below is already bathed in morning sunlight. I don't open the sliding doors but rest my forehead against the glass and let the grief I had been holding at bay take over my body once more. With a loud sob, I cry in earnest, feeling my father's loss deep in my bones. It doesn't matter that he wasn't my biological father. I push the knowledge to a dark corner in my mind. There will be enough time to deal with that later.

I don't know how long I cry, but my face is soaked and my

nose is stuffy by the time the tears have dried out. An unbearable weight presses against my hollowed chest, caving it in. Suddenly, the house feels suffocating. I have to get out.

Outside, I spare one glance at Max's sports car and decide against it. I need to feel the wind on my face.

The Vespa it is.

When I hop onto it, I remember the feel of Alistair's body behind me, how his arms wrapped around my waist and his warm breath tickled my skin. God, I miss him so much. I wish I had brought my phone so I could call him and hear his voice. Another tear rolls down my cheek, but I hastily wipe it off.

Revving up the engine, I take off down the path leading back to the winding road, going to the spot where I found Alistair stranded. It's only ten minutes from the villa. I don't know what I'm going to do once I get there, but somehow, I know that's where I have to be.

ALISTAIR

Max picks me up at the airport, looking as bedraggled as I feel. The first thing out of my mouth is to ask if he found Chiara.

"Yes. She took my car, and I finally remembered it has a GPS tracking system. She drove all the way to our family's villa."

"She's in Tuscany? I wish I had known. I would have flown straight there."

"It's only three hours by car. Here, I got you a rental."

"You're not coming?"

Max shakes his head. "No. I'm needed here. My mother is.... Well, I'd better stick around."

"I'm sorry about your uncle."

Chiara's cousin looks out in the distance. "Yeah, me too. Chiara was the one who found him. She—*Dio santo*—she was standing right outside his office when she heard the gunshot."

"Jesus." I rub my face, worry squeezing my heart in a merciless vise.

"Come on. I'll take you to the car. The sooner you get to her, the better."

Max got me a sports car. Maybe it's his hint that I should put the pedal to the metal.

It takes me a while to get out of the city, but once I hit the highway, I ignore the speed limit, praying I won't be stopped by the Italian police. I make the trip in two hours instead of three.

I'm about ten minutes from Villa Moretti when I spot a lonely Vespa parked on the side of the road. Pain twists my gut, and I can't draw air in. I recognize the spot. It's where I got my flat tire. I park the rental behind the Vespa and jump out. I'm about to call Chiara's name when I see her lying against a tree, unmoving.

No. No. No.

"Chiara," I say as I kneel next to her and shake her shoulder lightly. When she blinks her eyes open, a wave of relief washes over me.

She turns her face to mine, her gaze confused. "Alistair? Is it really you?"

I lift her up, bringing her to my lap and cradling her like a baby. "Yes, my love. I'm here."

She curls her hands in my shirt, burying her face against my chest. Her entire body is shaking as she cries. I kiss the top of her head, holding her tighter.

"He's gone. I couldn't save him," she says between hiccups.

"I'm so sorry, Chiara."

"If I had gotten home a minute earlier, he'd still be alive."

"No, you can't think like that. What happened is not your fault."

She cries harder, and I can't do anything besides let her. It kills me though. I wish I could take away her pain and guilt.

A few minutes pass before she speaks again.

"Then my mother came in and destroyed me."

Fuck that woman. I don't know what I'll do when I come face-to-face with her again. I can't understand how she can torture her own daughter like that.

"Come on. Let's get out of here."

I carry Chiara back to the car. I'll deal with the Vespa later. When I place her in the seat, she doesn't look at me, just stares at the road ahead, listless. Not knowing where else to go, I drive back to the villa. It's a silent and heavy ten-minute ride. She's no longer crying, but her expression is one of desolation. I don't know what her mother told her, but it must have been something awful.

As soon as I park in front of the house, Chiara gets out of the car. She only takes a couple of steps in the direction of the front door before freezing.

I touch her lower back and pinch her chin to turn her face to mine. "Goldi, please tell me what I can do."

"Kiss me, Alistair. Just kiss me."

I capture her face between my hands and bring our lips together. I taste the saltiness of tears on her lips, and there's nothing I want more than to make her forget, if only for a moment, the sadness that's crushing her heart.

Her arms go around my neck as our kiss turns into a clash of tongues and teeth. I lift her up by the waist, and she immediately wraps her legs around my hips. The skirt of her dress hikes up, and I move my hands so her sweet ass fills my palms. It wasn't my intention to sex Chiara up, but if that's what she needs, I won't object.

I stride into the house, and between kisses, I ask her where to go. She points at the hallway on the right, and I immediately guess where she wants me to take her: to the room where she caught me half naked.

Placing her down on the soft mattress, I make quick work of removing my clothes. Chiara just leans on her elbows and watches me with heavy-lidded eyes. Standing completely naked in front of her and sporting the mother of all boners, I wait for her signal. She licks her lips, then slowly pulls her dress off, revealing simple black lingerie. My mouth waters, and I lose the little restraint I had left. Like a starved wild animal, I pounce, fusing my lips with hers again as I cover her body with mine. She parts her legs for me, and I pump my hips, rubbing my erection against her already soaked panties.

"Alistair, I need you inside me right now."

Letting go of her mouth, I lean back so I can roll her panties down her legs. I would love a taste of her sweet pussy, but that can wait. I can't resist playing a little with her tits though. I open the front clasp and cover one hard nipple with my mouth before she can protest. While I'm busy sucking and kissing one, I tease the other with my hand.

Chiara's fingers are in my hair, pulling at the short strands. She doesn't let me play with her breasts for too long before she urges me to fuck her already.

"As you wish, Goldi."

I'm inside her with a hard thrust, sheathing myself in her tight heat with ease. Chiara hooks her legs behind my ass, and I ram into her harder and harder with each push. I'm ready to explode, but I hold my release off for as long as I can. My balls are tight as a tendril of pleasure curls around my spine.

Chiara's long nails scratch my back when her body finally shatters under mine. I lose the fight, grunting as I fill her with my release. Even after the tremors are gone, I keep pumping because she feels too damn good.

She unhooks her legs from behind me, making me stop. I

lean back so I can stare at the most beautiful woman on the planet. Her sad eyes stare back at me, and in that moment, I make a vow to spend the rest of my life making sure I don't see that glint in her gaze again.

48

CHIARA

I stretch out on the comfy bed, and Alistair's arm around my belly holds me tighter. I experience two seconds of bliss before the reality of what happened yesterday barrels down on me, annihilating my bubble of happiness. My chest becomes tight, and the urge to cry renews. But I fight the tears because crying won't change the fact that my father is dead.

"Good morning, my love," Alistair whispers in my ear.

I focus on him, on his voice, on his warmth as I fight the sadness that wants to drag me down. He came to Italy even though his life is also falling apart. He dropped everything for me, and that means more than a thousand love declarations. I don't know how he found me, but he did, and I'll never be able to thank him enough.

"Good morning," I reply.

My stomach grumbles, and I remember I didn't eat anything yesterday. After Alistair distracted me with his love-making, I fell asleep in his arms.

"Is there any food in this house?" he asks.

"Probably not."

"Are you up for a trip into town?" He nudges my neck with his nose while pressing his erection against my butt.

I arch my back, twisting my neck so I can kiss him.

It's sweet and unhurried. He runs his hand down my belly until he finds my aching spot. With deft fingers, he parts my folds, then begins to play with my bundle of nerves. He has me panting in seconds, and I rejoice in the fact that he's not being an insensitive jerk for me wanting sex. Yesterday, I made it obvious that's what I need, a distraction from the overwhelming sadness that's swirling in my chest.

Letting go of my lips, he places sweet kisses on my neck while he inserts a finger inside me. He doesn't rub his erection against me; in fact, he's lying completely still besides his hand and mouth. He inserts another finger at the same time he applies pressure on my clit with his thumb. The pleasure builds faster than lightning, making my head spin. I close my eyes, curling my fingers around the tangled sheets before I cry out. Alistair increases his pace, milking my orgasm to the max, and it takes me a couple minutes to get back down to earth.

He kisses my shoulder before I turn to him. Caressing my cheek with his fingers, he stares at me like I'm the most beautiful thing he's ever seen. My shattered heart begins to beat faster as it tries to reconcile the feeling of elation with grief.

"Thanks for coming," I say.

"Goldi, I would go to hell to find you. To be honest, I've never been more scared in my life."

"What do you mean?"

"When I saw you asleep by that tree on the side of the road, I thought the worst had happened."

I frown. "I'm so sorry. I didn't mean to make you worry. I don't even remember falling asleep. I guess exhaustion just took over."

"Please promise me you'll never do something like that again."

I close my eyes and take a deep breath. "I couldn't bear to stay in my parents' house after what happened. After what my mother told me."

"Let's not talk about her."

I open my eyes again. "No, I want to. I have to get this off my chest." I pause, needing to take a deep breath first. "Max is my brother."

Alistair stares at me speechless for a couple of seconds before he furrows his eyebrows. "How?"

"It's awful. His father raped my mother, and I'm the result. Dad never knew the truth, but that explains why she hates me so much."

Alistair pulls me against his chest. "I'm so sorry, Chiara. Where is he now? The scumbag, I mean?"

"In jail for beating Max within an inch of his life."

"Jesus."

"I'm fucked up, Alistair. Are you sure you want me around?"

He laughs against my hair, but it's a sound without humor. "You're not fucked up, my love. I am."

He must be thinking about his friend Jamie and his reckless past. I touch Alistair's face, wanting to offer him comfort. It's not enough—those scars will never vanish completely—but I'll try my best to make the burden easier for him as long as he'll let me.

He grabs my hand, turning it around to place a soft kiss on my palm.

"I didn't mean to make it about me. I'm sorry," he says.

"Please don't apologize. Misery loves company."

My stomach decides it's been ignored long enough and growls even louder.

"Okay, let's hop into the shower and go find something to eat," Alistair says.

"Together?"

"If you want to."

I grin. "Yes, I need help reaching some hard places."

49

ALISTAIR

W e headed back to Milan yesterday, and I checked us into a hotel. Knowing something bad had happened between Chiara and her mother, Max brought her clothes to us. He didn't linger, and it didn't take a genius to see the guy was battling his own problems. With red eyes and a scruff, he looked nothing like the young man I met before.

I noticed how tense Chiara got when Max gave her a hug, how she watched him with guilt in her eyes. Not that she has anything to feel guilty about.

The wake and the funeral aren't being held in Milan but at a family property in Lake Como. When Chiara mentioned the Moretti name had weight, I didn't realize they were that important. It makes it even more appealing to the media that a member of one of the most prominent families in Italy was part of a huge financial scandal. No doubt the entire family will be under scrutiny now.

Heads turn when Chiara and I walk in together at the lakefront mansion. I clench my jaw and place a protective hand on her lower back. People stare and talk about us, not even bothering to whisper. Chiara's spine is taut, so I lace our hands together, squeezing lightly. She turns to me and smiles a little, her eyes dimmed by sadness.

Due to the manner in which her father died, the coffin is sealed shut. Chiara makes a strangled noise in the back of her throat when we get near it, but she stops halfway toward the front row.

"What's the matter?" I ask.

"I don't think I can do this."

"Maybe we should go outside for some fresh air."

"Yes."

I guide us to the double doors I spotted earlier. The path leads to a garden that seems to wrap around the house. A few people are milling about, mostly more interested in smoking than the scenic view of the lake.

"Oh God," Chiara whispers so low, I almost don't hear it.

I follow her gaze. A young couple is veering our way, both dressed to the nines and sporting an arrogant expression on their faces.

"Chiara, I see you finally decided to show up," the woman says.

"Be nice, Paola," her companion chimes in.

Ah, so this is the infamous cousin, which means the guy with her must be Pietro.

I wrap my arms around Chiara's waist, bringing her closer to me. His eyes don't miss the movement, narrowing in the process.

What a fucking toad.

"I'm not going to be nice. Chiara totally bailed on her own mother when she needed her the most. If it weren't for m—"

"Shut your fucking mouth, Paola, or I swear to God you're going to need a plastic surgeon to fix your face," Chiara retorts.

The woman makes a distressed noise while her eyes turn as round as saucers. Her husband's jaw slackens. I have to fight the urge to laugh, but I'm loving the fierce side of Goldilocks.

"That was uncalled for," the idiotic man says.

I can't keep my mouth shut any longer. "What's uncalled for is this bullshit. Chiara just lost her father. And here you are, trying to make her feel guilty. You should be ashamed of yourselves."

"Who the hell are you?" Paola asks, obviously recovered from the burn.

"He's my boyfriend," Chiara replies. "Come on, Alistair. The air has become toxic out here."

She drags me away, which is good, because another minute in front of the duo and I would probably be called an American savage.

Back inside, we find the bar. Chiara orders us two glasses of whiskey and drinks hers as if it were a shot.

"Whoa, take it easy there, sweetheart."

"I need liquid courage to survive. Let's take our places. I can't wait to introduce you to my mother."

Knowing all I know about the woman, I'm not looking forward to the introduction. I try my best to feel empathy considering what happened to her, but she's tortured Chiara her whole life; I can't bring myself to feel anything for her but contempt.

The introduction happens, and to my surprise, no barbs come our way. In fact, I believe her mother is heavily medicated. I guess it's better this way.

I sit next to the woman, giving Chiara a little buffer. She's tense throughout the entire service though. Our hands are fused together, and from time to time, I squeeze hers to let her know I'm there for her.

I'm usually not overly emotional, but I do shed a few tears for the man Chiara loved so much. I wish I had met him.

Later, I'm introduced to the rest of the family. Before

meeting each of them, Chiara gives me a quick rap sheet. I make sure to glower at all the cousins who gave her grief growing up. Unfortunately, no one misbehaves in front of me, so I have to be polite as well.

I catch Pietro staring in our direction a couple of times, and I make sure to stare right back at him. He always looks away first.

That's right, buddy, you should be scared.

By the time we get back to the hotel, it's already past midnight. Chiara is exhausted, so I tuck her into bed, content with just holding her against me.

My phone rings right before I'm about to doze off. With a quick glance, I see it's Enzo calling.

"Hello?"

"Ciao, Alistair. How's it going?"

"You sound awfully chipper."

"I have great news. Congratulations, my friend. You're officially a free man."

"She signed the papers?"

"Yes, she fucking did. Now, please promise to enjoy your freedom for a while, okay?"

I glance at Chiara, who's sound asleep in my arms. "Not a chance in hell I can make that promise."

CHIARA

When I wake up, I find the other side of the bed empty. I sit up and search the hotel room. It's morning outside, but the curtains are drawn, so only a few rays of light come through.

"Alistair?"

"I'm here, Goldi," he answers from outside our suite. A

moment later, he comes in, holding a tray with breakfast. "Good morning."

"What time is it?"

"A little past eight. Are you hungry?" He sets the tray on the nightstand and sits on the edge of the mattress.

"Not really."

Alistair frowns. "Goldi, you have to eat. I don't want you getting sick on me."

"Okay, I'll drink some orange juice." I reach for the glass.

His lips are still a thin flat line, but at least the V between his eyebrows is gone.

"When do you want to fly back to LA?"

His question makes my stomach queasy. I have to tell him about not being able to return to DuBose.

"I don't have good news, Alistair." I drop my gaze to my lap, unable to withstand his stare.

"Goldi, you're scaring me."

I take a deep breath and blurt out, "I can't afford to pay for DuBose anymore. My father's assets are still frozen even after his death."

He places his index finger under my chin and makes me look at him again. "I'll cover your tuition, Goldi. And if you want to keep living at Brandywine Hall, I'll pay for that too, although I'd prefer if you moved in with me."

"Alistair, I can't ask you to do that. It's not right."

"Why is it not right? You're the woman I love. Why can't I help you graduate from the school of your dreams?"

"Because we've only been together for a short period of time, and I'm not a leech."

He furrows his brows again. "Goldi, I know you're not a leech. If it makes you feel better, you can pay me back once you're taking Hollywood by storm."

I bite my lower lip, fighting to keep the tears at bay. "This is too much. I don't deserve it."

"What are you talking about? You deserve everything and more. You're the kindest, loveliest person I've ever met. If you wanted the moon, I'd find a way to get it for you."

With a shudder, I wipe the tears from my cheeks. "I don't want to be a burden to you."

He touches my shoulders and looks deep into my eyes. His gaze is brighter and a little red as if he's been crying or is about to.

"You're not a burden. You're the reason I wake up with a smile on my face. You're the ray of sunshine that keeps my monsters at bay. You're it for me, Goldilocks. I'm asking you—no, begging you to let me do this for you if it's what you want. If you want to stay in Italy, that's fine too. I'll move."

My eyes go rounder. "You'd give up your entire life in the States to move here for me?"

"In a heartbeat."

I throw my arms over his shoulders and crush my lips to his.

He kisses me back, hard and fast, before easing off. "What's it going to be, my love? LA, Milan, Tuscany? You tell me."

"LA first, and then we'll see. As long as you're with me, I don't care where we live, Alistair. I love you."

"I love you too, Goldi. So damn much," he says in a husky tone before he pounces, pushing me on my back to show me how much.

50

ALISTAIR

Seven months later

I haven't set foot in DuBose since I got fired, but nothing would keep me away from coming to Chiara's graduation. She returned to school after the tragic death of her father and flourished academically despite all the drama. She graduated with honors and earned a coveted scholarship to UCLA.

I'm hanging out with Monica, Tessa, and Caio as we wait for Chiara and Robbie to finish saying their goodbyes to their friends. The ceremony took place on the football field, and we're all glad the temperature remained in the seventies or we'd be melting. There isn't any shade around here.

"How are your parents, Alistair?" Tessa asks.

"They're well. The last time they checked in, they were in Argentina."

"Oh, Buenos Aires is one of my favorite cities in South America," Monica pipes up. "So romantic."

"I'm considering taking my parents up on their offer and meeting them there with Chiara."

"I'm sure she'd love it," Tessa replies. "It warms my heart to see you happy again, Alistair."

Caio groans. "Can we stop with the sappiness already?"

Monica hugs her brother sideways. "Don't be a hater because you can't keep the door to your bedroom from revolving."

He rolls his eyes, something I only see him do when he's with his sister.

Tessa looks over my shoulder and turns serious. "Principal Forrester is coming our way."

I turn, body tense. I haven't seen or talked to him since he fired me. He greets my companions and then focuses on me.

"Alistair, may I have a word with you?"

"Of course."

We walk away from the others to a spot on the football field that's less crowded. I shove my hands in my pockets, trying to appear relaxed, but it's hard to do so with him. We have too much history.

"Thanks for letting me come to Chiara's graduation, Forrester. I appreciate it."

He nods. "I don't like how things went the last time we met, Alistair. I said things I shouldn't have."

"You were right to be angry with me. I broke your trust."

He seems pained, but he isn't one to share a great deal about himself.

"Are you happy?" he asks.

"Yes, yes I am."

"I'm glad to hear that. It's what matters, isn't it?"

"Absolutely."

I spot Chiara and Robbie coming over, so I say my goodbyes to Forrester and return to the group. When she's within reach, I pick her up and twirl her around.

"Congratulations, Goldi."

She laughs. "Alistair. Put me down."

I do so, sealing my lips to hers. I keep it brief, but only in consideration of our friends. They don't need to witness me ravishing Chiara's mouth like a savage.

It's no surprise I find everyone watching us with stupid grins on their faces.

"I was about to tell you guys to get a room." Robbie smirks.

"Oh, they will soon enough." Caio snorts.

I glance at Chiara, finding her cheeks bright red. I can't believe she hasn't gotten used to Caio's comments yet. He, like my parents, doesn't have a filter.

Robbie's expression changes when he notices Phillip approaching. As far as I know, they're still keeping their relationship a secret. He says hello to us all and then stops in front of Robbie.

"What are you doing here?" Robbie asks.

"Do you think I'd miss your graduation?"

"Yeah. Isn't it what we've been doing the entire year? Pretending we're just casual friends?"

"I'm done pretending." He steps into Robbie's space and kisses him in front of everyone.

Caio whistles. "Whoa. I did not see that coming."

When Phillip steps back, Robbie's face is flushed. The poor guy looks stunned. He then turns to Monica and Tessa and introduces Phillip as his boyfriend.

I can't help but smile from ear to ear.

"Aw, look at you," Chiara teases me. "You're not going to cry, are you?"

I pinch her waist. "Shush, woman."

"Don't you know, Chiara? Alistair is the biggest crybaby I've ever met," Caio pipes up. "Cries over cereal commercials."

Chiara loops her arms around my waist, smiling so hard, her eyes twinkle. "I was right all along. You are a big cuddly bear."

I lean forward, touching my nose to hers. "I can be whatever you want." I pause to bring my lips to her ear. "As long as I get to eat you."

CHIARA

After graduation and the following celebratory lunch with Robbie and his family, I expect Alistair to drive back to his condo, so when he takes the highway heading in the opposite direction, I glance at him sideways.

"Where are we going?"

"It's a surprise, Goldi."

"Oh, I'm intrigued. Are you going to give me a clue?"

He smirks. "I'm sure you'll figure it out soon enough."

"Is that so? Hmm."

When I see the sign to Sonoma, I understand his meaning. "We're going to wine country?"

"Maybe." He smirks.

I haven't been to Sonoma since the fire. Alistair didn't want me to see the destruction that devastated most of the valley. I saw plenty of pictures online though, so I'm a little anxious.

During the three-hour drive, I try my best to make him reveal his plan. I even offer sexual favors in exchange for clues, something he denies me vehemently for safety reasons. Thanks to that, I'm on pins and needles when we approach our destination.

I recognize the driveway that leads to his parents' property even though I've only been there once. I expect to find nothing but an empty lot, so when a brand-new construction appears in front of me, I gasp.

"Oh my God."

Alistair chuckles. "What do you think?"

"You rebuilt the house?"

"Yep."

He parks the car in front of the porch. It's not a replica of his parents' former home, but it's the same style.

"When?"

"As soon as I was allowed to. Do you like it?"

I'm stunned for a moment and don't answer right away. When I do find my voice, I smack Alistair's chest with the back of my hand. "And you kept this a secret from me?"

"It wouldn't be a surprise if I told you."

"I can't believe this."

"Come on. I can't wait to show you inside."

He gets out of the car, and I do the same. As much as it was a lovely surprise, I'm a little mad that he didn't share it with me. I could have helped him.

I wait for him to unlock the door, biting my tongue to avoid saying something that would ruin the moment.

He moves out of the way and says, "Ladies first."

I only take a few steps in before I freeze. The house is empty.

"No furniture yet?"

"I knew it was a gamble building the house without asking for your input. I wouldn't dream of decorating it on my own. I value my life." He chuckles.

I smirk. "Smart man."

"Come on. Let's check out the back porch."

He ushers me through the empty living room space toward the wall-to-wall sliding doors. The sun is setting, casting the valley in the most amazing orange hues. But the best part of the landscape is that there's no trace of the charred destruction the fire left behind. The land is ready for new crops.

While I was busy at DuBose, Alistair decided to take some time off to figure out what he wanted to do next. Rebuilding the vineyard was an option—one I was more than one hundred percent on board with. I can't believe he kept it a secret for so long.

"Oh, Alistair. This is amazing."

"Well, it's not as amazing as it can be."

"What do you mean?" I turn to him, finding him on one knee, holding a diamond ring in his outstretched hand. "Oh my God."

"I know it's soon, and we have our entire lives ahead of us, but I don't want to wait another second. You're it for me, Chiara. It may have taken me a few detours to find you, but I know you're the one I want to spend the rest of my life with."

"Do you want me to marry you?"

He chuckles. "Yes, I do. I was getting to the question part. What do you say, Goldi? Will you make me the happiest man alive and be my wife?"

I want to say yes from the top of my lungs, but I end up bawling my eyes out instead. It's ugly, and if Alistair were any smarter, he would run for the hills.

He doesn't. He gets up and hugs me tight instead, kissing the top of my head. It takes me a minute to get the hysterics under control.

Pulling back, I crane my neck to stare into his eyes. "Yes, Alistair. The answer is yes."

"Thank God. I was beginning to worry."

He puts the ring on my finger, and it feels like a dream. I keep staring at it in a daze.

"Goldi, are you okay?"

I lift my chin, meeting his stare. "I'm more than okay. I thought grand love stories only existed in movies, but you proved me wrong, Alistair."

"You proved me wrong too, sweetheart." He pulls me into his arms, kissing me so gently, as if he's afraid I'll break.

The toe-curling kiss ends too soon, but when Alistair pulls back and stares into my eyes, the most wonderful feeling spreads through my chest. My heart is overflowing with love for this man who I was lucky enough to rescue from the side of the road.

"Do you remember the name of the car rental company you used in Italy?"

He frowns. "Not off the top of my head. I'd have to look it up. Why?"

"I need to send them a thank-you card."

Alistair chuckles. "Okay, but why?"

"If it weren't for their incompetence, I'd have never met you."

His grin turns into a full-blown smile. "If that's your line of thinking, then we have more people to thank."

I see where he's going with this, so I stop him with a quick kiss and then whisper against his lips, "Just the car rental company will suffice. Now, I hope you brought some blankets or pillows."

"Why?"

"I want my fiancé to be comfortable when I ride him into oblivion."

*** THE END ***

Author's Note: You might be wondering why I didn't write the scene where Chiara tells Max they are siblings. The short answer is, Max will get his own book, and I felt that scene should be seen through his eyes.

ALSO BY MICHELLE HERCULES

Paranormal Romance:

Dark Prince (Blueblood Vampires #1)

Wild Thing (Blueblood Vampires #2)

Forgotten Heir (Blueblood Vampires #3)

Savage Vow (Blueblood Vampires #4)

Reckless Times (Gifted Academy #5)

Savage Games (Gifted Academy #6)

Contemporary Romance:

Wonderwall (Love Me, I'm Famous #1)

Sugar, We're Going Down (Love Me, I'm Famous #2)

Wreck of the Day (Love Me, I'm Famous #3)

Devils Don't Fly (Love Me, I'm Famous #4)

Love Me Like You Do (Love Me, I'm Famous #5)

Catch You (Love Me, I'm Famous #6)

All The Right Moves

Heart Stopper (Rebels of Rushmore #1)

Heart Breaker (Rebels of Rushmore #2)

Heart Starter (Rebels of Rushmore #3)

Reverse Harem Romance:

Wicked Gods (Gifted Academy #1)

Ruthless Idols (Gifted Academy #2)

Hateful Heroes (Gifted Academy #3)

Broken Knights (Gifted Academy #4)

Red's Alphas (Wolves of Crimson Hollow #1)

Wolf's Calling (Wolves of Crimson Hollow #2)

Pack's Queen (Wolves of Crimson Hollow #3)

Mother of Wolves (Wolves of Crimson Hollow #4)

ABOUT THE AUTHOR

USA Today Bestselling Author Michelle Hercules always knew creative arts were her calling but not in a million years did she think she would become an author. With a background in fashion design she thought she would follow that path. But one day, out of the blue, she had an idea for a book. One page turned into ten pages, ten pages turned into a hundred, and before she knew, her first novel, The Prophecy of Arcadia, was born.

Michelle Hercules resides in Florida with her husband and daughter. She is currently working on the *Blueblood Vampires* series and the *Rebels of Rushmore* series.

Join Michelle's Readers' Group:
https://www.facebook.com/groups/mhsoars

Join Michelle's newsletter and receive a free ebook!
https://BookHip.com/ZGZDPV

Follow Michelle on TikTok:
https://www.tiktok.com/@michelleherculesauthor

Printed in Great Britain
by Amazon

64212820R00184